THE SKULL AND THE LUTE

The De Veres, Book 1

Leslie Vollard

ARE YOU SIGNED UP FOR DRAGONBLADE'S BLOG?

You'll get the latest news and information on exclusive giveaways, exclusive excerpts, coming releases, sales, free books, cover reveals and more.

Check out our complete list of authors, too!

No spam, no junk. That's a promise!

Sign Up Here

www.dragonbladepublishing.com

Dearest Reader;

Thank you for your support of a small press. At Dragonblade Publishing, we strive to bring you the highest quality Historical Romance from some of the best authors in the business. Without your support, there is no 'us', so we sincerely hope you adore these stories and find some new favorite authors along the way.

Happy Reading!

CEO, Dragonblade Publishing

CHAPTER ONE

1174 A.D., Winchelsea

ASPIRING NUNS DIDN'T generally write love poems, but then, no one ever accused Carenza of being a rule follower. She didn't want love. In fact, she'd gone to great lengths to avoid it, but she *did* love the language of love.

Ignoring her mother's summons, Carenza smoothed the skirt of her modest black dress and pulled a quill from a drawer in her desk.

"I'll be down in a few minutes," she told her maid, Elaine, who was patiently standing by the door, tucking a strand of blond hair into her neat side buns.

"I'll tell her, but she won't like it, my lady."

"I had a new idea. Tell her I'll be there soon."

Elaine raised an eyebrow but left without another word.

Carenza brushed a wisp of errant hair behind her ear as she sat at her simple desk with an angled top, looking with longing at Saint Mary's Abbey across the harbor, absently tapping her cheek with the end of the swan feather quill. The day was so clear she could see the coast of France across the Channel.

Words began to coalesce in her head, and she dipped her quill, inspiration filling her, ready to burst forth, when the heavy wooden door creaked open.

Elaine was back, already?

"She wants to see you now, my lady."

"Of course, she does." Taking a deep breath, she silently prayed for patience and fortitude, touching the tiny, carved skull on her rosary.

"She asked that you come to her receiving room."

Carenza made her way through the bare stone castle corridors, lit by candle sconces, and descended the winding staircase to her mother's receiving room. It was decorated with cushions and tapestries in the vibrant hues of Aquitaine, her mother's former home. Two narrow windows with pointed tops let in shafts of afternoon sunlight.

The Baroness Isabella de Vere swept in after Carenza. Her mother was considered a beautiful woman, not that Carenza paid attention to such things. People said the two of them looked alike with their ink-black hair and penetrating eyes. But all Carenza could see was the stark contrast between her mother's ostentation and her own austerity. Her mother looked like a peacock with her jeweled hairnet and extravagant blue gown with richly embroidered bell sleeves that dripped down to the floor.

Carenza frowned. The fact that her mother remained standing was not good. It meant she was too agitated to be still and needed to lecture her daughter from a height. She sighed.

"I'll be brief," her mother said, her voice clipped and commanding. "Earl Raymond de Broase of Hawkhurst will be here tomorrow. He intends to propose an alliance that will provide significant economic benefit and protection to Winchelsea. To seal the alliance, he will seek your hand in marriage. Queen Eleanor herself suggested the match when your father and I saw her and King Henry in Dover last month."

Oh no. Not another suitor. It had only been a week since she scared off the last one.

"This time, Carenza, you will do your duty. You will not run away. You will not insult the man. You will not tell him you are a sea witch. You will not sermonize about death and mortality. You will not pretend to be mute. You will not show him your drawings of deadly sea creatures. Additionally, you will not place any of said creatures on his seat in a boat."

"How was I supposed to know the Baron of Sandwich was going to sit on—"

"Silence," her mother ordered, holding up her hand. "I'm not finished. You will not speak of your ridiculous aspiration to become a nun."

"But Mother—"

"You will not wear shapeless black dresses like the one you have on now, nor will you wear that skull rosary you're so fond of. You will not mention any other high ladies who might be better matches for him."

"Mother—" It was nearly impossible to get a word in edgewise when her mother was in high dudgeon, but she had to try.

"Be quiet, Carenza," her mother said, clenching her fist and turning to pace. "Here is what you will do. You will wear the dresses and jewelry I have chosen for you. You will be punctual to meals and entertainments at which I require your presence. You will speak when you are spoken to. You will limit your responses to what has been asked of you, and you will be polite and demure and everything that a courtly young lady should be. Am I understood?" Her mother turned to face her and glared.

"Mother—"

"Am I understood?"

There was no point in arguing. She knew the best way to get out from under her mother's disapproving gaze was to accept without a word, but she couldn't let her mother stand there and try to destroy her lifelong dreams without a fight.

"And I suppose you are to be my model for polite and meek behavior, Mother?"

"How dare you!"

"How dare I? I'm your daughter, that's how. If I'm stubborn, difficult, and opinionated, where do you think I learned it? No one who has met you would ever call you meek, Mother, and it doesn't come naturally to me any more than it does to you."

"Carenza, now you—"

"I'm not finished," she said, raising her voice. "All my life, you and Father promised me a choice. All my life, you swore you wouldn't make your daughters marry strangers as you were forced to do when your family came north with Queen Eleanor's court. I was going to be a nun. You agreed to let me follow my calling, and now you think you can change your mind, and I'll accept it?"

Her mother pressed her lips into a thin line, and her clenched fist shook as she squeezed it even tighter.

"You know that everything changed when we lost your brother," her mother whispered in cold fury. Unconsciously, Carenza touched the skull on her rosary. "Circumstances change, and you must adapt. What I ask of you is nothing more than what was asked of me. You are nineteen years old, several years older than I was when I had to marry. You will do your duty, Carenza. I am finished discussing it. You are dismissed to go see your father. He would like to speak with you as well." With a swing of blue silk, she pointed an imperious arm at the door and pressed her lips together in a thin line.

With an outraged grunt, Carenza stood up and left, slamming the heavy wooden door behind her with an effort. The resulting boom rattled the nearby candelabra. She knew she shouldn't have dignified her mother's lecture with a response. Her mother always got under her skin. Though she always intended to stay cool and collected, her mother had a special talent for needling her. She never managed to hold her tongue and keep the high ground.

If only she could learn her father's trick of listening to her mother indulgently and then declaring quietly, "Enough, Isabella!" thereby bringing the conversation to a dead stop. Her mother almost seemed to enjoy it when her father did that. If they weren't her parents, she would have said the look that passed between them on such occasions was flirtatious. She'd tried "Enough, Isabella!" once, and the result had been cata-strophic. No, her father had magical powers.

Or love had magical powers. That was why Carenza feared it. Love made people capitulate and compromise. She vividly remembered her friend Genevieve from the abbey, who was like the older sister Carenza never had. They were going to be nuns together. Genevieve had a sharp and active mind, always challenging Carenza to learn more and think harder. But one day, Genevieve came back from a visit to her parents, changed. She couldn't be bothered with Carenza or her studies. All she cared about was Benedict, the Baron of Hythe. It was like watching a dear friend take ill.

Before long, she married Benedict. The first time Genevieve visited Winchelsea after her marriage, she'd seemed deliriously happy, but the next time, it was like the light had gone out in her eyes. Genevieve wouldn't say what had gone wrong, but to Carenza, it was clear: Love was a sickness that had changed her friend for the worse and led her to woe.

Carenza did not want love, and she certainly didn't want marriage, with or without love. It was all a trap to cage the soul.

Still seething, she knocked on the door of her father's study, then, without waiting for an answer, entered the familiar room with its haphazard clutter of books and maps and model ships on every surface. It had plain stone walls and several unadorned shelves packed with parchment scrolls. There was a heavy, round table in the middle of the room with legs carved to look like krakens and leviathans, where her father sat poring over a map. He was a portly man, slightly shorter than average, with a jolly face and a long, curling mustache. As usual, he wore a navy blue wool jerkin over a plain, white linen shirt and navy wool breeches. He dressed like a simple sailor whose clothes just happened to be of the finest fabric and cut.

"Carenza." Baron Martin de Vere stood up and beamed at his daughter, pulling her into a warm embrace. "From the look on your face, I'm guessing the conversation with your mother didn't go so well?" He invited her to sit with a gesture.

"Does it ever? We've had this same conversation at least half a dozen times in the last year. It never seems to change from one time to the next. We're always at each other's throats by the end." She looked her father in the eye. "I don't want to marry, Father. Please don't make me. All my life, you've told me I wouldn't have to, and nothing, nothing is going to change my mind."

Her father looked at her with sad resignation. "Nothing, daughter? Not even our people starving in the streets?"

She looked up in alarm. "Of course, I would never choose my own good over that of Winchelsea. But has it truly come to that? There must be another way. I know if we put our minds to it, we can find a solution."

Her father looked so very tired. "We never had much farmland under our authority, as you know," he said, indicating the map, "and recently, floods have been wreaking havoc, destroying crops. In addition, pirates have been plaguing our trading vessels. Countess Helisende of Hastings claims she can't afford to send help, and Baron James of Sandwich won't speak to us after the jellyfish incident. We must turn to Lord de Broase for aid. We need his grain to feed our people. He wants favorable terms for exports of wool and iron through Rye Harbor. He wants this alliance, and we need it, my dear."

Carenza swallowed. She didn't know things had gotten so bad. However firmly she believed in her own calling, she could not bring herself to cause suffering for others to follow it. "He won't ally with us without a marriage? Surely, there are plenty of other noblewomen for him to marry."

Her father shook his head. "His negotiators were firm on that point."

"And it has to be me?" She felt the walls closing in.

"Alais is still too young, however grown up she may think herself. Anyhow, Lord de Broase is my age," he said, his face reddening. "He specifically asked for the hand of our oldest unmarried daughter. He doesn't want to wed a child."

All she could manage was a soft, "Oh."

"I'm sorry, Carenza. Truly, I am. I know this is not the life you hoped for. It's not the life I wanted for you, but we have no choice. You need to do your duty to your people." He put a firm but kindly hand on her shoulder.

She didn't think her father could possibly make her feel worse than her mother, but this… She couldn't shirk her duty. If, in the end, she couldn't find another solution, she would have to do as her parents asked. When her brother Charles died, she knew things had changed. They'd told her that she had to consider marriage, but until now, it hadn't really sunk in.

Still, there had to be a loophole, and she was determined to find it. There had to be a way to save Winchelsea without her marrying. She wasn't ready to surrender yet.

"Carenza?" Her father furrowed his brow, and his eyes shone with deep concern.

"I'm going to pray on this," she answered, without looking directly at him, and went straight to the family chapel to pray for deliverance.

She needed time in the beloved space, breathing in the lingering scent of incense, kneeling before the painted statue of the Virgin Mother in the flickering candlelight to calm her thoughts and concentrate her mind. Shafts of afternoon light poured through the stained-glass windows, making colorful pools of light on the stone floor.

Christ looked down on her from the crucifix on the velvet-covered altar, reminding her how insignificant her suffering was compared to his. If he could make such a sacrifice to follow the will of his Heavenly Father, surely she could find a path to follow God's will as well. Would God have put it in her heart to become a nun if she was meant to marry? She had to trust in the Lord to show her the path forward through these tribulations.

That evening, she asked to eat dinner in her room. She couldn't face the rest of the family. Her sisters stopped by after the meal was finished.

Alais barged into the room and did a little dance of glee. She wore a blue gown that fit her sixteen-year-old form a bit too closely, displaying her curvaceous shape in a way that made Carenza purse her lips in disapproval. "Ooh, I'm so excited for you! Once you're married, it will finally be my turn. There are so many handsome young lords to choose from. I can't wait, I can't wait, I can't wait!"

Iselda, her youngest sister, came in and tried to drag Alais away. "Leave her alone. Not everyone is as excited to get married as you are."

Her two sisters couldn't be less alike. Only a year separated them, but Iselda had all the meekness and innocence of a child. Unlike Alais, who was currently driving her mad.

Carenza pierced Alais with a sharp look. "Leave." The last thing she needed right now was her little sister's man-crazed chatter.

Alais rolled her eyes and complied with a huff.

"Are you going to be all right?" Iselda asked, putting a hand on Carenza's arm. Carenza looked at her sister's soft brown eyes and sympathetic face and couldn't help but tuck a wayward strand of hair into the long, brown braid hanging over her slim, boyish shoulder.

"I could use a miracle about now." There had to be a solution that would allow her to follow her calling to live a life of study and contemplation, free of the constraints of marriage. If only she could find it.

Iselda nodded silently and squeezed her arm, then left her in peace.

Carenza picked up her quill, as she always did when she needed comfort and looked out at the lights of the town. Candles, torches, and firelight illumined cozy windows. In the pale moonlight, she could still make out the silhouette of the abbey across the water.

Closing her eyes, she felt for the music of the harbor in her mind, letting memories of images and sounds wash over her as the sea breeze caressed her face. She'd tried to set this down in verse so many times and never seemed to get it right. There was no forcing it. She had to let the music ripen and grow within her until it spilled forth of its own accord.

She always imagined that her home, the town of Winchelsea, and Saint Mary's Abbey gazed upon each other across the bay like a cavalier and his lady. Winchelsea was the cavalier, standing proud with a tall castle and a cape of stone buildings and thatched roofs, draping down to the busy port. The abbey was the lady, standing aloof on a small isthmus across Rye Harbor, her delicate stonework echoing that of the town but more modest in scale and more graceful. Carenza liked to think of them singing to each other across the water in a complex duet of syncopated rhythms and varied harmonies, music beyond any earthly musician. But this was no music of the spheres. This was an intertwining of the sacred and the profane. The nuns marked the hours with their prayers, and the raucous port answered with shouts and bangs and ribald songs.

The flow of composition soon gave way to the venting of her feelings, and her poem quickly turned into an extended diatribe on the evils of marriage.

She continued to write as the lights winked out one by one, and the town went to sleep, not stopping until Elaine came in to help her prepare for bed.

"How will you get out of it this time, my lady?" Elaine asked as she brushed and braided Carenza's hair.

"I don't know yet." She put down her quill. "Father said we need the alliance to keep our people from starving after all the floods and piracy. I'm not so selfish that I'll let anyone starve for the sake of my calling."

Elaine squeezed her shoulder. "I'm sorry, my lady. I know you'll do what's right." She took Carenza's hand to help her stand so that she could take off her dress. "You know, you might ask the abbess for guidance. She was the one who planted the idea of you taking holy orders in the first place."

"The abbess?" Carenza shrugged out of her dress. "She was quite clear about my duty to my parents when we last spoke."

"True. I was just wondering if you'd used every last argument at your disposal. Perhaps the abbess might have an idea that you haven't thought of yet? She's very clever."

She sighed as Elaine helped her change into a clean linen shift, sliding her arms into the long, narrow sleeves. "Even if she does, I don't know if my parents will listen. They'll say I have a duty to the people. I don't see any way around that. At least not yet."

"Well, think on it, my lady. Perhaps something new will come to you in the morning. If anyone can find a solution, it's you."

Perhaps seeing the abbess wasn't such a bad idea. What was the worst that could happen? If Carenza failed, at least she would have delayed meeting her fiancé.

She turned to Elaine with a sly grin. "By any chance, could I borrow a cloak tomorrow?"

CHAPTER TWO

D ANIEL RAN HIS hand along the smooth, rounded wood shaft that would become a ship's mast as he rubbed a glistening, sticky mix of linseed oil and pine tar into its surface. The afternoon sun lit the stone warehouse with rays of golden light from high windows, and the sweet smell of fresh wood pervaded everything as chips and shavings covered the floor.

As he stepped back to grab a clean rag, a familiar older gentleman with short white hair, a leathery, wrinkled, clean-shaven face, and sad, hazel eyes looked straight at him. The man was wearing a sword and a fine, gray woolen cape with a silver clasp; he looked entirely out of place beside the rough workers, stripped to the waist, nailing together the final pieces of the hull of a merchant vessel. What was John doing here?

"Marcel," Daniel yelled above the din to a man sanding a tiller, "I need to step out." He tilted his head toward the visitor. "I'll be back as soon as I can."

Marcel nodded.

Daniel washed his large, calloused hands in a basin and brushed sawdust from his short-cropped curls and the thick bristles of his beard. He pulled a rough brown homespun tunic over the chiseled muscles of his chest and thick corded arms that glistened with sweat from his work. Years of heavy labor had changed him from the skinny youth who fled to Dover nearly a decade and a half ago into a towering bear of a man.

He would be unrecognizable to any who hadn't watched the transformation, and this man before him was the only person who had seen it from the beginning. Those eyes had watched his first steps, his first ride on a pony, his first bull's eye with a bow and arrow. And they had seen him grieve, time and time again. What does your arrival portend this time, my friend? Good or bad?

He motioned to John to join him outside. Once they were away from the loudest of the noise, he clapped the other man's back and gave him a hug.

"I've missed you," he said, seeing how John had grown thinner and wirier since their last meeting. "It's been—what—five years since I last saw you? What brings you to Winchelsea this time?"

John looked around warily, his face pained. "I'm here to prepare for your uncle's arrival. He'll be here tomorrow. If all goes according to plan, he'll marry one of the de Vere daughters and form an alliance with Winchelsea."

Daniel stifled a curse. "Then you're here to tell me I must leave. Again."

John gave him an apologetic look. "I felt it was only right to warn you, my lord."

"Don't call me that. It's been seventeen years since I left that behind. I'm Daniel, plain and simple," he said in a harsh whisper.

"Of course...Daniel." John bowed his head. "Is there somewhere quiet and private we could sit and speak?"

"How about somewhere loud and public? There's a tavern near here. The noise from the patrons will drown out any possibility of being overheard."

John nodded his assent, and Daniel led the way to the Juggler on Silver Street, which also happened to be his current home. It was a squat building close to the western wall of the city with a long, dark common room with a floor covered in straw. He greeted the plump, middle-aged proprietress as they entered and asked for two ales. As promised, the ambient noise was raucous. They found a table in the corner where they could hear each other without yelling.

"My lord," John began.

Daniel winced, then looked around quickly to ensure no one was listening.

"My name is Daniel."

"Sorry. Daniel. It's a hard habit to break, even after all these years." John rubbed his sunburnt, balding scalp. "Your father would be so proud of you, my boy. I can't tell you how much you look like him now that you're grown."

"I can't imagine he'd be too pleased with my current circumstances," he said, looking down at his rough attire.

"Your father respected hard work and perseverance in the face of adversity. You've built a life for yourself against overwhelming odds."

"And you're here to tell me I have to scrap it and start again." Daniel leaned back and shook his head. "I like it here, John. I'm content, or as content as I can be, after everything that's happened."

John considered him. "I suppose you could stop running. You're a grown man now. It's not like when you were a lad of nine and had no choice but to flee. The men would follow you if you came forward. Your uncle is feared but not respected. If they knew you'd survived…"

"No." The hated face of his uncle flashed in his mind's eye. He would never return to that life. How could he? Some of his ale splashed on the table as he slammed down his mug. "I'll take my revenge on my uncle for killing my family if I have a chance, but I refuse to become him."

"Not your uncle," John objected. "Never your uncle. Your father. You could take his place, restore Hawkhurst to what it once was, restore our honor, restore decency."

"I'm a shipwright, not a lord of men. I gave a solemn oath to foreswear my name and title for good when I married Adele."

The pain of losing her was never far from the surface. Even saying her name made his chest ache with longing. He took a long drink. "God rest her soul," he whispered into his cup, crossing himself.

John shook his head. "If you stay and you don't take him down, he will come after you. He let slip that he's heard rumors you might be here. He'll be looking for you. He knows you're a shipwright. The only way you'll ever have peace is if you stand up to him. Earl Daniel might stand a chance. Daniel the simple shipwright? He will chase that man until he's dead."

"Or until I kill him," Daniel said with a sigh, staring into the dregs of his cup, swirling them around. John might be right. The answer he sought wasn't in the remains of the cheap ale, no matter how hard he looked. After a long moment, he looked up and asked, "If I wanted to take revenge while he's here, but without claiming my title, what would be the best way to do it?"

John's eyes bored into him. "Why won't you take up the title?"

"Because it's poison. It's a curse. Look how it has twisted my family. It killed my father and turned my uncle into a monster. I refuse to let Hawkhurst destroy me, too."

"It's your uncle, not the title, that is poison."

Shaking his head, Daniel answered, "Both are tainted beyond repair." Enough of this foolishness. It was dangerous to have this conversation in public, even amidst the din surrounding them. Besides, he needed to return to the warehouse. That mast wasn't going to finish itself. He fixed John with a stern stare. "Are you going to tell me how to get at my uncle or not?"

"You'd need to find a way to get to him in the castle," John said, now grim and impassive like the military commander he was. "He's too heavily guarded while he's traveling, but I've told him the danger is minimal while he's staying with the de Veres. His man, Richard, will be with him, as usual, but I'm sure you wouldn't mind an excuse to dispatch him too. You'd need to stay out of sight if you want to avoid recognition. While you look nothing like the lad who ran away, you still have the de Broase face. You'll have to be careful."

Daniel nodded slowly. Perhaps the time had finally come. He'd laid low all these years, but he knew what John said was true. His uncle would never stop until one of them was dead. He was tired of running and hiding. He'd been preparing for this fight since the day his father died. This wasn't a fight he invited, but he'd put it off as long as he could. Revenge wouldn't make him happy. There was no happiness without Adele, but perhaps he could at least be free and find some peace.

"I can find a way into the castle," he said, his mind spinning. "I'll let you know as soon as I have a plan. My friend, Gerard, is up at the castle regularly as a troubadour. He'll find you, and then we can meet again to coordinate."

"Of course. Though I must remind you that I can't assist you openly unless you declare yourself," John said with wary eyes and a furrowed brow. "I would be honored to lay down my life in the service of the true earl, but as long as you are in hiding, I have to maintain the pretense of loyalty to your uncle for your own safety, as well as that of my family."

"I know. I would never want to endanger your family. We'll be discreet." He clenched and unclenched his fist beneath the table. Getting in the castle would be difficult, even with Gerard's help. Was there a way to lure his uncle out? Though his uncle was unlikely to leave the castle without ample protection. He would have to sneak into the castle, then. But with what disguise? "So my uncle is coming here for a bride? This would be…what…his third wife?"

John nodded.

"I've never met the de Vere daughters. Whoever he's courting has my pity. Perhaps there's some way to use the wedding to get to him." He paused and stared at the ceiling. It would be a highly public event, which would make it easy for him to slip in but difficult to get his uncle alone.

John narrowed his eyes. "Better if you can get to him before.

There will be too many people at the wedding. You'll have better odds if you can get him alone."

Daniel was glad to see John was thinking along similar lines.

"He's a coward, always has been," John continued. "He relies on the strength of others to carry out his will. When he's alone, he's vulnerable."

"Good point. And it's probably best to spare his poor bride-to-be from going through with the ceremony anyhow."

"Agreed."

He'd have to give this some thought. There were several options, but he needed to talk it through with Gerard before deciding on a course of action.

"Enough plotting for now. How are you and your family? Are you well? How are your grandchildren?"

With a smile, John shook his head. "It's kind of you to ask, Daniel. My grandchildren aren't children anymore. Lucinda just got married."

"No!"

"It's true!"

Daniel laughed. He wished he could have gone to Lucinda's wedding and raised a glass with her cousins, who had been his childhood playmates. But no. Such simple pleasures were not to be.

"Speaking of weddings, have you met anyone special?" John asked with a careful smile.

"You know I'd never risk it after what happened to Adele," he said, trying to keep his voice even. He knew John meant well, but he would never risk another woman's life, at least not while his uncle lived. To dispel the awkwardness, he asked, "Any news of my sister?"

"Oh yes, my…I mean…Daniel." John positively beamed. "Your sister is doing well. She married the Earl of Ashford. She's out from under your uncle's thumb at last, and she seems quite happy. She has two children now, a boy and a girl, named Abelard and Emmeline, both very sweet." John paused. "You should go visit her."

Daniel's heart squeezed. Oh, how he would love to, but did he dare? "No, I won't put her in danger," he said in a gruff voice, shaking his head.

"Your uncle would hardly harm the Countess of Ashford."

There was no limit to the atrocities his uncle was capable of when provoked. "He killed my father."

"She doesn't even know you're alive," John pleaded. "Don't you think she deserves to know?"

"She deserves every joy that life can provide, but I won't put her in danger by making contact. Perhaps when my uncle dies," he said, relenting slightly at John's gentle remonstrance.

"All the more reason to bring that about quickly. I know you don't want to hear it, but I still think you should declare yourself. He'd be deposed in no time."

At that, Daniel huffed and rubbed his forehead. Not this again. "No."

John sighed and shook his head, pushing his chair back from the table. "It's been good catching up with you, my boy, but I should get back to the castle before I'm missed. I'll keep an eye out for Gerard, and hopefully, I'll see you again soon."

Daniel gave a curt nod.

"Is there anything you need? I know you always refuse my coin, but if there's any way I can be helpful..."

He shook his head.

The two men stood and embraced briefly. Then John went on his way.

Emotions churning, Daniel sat quietly for a long time, then went over to the bar. His uncle had to be stopped. The nightmare had to end at some point. There would be no better opportunity to bring it about if only he could figure out how.

And then what? That was a question for another time. He didn't dare dream of what life would be like after his uncle was gone. It would only lead to heartbreak, as he had learned time and again.

For now, it was best to focus on the problem at hand. He needed a way into Winchelsea Castle.

"Franny, have you seen Gerard? I need to talk to him."

Franny chuckled over the glass she was polishing. "He's up at the castle with Mistress Elaine."

"Which means heaven only knows when I'll see him again. Thank you, Franny. I've got to head back to work. If you see him, tell him to find me."

He left a few coins on the counter and headed out, wondering how long it would be before he felt a knife at his throat.

DANIEL WAS EXHAUSTED when he returned that evening to the small attic room he shared with Gerard at the Juggler. He looked around his humble home, shaking his head. It was a far cry from the castle he grew up in. There were two narrow beds, two trunks, a wardrobe—which was entirely taken up with Gerard's outfits for performing—and a small writing desk, which was Daniel's private domain. He had three precious pages of palimpsest parchment that he had purchased from a penny-pinching notary at the custom house, and he'd reused them, scraping them time and again until he could no longer make out the new writing. The rest of the attic was given over to wine and ale barrels and provisions for the tavern below. The entire attic smelled of hops and cured meats.

The tavern's enormous tabby cat wound around his legs affectionately, and he bent over to scratch its head. "Sorry. I don't have any fish for you this evening. You'll have to be content with catching mice."

Daniel had rescued the cat from a fishmonger who'd been trying to hit it with a stick, calling it a demon spawn. It had fled to Daniel to escape its attacker and refused to leave his side after he'd shooed the other man off. Franny only let the cat stay because she was a good mouser. Cats were supposed to be omens of ill luck, but Daniel didn't believe a word of it. How could such a sweet, soft thing bring anything but good?

As he lay down, the cat curled up by his side, its low purr an irresistible lullaby. Sleep took him, and his mind settled into its accustomed groove of memory and dream, replaying a past that would never stop haunting him—his father's unnatural stillness in death, a ride through the night and into the next day with John at his side, not knowing if he would ever see his mother or sister again. Then there was a farm, a man with his two children, a little boy and a girl his own age. Adele, gawky with golden braids and a teasing smile, whispering secrets in his ear up in the branches of an old elm tree.

Adele, older now, no longer gawky, a budding beauty with mischief in her blue eyes, confiding her dreams of adventure and dread of domesticity. A stolen kiss. A promise made. An agonizing wait. He'd built a boat for her, piece by piece, to give her the freedom and adventure she craved when they were finally able to wed. At last, Adele had stood beside him in church, eyes shining with love. He felt the sweet desperation of her body against his own after years of waiting. Oh yes, Adele, please I need you, I love you, it's too much, oh God!

And then—

Gerard stumbled over a trunk and cursed, rousing Daniel from his dreams. Daniel pushed himself to sitting, sending the cat scurrying across the room. He ran his hands over his face and lit a candle.

"Adele again?" Gerard asked, trying and failing to focus on Daniel's face.

Daniel nodded. It was always the same dream. He never escaped it. "You're drunk," he grumbled. "Again."

"M'not." Gerard pitched himself face-first onto his bed.

"I need to talk to you," Daniel said, yawning as he pulled Gerard's muddy boots off with disgust. Clearly, the man wasn't going to do it himself.

"Now?" Gerard asked the pillow.

"Now." He flipped his friend onto his back as if he was a sack of grain.

"Whatizzit?" Gerard shielded his eyes from the candle and burped loudly.

"You smell like a rooting hog."

"*Pfffft.*"

"If your father could see you now, he'd have my hide for what I've let you become." It was a low blow, he knew, but Gerard was doing this altogether too often.

"I'm a grown man, Daniel, an' my father's dead." Daniel was grateful that he didn't add "because of you." Not that Gerard would ever go that far, but he heard the implied accusation, nonetheless. "An' yer not my father, s'leave me alone," Gerard finished. He threw his pillow at Daniel.

Sighing, Daniel shook his head. "John came to see me today. De Broase will be here tomorrow. He's planning to marry again, apparently."

At that, Gerard propped himself up to a sitting position, his eyes almost focused. "De Broase? Here?" he asked, suddenly sounding more sober. He squinted at Daniel, who nodded.

"You're going to tell me we're leaving again, aren't you?"

"No," he said, looking Gerard in the eye. "Not this time. I'm tired of running."

"Are we finally going to kill him?" Gerard cocked his head, a little too much excitement in his bleary eyes.

"Not we. I am going to kill him. You are going to keep being the castle's favorite songbird and avoid arousing any suspicion. If this all goes wrong, I need to know you'll be safe."

Gerard used the heels of his hands to rub his eyes. "Worried about me, are you? I'm touched." He grabbed Daniel's hand and gave him a mocking, soulful look.

Daniel pulled his hand away and waved it in front of his nose. "You reek."

"Well, I'm glad we're not leaving. I had the loveliest time

with Mistress Elaine this evening after her mistress went to bed. I think I'm in love!"

Daniel was unimpressed. Gerard fell in love every five minutes and had no compunctions about romancing half a dozen women at a time. Try as he might to have a tempering influence on his honorary little brother, he never managed to change Gerard's ways. His brother-in-law had a thin, pale face with cheekbones that made women weep in envy and soft, brown, curly hair that was just a touch too long. He had perfected the lovesick poet pose, and his smokey voice sent women into transports of rapture. With Daniel, however, he didn't bother with the act, and his eyes were pure mischief.

"She loves your poems, by the way," Gerard drunkenly enthused. "Can't get enough of them. Thank you so much for helping me seduce her."

Daniel shook his head. "I'm not helping anyone seduce anyone. I'm composing poems so you can make a living earning patronage as a ruddy troubadour, you complete ass."

"Thank you," Gerard replied, with a ridiculous grin that reminded Daniel of the seven-year-old he'd met all those years ago.

"Now get some sleep. I need you sober in the morning so that we can plan."

Unable to sleep himself, Daniel sat down at his desk to write, the cat curled up at his feet. By candlelight, he let soaring words carry him away from the dark dreams that haunted him.

Chapter Three

As the church bell rang noon, Carenza covered herself in Elaine's old cloak and fled down Castle Street, past merchants, taverns, and inns until she reached the docks. The streets were crowded this time of day, and no one gave her a second look. Hoping to buy herself a few hours, or better yet, a few days, she went to catch the ferry to the abbey. She knew her duty, but try as she might, she couldn't bend herself to it. There had to be another way to save the town. She wasn't ready to surrender just yet.

Rosary in hand beneath her cloak, she slipped into a dark stone warehouse by the ferry on Fish Street, hoping her father's marshal hadn't seen her. She peered out from the shadow of the doorway into the bright sunshine where a dried-out raisin of a man, wearing a leather jerkin tooled with the de Vere coat of arms, was scrutinizing every moving shape in his field of vision. His bony face, fringe of white hair, lean, muscular figure, and proud carriage were unmistakable. Unfortunately, Bertrand was good at his job, which meant eventually he'd catch up to her. She'd prefer to be safely within the abbey by then. The abbess would understand that she wasn't running away, just delaying things a little bit to strategize. She had to.

Carenza looked around at the warehouse as her eyes adjusted to the dim light. She'd seen it countless times from the outside but had never been inside before. Standing behind a large pile of logs, she peeked out at the numerous planed wood boards leaned against the wall beside her, some of them as tall as the rafters. High windows allowed shafts of sunlight to illumine the lower reaches of the building in bright patches that made the shadows seem deeper. A large, open barn door at the back let in additional light, but none of it reached her. She was well hidden behind the wood in the darkest part of the warehouse. No one would find her here if she didn't want to be found.

A sound interrupted her reverie. Someone was there. Someone was…singing? She peered between the logs to see a man roughly the size of a bear, stripped to the waist, using a broad axe to carve a long board into a sinuous curving shape. A shipwright, perhaps? The space certainly suggested some form of woodworking. The muscles of the man's arms and back spoke to a life of hard labor. The stark contrast of sunlight and shadow played over every curve and sinew in his powerful frame. Shipbuilding required a unique blend of strength and delicacy, her father had said. One wrong cut and the whole board was ruined. The man's movements were smooth, assured, and efficient. Despite the coolness of the space, a sheen of sweat made him glisten in the shaft of sunlight and dampened his ebony curls and his full and tidy beard.

Suddenly warm, she slipped the hood of her cloak off in the shadows and leaned in for a better look.

Much to her surprise, she recognized his song as a troubadour lyric. It was a new composition. The singer that performed it at the castle earlier in the week had the pale and sickly pallor that was all the rage amongst courtiers these days, a wastrel for certain. He sang incongruously about refining his song with plane, file, oil, and wax as if he were sculpting wood. The singer had never done a day's manual labor in his life, by the look of him, but there was a plaintive catch in his voice and a cleverness to the rhymes that gave an unexpected substance to his performance.

How in heaven's name had a shipwright learned it? Certainly, this particular song, with all its carpentry metaphors, fit the man she saw before her better than the milksop that had performed it, but the man in front of her had no business knowing it.

The man interrupted his singing and tried a modified version of the last stanza. He shook his head and tried again, changing just two words. This time, he nodded in satisfaction. Could he be composing? His revision sharpened the rhymes and multiplied the meanings. She was impressed. This man was too clever by half unless perhaps he'd overheard another version somewhere. But where? This wasn't a tavern song. More puzzling still, there was an intelligence in his eyes that made her certain the innovation was his own, but what could explain such a man in such a place? Why would he wield an axe if he could spin a verse?

She could never resist a puzzle, a mystery, or unknowns of any kind. How many times had the abbess lectured her on the perils of excessive curiosity? But her mind was not a tame thing, nor had she ever met with success in her feeble attempts to rein it in. Why would the Lord in heaven have blessed her with such a mind if she was meant to tie it down? And the puzzle before her was too delicious to resist.

"Did you compose that song?" she asked aloud before she could stop herself. Holy Mother, full of grace! She should not have said that. There was enough to worry about without having to extricate herself from the clutches of a rough laborer in a dockside warehouse. But having spoken, she had to say something to get herself out of this mess.

Pulling her hood back over her head, she stepped out of her hiding place, knowing it was probably a mistake to reveal herself. But it was too late. She really shouldn't have said anything. It was foolish. The man could be dangerous or, worse yet, he could know her father. Sometimes, it seemed like everyone in Winchelsea knew her father personally. She kept the rough woolen cloak wrapped around her to hide the silk dress beneath, and she kept her face hidden within the deep hood.

The man stood silently, staring at her, frozen in his action.

"'Joining tongue to groove, my words a perfect fit, I smooth and then improve each verse with whetted wit.'" She sang his opening verse back to him in her clear, rich alto voice. "Is it your composition?" It was none of her business, but she had to know. Singing again, following the same melody, she continued, "Are you a songbird, sir? It sounds as if you are. Your words could make a stir. Your verse could take you far."

His intelligent, chestnut-brown eyes went wide, and he clenched his jaw as she sang. He shook himself and demanded in an unfriendly growl, "Who are you, and what are you doing over there?"

"My name is…Ann, and I'm…hiding from my father." She cleared her throat and squared her shoulders, pretending a confidence she did not feel. "He's a wine merchant, and he wants me to marry someone I don't like. I'm trying to get to the abbey. I want to be a sister." Close to the truth. With a few minor modifications. Had she overexplained? She always overexplained when she was nervous. If only she was a better liar.

"I…I came in here to hide, and then I heard you singing. It…It seemed like you were composing. You're really very good. Have you ever considered performing at the castle? My m…I mean, that is to say…Lady Isabella gathers troubadours for an evening of songs every so often, and she gives a prize to the best performer. I know someone who might be able to get you an invitation. You might win some silver if you went." He tilted his head at her words, the intensity of his gaze sharpening, though she hardly knew how that was possible. She tapered off into silence, holding her breath as warmth suffused her body. What was she thinking even talking about the castle, let alone her mother? A foolish thing to do.

"Who are you really? You're no wine merchant's daughter." He put down his axe and started to walk toward her.

"I—I'm sorry," she stuttered, backing away. "I'll just… I'll just go see if the ferryman has returned so that I can be on my…Ow!"

She tripped over something in the dim light, and a sharp pain shot through her ankle as she tumbled down. Foolish, stupid. How would she get out of this?

The man was by her side in a flash, grasping her arm to help her up. Heat radiated from him as he leaned over her. She'd never been this close to a man's bare chest. It made her feel nervous and unsettled. He was so close she could smell his scent—the sweetness of wood and wax mixed with the salt of his sweat and an animal musk that made her head swim. She was close enough to see the auburn hairs interspersed with the ebony bristles of his beard, matching the sparse patch of hair on his chest. He had two rings hanging from a chain around his neck, one a plain gold band and the other bulky, like a signet ring. She couldn't help wondering why he had them.

"Are you all right? Where does it hurt?" His arm wound around her, supporting her. She felt burned by his touch and jerked away.

"I'm fine," she said through gritted teeth. "I just twisted my ankle." She tried to push herself up to standing but lurched sideways as she tried to put weight on her injured foot. So much for getting away to the abbey. It was hopeless now. The man caught her before she fell again. She was forced to lean into him, to accept his support, even though all she wanted to do was run. He swept her feet from under her and carried her over to a wooden bench.

As she was pressed against the sculpted muscles of his chest, his beating heart pounded in her ear. The heat of him made her feverish, thirsty. The pressure of his arms filled her with a hot, prickly sensation she'd never felt before that spread to parts of her body she avoided thinking about.

After putting her down, he stood back and looked her up and down with an intensity that made her feel as if her skin was on fire. What right did he have to look at her like that?

But then, what right did she have to even be here? If Bertrand found her here alone with a man and worse yet injured, things would go very badly. She heaved in a long sigh. She was going to have to find a way to get them both out of this.

"Now, will you tell me the truth?" he asked, taking in her silk dress and pearl rosary, the cloak having fallen back when he picked her up. Her dress was a form-fitting, deep-red silk gown with gold embroidery adorning the edges. She was embarrassed by the low cut in front, displaying the ample bosom that she generally hid from sight beneath the demure, shapeless dresses she preferred. She would never have chosen something so immodest for herself. Her mother wanted her to wear something enticing for her prospective suitor. And now, here she was, exposing herself in front of this strange man.

She turned her gaze to the floor. "My name is Carenza. My father is Baron de Vere."

The man sucked air between his teeth and took a step back. "My lady, I'm a dead man if someone walks in here. They'll think I attacked and compromised you."

She stared harder at the floor, gritting her teeth. How embarrassing this all was. "I'm very sorry. I didn't mean to..." she trailed off, not sure what to say.

He stood still, staring at her, assessing her.

She slowly raised her gaze to his, grasping her rosary for strength.

"That's an unusual necklace for a young woman," he said with a frown. Why was he commenting on her jewelry at a time like this?

She looked down at the string of pearls with the tiny, delicate skull and crucifix carved from leviathan bone by her grandfather. "My grandmother gave it to me when my brother died. It reminds me that death can come at any time and life should not be wasted."

The man took a deep, shuddering breath. Intense emotion flashed across his face, then was stifled as quickly as it had come. He shook his head and ran his hand through his hair. "You should never have come in here, Carenza de Vere. Death can come at any time, and you should not invite it. Nor do you have the right to waste my life for your foolishness."

He glanced out at the street. The passersby were all going about their business. None of them appeared to have noticed anything unusual in the warehouse, at least not yet. He shook his head and grunted.

"Wrap your cloak around you and hide your face."

She complied immediately.

"I'm going to a tavern nearby. The matron is a friend of mine. I'll bring her back, and she'll stay with you while I find someone who can take you home to your father."

She started to object, but he interrupted. "My friend will say she saw you trip and fall on the street and brought you in to sit down. Obviously, no one can know we were alone together. You'll go home to your father, and you'll forget we've ever met. Is that understood?"

"I don't suppose you might be willing to take me to the abbey instead?" It was unlikely he would agree, but it was worth a try.

He gritted his teeth and looked at the ceiling as if praying for patience. "No, my lady. I would not. Now, can I have your promise you won't try to move while I go get my friend?"

She nodded slowly. He was right, of course. It was the only option. She couldn't flee with a sprained ankle.

"Good." He grabbed a rough brown tunic from a peg on the wall and pulled it on. She should have been relieved that he covered himself, but she felt oddly bereft. Oh dear. What was happening to her? How could she even think something like that? "I'm going," he announced as he marched toward the door.

"Wait," she called out. He stopped and gave her a look of pure fury.

"What is it?"

"I don't even know your name. Pray, good sir, tell me who you are?"

He gave her a dark look and shook his head. "They'll have a harder time putting a noose around my neck if you can't tell them who I am. Forget me."

He disappeared into the street, and she stared after him, certain she would never forget a single moment of their strange meeting. She was still staring several minutes later when a middle-aged woman waddled in the door and made a curtsy, glancing around quickly to make sure no one saw.

"My lady, my name is Franny. I'm so sorry about your foot. We'll get you back to your father right quick."

Carenza offered a wan smile in return. This ruse may get the shipwright out of trouble, but she was in for it when Bertrand found her. Or really, when her mother got hold of her. The one would lead to the other, but Bertrand wasn't really the problem. It wouldn't do for her to blame him for doing his job.

Franny sat down next to her and gave her a friendly pat on the knee. "You aren't the first runaway I've run across headed for the abbey, nor will you be the last, though you're the first I've found that lives in a castle. Marriage isn't as bad as you think, my lady. You might find you like it better than you expected. And I'm sure it can't be all bad wearing fancy dresses and living in a castle and all."

Franny's face was friendly and obsequious, but Carenza knew when she was being admonished. After all, her life was far from terrible. Even with a husband she didn't like, she would still live better than most women could ever dream of. This whole situation made her want to crawl into a hole.

A young boy walked in, with Bertrand following close behind. "She's in there, sir! She tripped and fell, and Franny brought her in to rest her foot!"

Carenza had half-hoped the shipwright might be the one to bring Bertrand, but no. It would have been foolish for him to involve himself in any way. She would never see him again. She would never solve the mystery of who he was or why he knew a song that he shouldn't. What an infuriating puzzle of a man!

Bertrand planted himself in front of her with a long-suffering look. "You've led me on a merry chase, my lady," he said in his usual deep, funereal tones. "I must take you home to your mother. She'll know what to do with you."

Was he gloating? Good heavens, he was gloating.

Soon, Bertrand had her bundled onto a horse for the ride back to the castle. She thanked Franny for her help, and Bertrand gave the woman a silver piece for her trouble. With a sigh, Carenza turned to ride back up Castle Street with Bertrand at her back. She took one last look at the warehouse and saw the shipwright leaning against a wall in the shadows. He was watching her with dark, brooding eyes. He didn't look away when she met his gaze. Blood rushed to her face, and she turned away, squaring her shoulders, looking straight ahead, and touching her necklace. She would never see him again. Never.

CHAPTER FOUR

D ANIEL WATCHED CARENZA ride away up the hill, wondering why he felt like his whole world had turned on its head. The foolish woman could have gotten him killed, still could. But he couldn't stop picturing her turning, with a straight back and square shoulders, to face her fate, ink-black hair escaping its pins to fly behind her in the wind. Her vitality moved him, and it was unnerving the way she saw right through him. He'd dodged her question about composing, but she'd known. She'd definitely known.

And then there was her own little snippet of verse. For years, he'd been faithful in thought and deed to the memory of his beloved Adele, but a spear of raw desire pierced him as she'd improvised, followed quickly by guilt and anger at his own reaction. He'd heard about women who composed, like the Countess of Dia, who held their own with the best troubadours of the time, but he'd never actually met one. He never thought he'd encounter a woman who could truly match wits with him. Even Adele, with her quick mind, had never been able to keep pace. She'd loved his poetry but had never attempted to compose her own.

Carenza de Vere's teasing little verse filled him with a ferocious hunger unlike any he'd ever felt, and he was so deeply ashamed.

He knew his angry response was unwarranted, but he couldn't see straight, drowning as he was in hunger and self-loathing. He may have scared her, but not nearly as much as she'd scared him. Six years, resisting the temptation to seek comfort with a woman for fear she would end up paying with her life. Six years of exhausting himself with hard labor to reduce his natural urges. Six years of sublimating his passion in verse. Was he so easily undone?

No. He loved Adele, only Adele. This was just a moment of feeling unbalanced. He was only human. It was inevitable he would have moments of weakness. He needed to compose a song. Yes, that was all it was. He'd vent his feelings in verse and be done with them. No one ever had to know.

Then, he had a darker thought. Was she the woman his uncle was planning to marry? Carenza de Vere was the oldest of the sisters and the most likely match. The thought of his uncle laying his disgusting, murdering, blood-soaked hands on her made him sick. Might there be some way to use this chance encounter to get to his uncle and save her at the same time? No one deserved to be married to that monster, least of all an innocent and captivating young woman like Carenza.

Perhaps he could use her interest in his verses to coax from her an invitation to the castle. He could tell he had piqued her curiosity.

A plan began to form in his head. He could write a song for Gerard to sing, craft it just so, hinting without disclosing, evoking without declaring. She would know it was from him, but no one else would. Hopefully, it would provoke a response, and he could parlay it into the invitation he needed.

Then he sighed and shook his head. "What I need is a tankard of ale," he mumbled to himself.

He followed Franny into the Juggler and sat down at the bar. The cat immediately jumped in his lap as Franny poured him his drink and herself a flagon of wine.

"Watch yourself, Daniel. That could have gone very badly.

Still could, if the young lady isn't discreet." She took a gulp.

"Thank you, Franny. I am in your debt." He raised his tankard to her and drank deeply, absently petting the cat with his other hand.

"Pretty young thing," Franny said, the corner of her mouth quirking into a smirk. "Foolish, but pretty."

Daniel grunted and took another long sip. Franny had no idea. "Could have gotten me killed. Could have gotten herself killed too if she'd wandered through the wrong door, a woman alone wandering the docks in silks and pearls…. She's lucky the worst that came of it was a sprained ankle."

"Listen to you, worrying over a girl that nearly put your neck in a gibbet! She turned your head good and proper, didn't she?" Franny's smile was all too knowing.

"Don't know what you're talking about," he said, putting on the most innocent expression he could muster.

"If you say so," Franny said with a wink.

"I have to go." He drained his cup and lifted the cat off his lap. "Work to do."

He left a coin for his ale and exited the premises as quickly as he could and still maintain his dignity. New verses were already forming in his head, new verses about his uncle's intended, if his guess was correct. The rest of the afternoon flew by in a blur as words appeared and rearranged themselves as some unseen hand wove them together into a delicate lace. All the while, his hands continued their rough work of cutting, honing, and planing wood. The work required no thought, only muscle memory, leaving his mind free to pursue its craft.

The words flowed with unexpected ease. This burst of inspiration had little to do with her. Perhaps she was a catalyst—her beauty, her innocence, her pitiable situation—but, he told himself, his passion was for words, not for her. She just happened to bring to mind new turns of phrase, new metaphors, and images that heightened the impact of his verse. It had nothing to do with her hair streaming behind her like the fresh stroke of a quill before the ink has dried. He'd hardly noticed she smelled of roses, cardamom, and almonds like a spice trader's cake. If he kept thinking about the way that death's face nestled between her breasts, making her seem to pulse with life, it was only because images evoking mortality lent gravity and urgency to a lover's lament. He was just immersed in the flow of composition.

Composing was a vice, a habit he couldn't break, almost a nervous tic. His arrangement with Gerard was harmless enough, and it gave his wastrel brother-in-law an income. Who would ever suspect a shipwright might be feeding lines to the great troubadour Gerard? He had never dared to go to court and perform himself. Too many people knew his poetic tendencies growing up. Too many people might notice a family resemblance despite his beard and draw dangerous connections. And so, he had always settled for living vicariously, feeding someone else his songs. But he would willingly cast aside his comfortable anonymity for the chance to end his uncle's tyranny and live in peace. All he needed to do was coax an invitation out of a pretty girl. How hard could it be?

The light grew too dim for woodwork, and Daniel closed up shop. As he headed back to the Juggler, he spotted Gerard walking toward him.

"Daniel, where have you been? I need you. Now." Gerard ambled toward him in an eye-popping red and white outfit with a clashing floppy green hat askew on his head and Daniel's lute hanging behind his back.

"Oh?" Daniel raised an eyebrow. Gerard hooked an arm around his friend. Clearly, the bard was already three sheets to the wind.

"I've almost gotten Elaine to bed me, but I need another song. Got anything new for me?"

Daniel smiled. "Maybe I do."

He knew he shouldn't encourage Gerard, but he did want to try out his new song.

"I knew I could count on you," Gerard said, clapping him on

the back. "She let me inside her bodice today. Her breasts are like melons. And—"

"Melons? So unoriginal," Daniel said, shaking his head. "How is it again that we convinced everyone you're a poet?"

Gerard slapped him on the back too hard. "You always come through for me, Daniel. Don't think I don't appreciate it!"

Daniel guided Gerard to an empty table at the Juggler and asked Franny for dinner and ale. Franny gave Gerard a disapproving side-eye. "Drunk already, lad?"

"It's Elaine's fault. I had nothing to do with it." He settled his face on his hand and fluttered his long, curled lashes at Franny. "I was comforting her, if you must know. Her lady is to be wed, and Elaine will have to go with her to her new home. She's going to miss me. Isn't it tragic?"

Daniel stiffened as he realized who Mistress Elaine must work for. Franny shook her head and walked away. She was a good woman, taking care of them like a mother of wayward sons. Daniel supposed they both fit that description today, though most days, he thought himself wrongly accused. And today, it didn't matter one whit. Not if what he thought about Elaine's mistress was true.

"Can you remind me which lady it is that Elaine works for?" Daniel tried to keep his voice even and casual.

"The nun," Gerard said with mocking gravity.

"The nun?"

"Carenza. Not quite a nun but wishes she were. Tried to run away to the sisters today, according to Elaine." Gerard yawned without covering his mouth. "She's a scary woman, Daniel. Did you know she wears a skull necklace all the time to remind her of death? I don't like the thought of Elaine moving to a strange castle with just skull lady for company."

There could be no doubt. Carenza's intended was Lord de Broase. She was going to be married off to that murderer. "You do realize who Lady Carenza is marrying."

"What? Who? Oh no, not..." Gerard stared. "You mean

Elaine would be trapped in Hawkhurst with skull lady and him?" He paused, his eyes wide. "We have to kill him before the wedding."

"I'm glad you agree," Daniel said with a grim laugh.

"Oh, Elaine is going to be so grateful! Might even pleasure me with her mouth. I would like that, you know…" Gerard rested his head on his arms and started to drift off to sleep.

Daniel kicked his friend's chair under the table. He wanted to kick Gerard, but of course, he couldn't. He could never hurt the man. "And whatever happened to Philomena? Weren't you and she…"

"Her husband came back from the Crusade."

"And Joan?"

"Found a husband in haste. I offered, you know, but the woman wouldn't have me. Found out about Philomena and jilted me, even after I'd gotten her—"

"Stop. Just stop." Daniel took Gerard's ale and moved it out of his reach. "If you tell me more, I might have to hurt you. You are an unprincipled pig, you know that?"

Nodding in agreement, Gerard pulled a tragic face, his eyes dramatically fluttering. "Alas."

"I should find someone else, someone who won't use my verse for evil." Resisting the urge to roll his eyes, Daniel focused on his mug of ale and rubbed his thumb over the rim reflectively before turning back to the bard.

He was gladdened to see his ruse had worked. Gerard was suddenly sober and alert. "You wouldn't!"

"I might."

"You don't…" Gerard gulped. "You don't really mean that."

Daniel sighed. "No, I suppose I don't. But I don't like you using my poems to seduce innocent—"

"Innocent? I swear to you, Daniel, there isn't an innocent one in the bunch. I do have some honor, after all. Never had a virgin, never will. On my honor, I swear!"

Daniel burst out laughing. Gerard's honor! That was rich.

"Well, I do have a new song for you. It goes like this…"

CHAPTER FIVE

"ELAINE, ARE YOU drunk?" Carenza was late for dinner with the man her parents had chosen for her, and it was made worse when Elaine kept dropping hairpins on the floor.

It wasn't bad enough that Carenza's ankle was wrapped tightly and splinted, making everything even more awkward. Not only was she about to meet the man she had to marry against her will, but she could hardly stand and had to use a cane to walk.

Elaine's head dropped apologetically. "I'm sorry, my lady. It's that man. I can't resist a fop with a silver tongue."

"Gerard, is it? The one my sisters go all moony-eyed over?" Especially Alais. If her flirtation got any worse, Carenza might have to have a talk with Mother.

"The very one. He's just so pretty, and his songs make me want to do things I shouldn't. Please don't tell your sisters." Poor Elaine was bright red.

"Perish the thought." How could she ever begrudge Elaine? She remembered how wrecked Elaine was after her husband's sudden death two years ago. "If Gerard gives you joy, or even amusement, then I'm happy for you. It's Alais that I worry about."

"I don't think he'd ever dally with a lady."

"You're a lady."

"Barely. I may have married a knight, but now I'm only a

lady's maid and a widow." Elaine finally got Carenza's hair pinned up right and heaved a sigh of relief.

Carenza took Elaine's hand and squeezed it. "You're much more than a lady's maid and a widow to me. I'm just glad we were able to save you from penury and give you a good home when your husband passed."

Elaine patted her shoulder. "Thank you, my lady. I am forever in your debt."

"Nonsense. I'm forever in yours for saving me from the cook's son when we were children, and he tried to make me eat worms. And besides that, you may regret that I saved you when my parents marry me off, and we're forced to move somewhere strange and new."

Carenza looked around her bedroom, not for the first time wondering what it would be like to live somewhere else. The stone floor was strewn with rushes and fresh herbs. The walls were hung with tapestries of unicorns and maidens in gardens, the sort of nonsense her mother thought belonged in a daughter's room. Her mantle was bare except for a crucifix and her Bible. Her bed was covered in a plain, undyed wool blanket, one of her mother's few concessions to her preference for monastic austerity.

A heavily carved vanity with a tall mirror dominated the far wall of her bedroom. It was a bulky, gaudy piece. She hated it. It was her mother's addition, of course. For all her complaints about the furnishings, however, she was far from ready to leave this room behind forever. She heaved a long sigh as she reluctantly removed her pearls and skull and put on the sapphire necklace her mother had sent with Elaine and insisted be worn instead.

"Thank you for covering for me earlier, even if it didn't work out." She gave Elaine a quick hug. "But please don't make a habit of getting drunk in the middle of the day."

"I won't, my lady," Elaine said, staring at the floor. "But in my defense, I really didn't think you'd be back so soon. Last time, you were gone three days before they found you."

"Fair enough." As escape attempts went, this was definitely one of her worst.

"And I confess I don't fancy moving to Hawkhurst, my lady," Elaine added, a pleading look in her eye.

"Nor do I, Elaine." She sighed and shook her head.

"Well, you'd best get downstairs. The earl will be waiting." Elaine gave Carenza another hug, and Carenza put one limping foot in front of another, praying in her head: Dear Lord in heaven, let me remember death that I may take joy in life and the promise of eternity in Your presence. Amen. She hid her rosary in a pocket, clutching it for courage.

The great hall was brightly lit with ornate candelabras and braziers. Three tapestries hung on the northern wall, each showing a man and a woman holding hands, surrounded by an impossible abundance of evenly spaced, colorful spring flowers, piled one on top of another into the sky. The head table had three heavy candelabras, fully lit, and a roaring fire burned in the enormous hearth carved with mythical monsters. The spring air had not yet lost its chill.

The heavy wooden table could seat twenty, and the back of each seat was carved with the House de Vere coat of arms. Two other equally long tables extended perpendicular to the head table, Lord de Broase's men seated at one and her father's men at the other. Their voices echoed from the rafters of the high, vaulted ceiling. The head table's places were set with gleaming silver plates and filigreed silver goblets. Carenza's mother's family had brought those with them from Bordeaux and given them to her when she married.

Carenza's mother frequently picked up an empty goblet from her homeland and reminisced, reminding her daughters that she met her husband for the first time on their wedding day, and the following day, they set out for Winchelsea, a fifteen-day journey from her family's new home in Northumbria. Her daughters expected too much of life and didn't respect their duty to their family nearly enough. Carenza knew the lecture by heart.

So here she was, and there was the man she was to marry. And there were her mother and father. She had dressed. She had arrived. She couldn't bring herself to do anything more.

"Carenza, my dear!" Her mother stood up from the table with a false, ingratiating smile and wafted over to Carenza, who stood frozen in the doorway. "So glad you could join us!" She put her arm around Carenza and propelled her forward to meet Earl Raymond de Broase of Hawkhurst, supporting her to make the limp less obvious. Carenza managed a respectful, if awkward, curtsy and looked up for the first time at her husband-to-be.

He was a large man with a powerful build and dark, curled hair streaked with gray. He looked of an age with her father, as she expected. Though the man wore a smile, there was no warmth in his eyes. There was something familiar about his face, though she couldn't figure out who he reminded her of.

This was the man who would be her husband, who would end her aspirations to take holy orders. This was the man who would carry her off to a cold and distant castle where she knew no one. He would own her. She would have to lie with him and bear his children. The thought of him touching her sent a shiver down her back. There was something cold, almost reptilian, in his eyes. She froze beneath his gaze like a rabbit facing its fanged, slithering doom. I'll find another solution. I will. There has to be another way.

He rose and placed a perfunctory kiss on her hand, looking her up and down like she was prey. The touch of his lips made her want to flee as fast as she could, despite her injured ankle. Her heart beat wildly with fear, and cold sweat dripped down her back.

Maybe he'll find me wanting. Maybe he'll change his mind and decide he doesn't need a wife after all. He might not like me any more than I like him. Who would want a miserable wife?

"She'll do," he said to her father. "We'll marry in one month."

She couldn't stop herself from shuddering. Fortunately, no

one noticed. She had only one month until her life would cease to be her own. One month until she had to surrender her body to his invasion. One month until she became the third Lady de Broase, his broodmare for babies. Her dreams were dead.

She curtsied again and said, "My lord," unable to bring herself to say anything more. He ignored her completely.

Her mother clapped her hands together and made doe eyes. "Wonderful! I do love weddings. Let's eat and celebrate."

Her father gave Carenza a rueful look when her mother wasn't looking. She nodded back reassuringly. At least he felt bad about this.

She sat and pretended to eat, unable to settle her stomach and attend to the conversation. Her heartbeat roared in her ears, reminding her she was a living person with free will. She had a heart and a soul. Yes, she was being handed over like chattel, but her soul was still her own. She fingered the pearls of her rosary in the pouch on her belt, finding the skull bead and holding it tight as she prayed for the dinner to end.

The earl and her father spoke of trade and defense and the trouble with pirates, and not once through the whole meal did her prospective husband address himself to her. It couldn't be more clear. This marriage was not about a man and a woman. It was about farmland, ports, soldiers, and taxes. She was necessary for the sealing of the pact, but she had no part in its substance.

Was there any chance she could be wrong about him? Could he be a kind man? Would he be a good father to his children? Did he care about matters of the mind and soul as she did? Did he love poetry and song as she did? She suspected that the answer to all of these questions was no. He was a man who couldn't be bothered to say two sentences to his bride-to-be. At least, she prayed, let him not be cruel. Please let him not be cruel.

"Do you enjoy the entertainment of troubadours, my lord?" her mother asked partway through the main course of roast suckling pig.

"I'm afraid, my lady, that my responsibilities keep me far too busy to indulge in such things," he answered with a cold smile. "Once upon a time, I had a nephew that liked it, but I'm afraid he met with a tragic end."

"Oh dear. I'm so sorry, my lord." Her flustered mother placed her hand on her imposing chest in sympathy.

"Don't be. I loathed him." His voice dripped with disgust.

"Oh. Oh. Well."

Carenza had rarely seen her mother at a loss for words.

Attempting to recover herself, her mother squared her shoulders and smiled her most winning and artificial smile. "I hope that those feelings don't extend to troubadours in general. We're great patrons of the arts here, just like Queen Eleanor. You know I used to be a lady-in-waiting for her? I'm trying to follow her lead and enrich the troubadour tradition in England. Our local troubadours can't compare to the greats from my homeland, of course—Guillaume IX of Aquitaine, Marcabru, Bernart de Ventadorn… But they do quite well. I'm planning a little surprise for you tomorrow. I hope that you'll enjoy it."

"I'm sure I will, madame," he said with polite impatience, turning to her father. "Martin, you tell me that you've had difficulties with pirates and smugglers, but I don't see any heads on pikes around Winchelsea. Why haven't you made an example of any of these troublemakers? If I'm going to lend my assistance, I assure you I will not go so easy on them. A few public executions can do wonders when it comes to dissuading criminals."

The blood drained from Carenza's face, leaving her dizzy. She couldn't stay and listen to this. "Pardon me, Mother. I'm feeling unwell. May I be excused?"

"I'm sure our guest would prefer you to stay, my dear," her mother said with a strained smile.

Earl de Broase waved her away as if she were a fly. "She can go. In fact, both of you can go. I only want to talk with Martin."

Her mother turned crimson as she stood, ready to storm out.

"Isabella," her father said, catching her hand and giving it a squeeze. At least he was sorry about this, not that it changed a thing. Carenza's shoulders sagged.

"Goodnight, Earl de Broase," her mother said with a curtsy before she swept from the room without sparing Carenza a word or a look.

Fighting back tears, Carenza followed suit, desperate to escape. She limped back to her room to find a more sober Elaine waiting with open arms.

"That bad, was it?"

"I don't even know where to begin." She shuddered, remembering how casually he'd spoken of mounting heads on pikes.

"And did you speak to him? Maybe try to tell him you're a sea witch, as you did with that baron from Rye?"

Carenza sniffed and gave a small, sad laugh. "He didn't seem the sort to scare easily." She shook her head and wiped her tears. "Besides, Father made me promise I would do what's right for Winchelsea, at least tonight. It's going to take a miracle to get out of this."

"So then it sounds to me like you were very brave. You did your duty for your family and your people. You didn't run away."

"I ran away just hours ago." She was embarrassed by Elaine's kindness. Really, she didn't deserve it.

"All right, well, you didn't run away again," Elaine said, raising her eyebrows.

"I couldn't very well with this ankle."

"Take the compliment, my lady," Elaine insisted with a laugh. "You are brave, and you are doing your duty. You choose to do what has to be done even when it terrifies you. You may not be able to get out of this, but you can choose how you go about it. You'll be happier if you can find your way to choose this rather than being forced to do it."

Carenza thought about this as Elaine eased her out of her dress and jewels and into a clean shift. She clutched her rosary in her hand and lay down on the bed.

"Elaine, what is it like being married? What will my husband expect of me?"

Elaine turned bright red.

"No, Elaine, I don't mean that." As if she would embarrass poor Elaine with having to explain wifely duties! "Mother told me about that already. What I mean is—what does a husband want of his wife? What can a wife expect of her husband? How does a marriage of two souls come about when you start as two strangers?"

Elaine sat beside her on the bed and took her hand. "Well, I imagine the priest in the church will take care of your souls. And it seems your mother has discussed your...um...physical obligations. Most men want a woman to manage their home and bear their children. He'll expect you to give him your body from time to time. That's how the children come about. It can be quite pleasant if you are compatible. As for keeping his home and bearing his children, I expect you know more than enough about courtly life to run a high lord's house, and you've always had a way with children. I think you have nothing to fear."

Staring at the canopy, she couldn't help asking, "How do you know if you are compatible?"

Elaine turned bright red and was silent for a long time. "Well, I don't rightly know how to explain it, my lady."

"What about Gerard? Are you and he compatible?" She gave Elaine a mischievous smile.

Elaine patted her hand and smiled into her lap. "Now you're just teasing me, my lady."

Carenza feigned innocence and shrugged before she was overtaken by an equally false yawn. "I think I'll do a little writing before I go to bed. Thank you for everything."

Elaine curtseyed and left her alone.

Carenza wobbled over to her desk as soon as the door closed, pulling blank parchment from the drawer and turning the day's events over in her mind. She was betrothed. The man she was to marry was odious and cruel, but nonetheless, she was to marry him. She'd made one last attempt to escape, and it had failed. So here she was. She would sacrifice herself for Winchelsea and pray for fortitude. Or a miracle. Both would be nice. Perhaps the Lord might smite Lord de Broase. He seemed like the sort that could use a good smiting. She closed her eyes and mumbled a prayer, asking forgiveness for her un-Christian thoughts about her fiancé. Then, she humbly asked God for strength to follow the path He had laid out for her. Surely, He wouldn't have inspired her to pursue a holy life if He wished her to marry.

Taking a deep breath and tapping the feather of her quill against her cheek, she turned her thoughts to that curious encounter with the shipwright. He was hiding something, that was clear. Why had he been so angry about her hearing his verse? And how did a shipwright know anything at all about troubadour verse? Such a riddle, such a welcome distraction from her impending marriage.

Never in her life had Carenza been so grateful for a puzzle.

CHAPTER SIX

DANIEL SAT CROSS-LEGGED on the floor of the Juggler's attic, strumming his beloved lute, as Gerard fumbled the song lyrics for the fifth time in a row. The candle providing them with meager light had already burned halfway down, and Gerard still wasn't getting it right.

"It's 'The secrets of my heart were hidden in my art.' Not 'The secrets of my art were hidden in my heart.'" Daniel tried to keep his voice even, but his brother-in-law was truly on his last nerve.

"Why does it matter? Sounds the same to me." Gerard took a drink from his tankard and glared.

"Because it does."

Before Gerard could respond, Daniel plucked the opening chords again, a bit more loudly than he'd intended. Usually, playing the lute soothed him. He reveled in the delicate vibration of gut strings resonating in the lute's round, hollow belly. The shape of it was so comforting in his arms, almost like cradling a sleeping babe. And Gerard had a singing voice that could beguile the very angels in heaven. Daniel loved to hear his brother-in-law sing his compositions. But this evening, nothing seemed to settle him.

Gerard frowned. "You'd better give the lute to me before you break it."

Daniel would never break it. He'd made the lute himself when he was working as a shipwright's apprentice. The man he worked for had a brother who was a luthier, and after Daniel finished a day of hard labor, he'd spent many an evening learning the luthier's delicate craft. A lowly shipwright could never afford such a fine instrument otherwise. This was his most prized possession, and he would never let it come to harm.

"I'll give you the lute when you sober up enough to get the lyrics right."

"Maybe I'll get the lyrics right if you tell me why it matters so much." Gerard narrowed his eyes. "You aren't usually this fussed over a few minor mistakes. What's gotten into you?"

"Nothing." Why did he feel suddenly warm? "Nothing at all."

Certainly, it was not about a black-haired siren who had stumbled into his warehouse.

Gerard took another deep quaff from his tankard. "No, it's definitely something. Does this have to do with Lord de Broase? Do you have a plan to take him down?"

"Maybe." The cat wandered out from nearby barrels and rubbed up against Daniel's leg. He scratched its head absently as he pondered how much to bring Gerard in on the plan. It had been forming in his head all day. "I need an invitation to the castle, and I have an idea about how to get one. You see, I met someone today."

"Who?" Gerard's eyes sharpened.

Daniel took a deep breath in and then let it out slowly.

"Carenza de Vere," he said quietly.

Gerard's eyes widened until they looked like they were about to pop out of his head. "You're going to explain what the hell is going on right now."

Daniel picked up the cat and settled it in his lap, where it immediately curled up purring. Why was it so hard to tell Gerard about his day? It wasn't as if anything happened between him and Carenza. And perhaps she could be helpful to his plans to get into the castle. Yes, it would involve seeing her again, and no, he wouldn't mind that. But the point of his plan was to gain access to his uncle, not to spend time with a beautiful woman.

"Well? I'm waiting."

Daniel sighed and told Gerard about his meeting with Carenza de Vere the day before last and then revealed his plan to get an invite to the castle. He meant to stick to the facts but found himself meandering into dangerous waters. "She wasn't what I expected."

"What does that mean? Why would you expect anything at all? Since when did you have opinions about Baron de Vere's daughters?"

"I didn't, until I met her. She's too smart for her own good. I don't know how she saw through me so quickly, but from her first words, it was clear she knew I was composing troubadour lyrics." Daniel shrugged and shook his head. "For years, we've kept up this ruse, and no one has suspected, but somehow, she knew I was your poet after listening to me sing a few verses while I worked. And she is either incredibly brave or unbelievably foolish to wander around the docks like that, a beautiful girl in all her finery. Another man might not have been able to control himself in the face of such temptation." He tried to keep his expression carefully blank.

"You complete idiot!" Gerard groaned and took another deep drink.

"I can't help that the woman chose to hide in my warehouse! And how could I ignore the opportunity fate presented me to get an invitation to the castle?" It was no excuse, and he knew it.

"What's your plan? I can tell already I'm not going to like it."

No, he wasn't, but Daniel needed his help. "When you sing the song I'm teaching you right now, she's going to know it's from me." He paused to give Gerard a pointed look. Well, she would, if you could keep the words straight. I think she'll ask you, and you'll be able to talk her into giving me an invitation to perform as a troubadour."

Daniel looked up to see heavy storm clouds on Gerard's

usually insouciant face.

"Let me get this straight. You want to send me to sing her a bloody love song in front of her fiancé, who also just happens to have murdered both of our families." Gerard raised an eyebrow. Understandably, Daniel supposed.

He nodded slowly. "I'm sorry, Gerard. I know I shouldn't put you in this position, but it's the quickest way I can think of to get an invitation to the castle. My uncle will be too well-guarded when he goes out. This will give me the access I need."

They both took long drinks.

Gerard put his tankard down with a thunk. "Why not disguise yourself as a servant?"

Gerard had a point.

"The other servants would know immediately that I didn't belong," Daniel said after a moment. "Though maybe your Mistress Elaine might be able to help me?"

Shaking his head vigorously, Gerard said, "I'm not getting her mixed up in this." He sat back against a barrel, arms folded. "How are you sure Carenza will take the bait?"

Daniel couldn't be sure, but he strongly suspected she would. It terrified him how much he needed her to, not only because of his plan but because of how intoxicating it was to be seen. He was tired of being invisible. In the warehouse, she'd seen him for who he was, and it was thrilling after all these years.

"I think she will."

"Did something more than you're telling me happen in that warehouse?" Gerard cocked his head and raised both his eyebrows.

Daniel jerked his head back. "Of course not. Who do you think I am?"

"A very lonely man," Gerard said, shaking his head.

Closing his eyes, Daniel took a deep breath. Sometimes, Gerard saw altogether too much. "You know I can't afford friends or companionship of any kind. I can't put others at risk. My uncle would only use my attachments against me. Look what happened to Adele and your father."

"And yet you keep me close," Gerard said with a teasing smile.

His brother-in-law meant it as a joke, but the words cut him deep. Had Daniel not thought the very same thing on many an occasion? Was it caring or selfishness that made him keep Gerard close when he kept all others at arm's length?

"I do it to keep you safe. I couldn't leave you on your own when you were a boy of twelve who had just lost his family. It was my fault they died."

"Not your fault, as we've discussed a hundred times," Gerard said quickly. "Your uncle's fault. The blame lies entirely with him."

"Everyone I've ever loved has died." Daniel's father, his mother, his guardian, his wife…

"Thank heavens you don't love me." The sadness in Gerard's eyes belied his mocking smile.

Daniel met his friend's gaze and sighed. "Of course, I love you, you idiot. Why do you think I've worked so hard to keep you safe all these years? Who kept you fed when you'd lost everything? Who worked night and day to keep a roof over your head when you had nothing? Who taught you to play the lute and turned you into one of the most popular troubadours in Kent so that you'd have a means of supporting yourself in case anything ever happened to me? Lord knows you've never been cut out for manual labor."

Gerard rolled his eyes. "Not this again. Are you about to give me your 'wastrel' speech? Because I already know it by heart. I'm a grown man now, and it's none of your business how much I drink or who I tup. We can't all be paragons of virtue like you. And maybe you'd be a bit less grumpy if you indulged in a little company from time to time. There are certainly plenty of willing wenches. You should have heard what Cecilia said about you the other day. I—"

"Enough. I'm not tupping Cecilia, no matter how many times

she tries to corner me in the larder. It's for her own safety. My uncle wouldn't hesitate to dispatch a serving wench if he found out. Look what he did to your sister to stop her from producing an heir that might threaten him."

Gerard held up his hands. "All right. All right. But you're missing out. Sarding Cecilia is a pleasure and a joy. There's this thing she does with her tongue—"

"Stop. I don't want to know." It was a good thing Gerard was family. Otherwise, he might be tempted to strangle him about now.

"All I'm saying is that if you indulged in a little female companionship, you might not be panting after the baron's daughter right now, writing her love songs and risking your life to catch another glimpse."

"This isn't about her. It's about my uncle. If she invited me to perform as a troubadour, I'd be able to corner him alone and end his miserable life."

"Mmhmm." Gerard's grin was too knowledgeable and, especially, too annoying.

Enough of this. "Look, are you going to help me or not? Do I have to find another way into the castle?"

Gerard looked at him with narrowed eyes for a long moment, then sighed. "Yes, I'll help you. I want to see de Broase dead as much as you do, and it's not as if I have a better plan. But I still say your motives are highly suspect."

"I don't care why you help me as long as you do," Daniel said, picking up the lute and gently nudging the cat from his lap. "Now, let's try this again."

CHAPTER SEVEN

THE NEXT MORNING, Carenza joined her sisters for breakfast in the solar. The space was bright with morning light from the southern-facing windows. Her mother's loom stood against the wall with her latest tapestry half-finished. Embroidery projects lay haphazardly on a side table beside a basket full of threads of varied colors. Carenza's lute leaned against the wall in the corner. While her father had defiantly affixed a map of Winchelsea and the surrounding lands to the northern wall, he had otherwise failed to make a mark on this overwhelmingly feminine space. Long ago, he'd given up on using the solar for his own work, preferring his study downstairs.

No sooner did Carenza sit down at the simple, utilitarian table than she was immediately assaulted with questions.

"Carenza, what happened yesterday?" Alais demanded, as she dipped her bread in pottage. "I heard you ran away again. Who caught you?"

"I twisted my ankle down by the ferry, and Bertrand found me," Carenza said, taking a sip of watered-down ale. "It was fairly humiliating. And then I had to appear at dinner with Lord de Broase, limping like an old woman. Not my finest hour."

"What was Lord de Broase like?" Iselda asked. "Will he make a good husband?"

"It's hard to say," she said, choosing her words carefully. "We didn't really speak much."

"I saw him in the hallway, and he looked very handsome for an older man," Alais said.

Carenza gave Alais a level stare. "You marry him, then."

"Papa said I couldn't," Alais said, as if it didn't much matter. "Anyway, I'd much prefer someone younger."

Alais didn't mean to be cruel and thoughtless, Carenza knew, but it hurt how little her sister recognized the depth of the sacrifice she was being asked to make. A knot of frustration formed in Carenza's throat, forcing her to clear it loudly. "Well, I am hopeful that if I marry Lord de Broase, you two will get to make your own choices about who and whether to marry." Unlike me. "You should consider yourselves lucky. This marriage will secure your freedom to choose."

"Well, I'm not choosing to be a nun. I know that much," Alais declared, pointing her bread at Carenza.

"I didn't think you would." Carenza tried not to roll her eyes.

"I'm going to marry someone young and handsome who worships my beauty and covers me in jewels," Alais said dreamily. This time, Carenza did roll her eyes. "He'll be tall and slender with soft brown curls and big brown eyes and long lashes. He'll write poems, and—"

"Alais, it sounds very much like you're describing that troubadour, Gerard. Please tell me you're not pining after that pathetic rogue," Carenza said, pinning Alais with her most disapproving glare.

Iselda giggled. "Oh, she is. She talks about him constantly." She made kissy noises at Alais, who stuck out her tongue.

"Alais, you know how completely unsuitable he is in every possible way. He may be noble if his story about being the fifth son of a bankrupt baron is to be believed, but he is certainly penniless, and besides that, I have reason to believe his heart is otherwise engaged. You can't seriously think—"

"I never said anything about marrying Gerard, just someone who looks like him," said Alais, airily dismissing Carenza. "But tell me what you know about where his heart is engaged. Who is it? Tell me, tell me, tell me, pleeeeeeease!"

"It's none of your business," Iselda cut in. "I'm sure whatever she knows was told to her in confidence, and you have no right to pry." Carenza gave a grateful nod of agreement. "Carenza, can you pass me a piece of the pear tart, please?"

"Of course." She served Iselda a generous portion.

"Can I have some, too?" asked Alais.

"Get it yourself," she replied.

Alais gave her a withering look and cut herself a piece of tart. "Speaking of Gerard, his poems have been really good lately, haven't they? But I wonder why his performances are so uneven. Sometimes, he's simply brilliant, and sometimes, it's just one cliché after another. Something seems to make him lose his nerve." She chewed thoughtfully. "I know! It must be his lady love. I bet he loses his nerve when she is in the audience. We just have to watch for a pattern, and then we'll be able to figure out who this woman is." Alais looked inordinately pleased with her cleverness.

Carenza kept her mouth shut. Her own suspicions about Gerard's uneven performance were sharpening the more she thought about it, but she wasn't going to say a word about that to her sisters.

"Nerves must have something to do with it," Iselda mused, "though I'm not sure about your theory on his lady love. Remember that time Mother had Carenza challenge him to a rhyming competition? A child in leading strings could have come up with better nursery rhymes than he did. And there were no ladies there but the three of us and mother. It can't be one of us."

Alais gasped and dropped her spoon, her eyes wide. "Carenza, it's you!"

Carenza stared at Alais. "You must be joking."

"No, it fits! He's in love with you! He completely fell to pieces that day." Alais radiated triumph.

"No, it's not me," Carenza said firmly. "And for my part, I

think he's just very bad at improvising. Perhaps he needs time to refine his rhymes, and his poor performances are the result of lack of preparation."

"No, he's in love with you. I'm certain of it." Alais nodded with unshakable conviction.

"Well, it hardly matters one way or the other, as she's marrying Lord de Broase," Iselda said.

"And when has marriage to another ever dissuaded a troubadour? In fact, they seem to prefer married women," Alais said, narrowing her eyes.

"You're incorrigible," Carenza grumbled, rising from the table. "I'm going to go pray for your soul."

True to her word, she headed downstairs to the chapel and spent the remainder of the day in prayer, only taking a short break for lunch. She wasn't praying for her sister, though. She was praying for a miracle. There was no hope of saving herself from marriage to Lord de Broase without Divine Intervention. All other paths to escape had been cut off, but she could still pray and hope, however slim that hope might be.

Dear Lord in heaven, let me remember death that I may take joy in life and the promise of eternity in Your presence. Let me live a life that pleases You. I feel the calling that You have put in my heart to dedicate my life to You. Please help me find a way to follow the path You have laid out for me without shirking my duty to my family and my people. Was it a sign that I tripped and twisted my ankle on my way to the abbey? Do You want me to follow my parents' will instead of taking holy orders? I humbly place myself in Your almighty hands. Amen.

Again and again, she prayed, her rosary beads clicking through her fingers at a slow and steady pace. Her knees ached from kneeling. Her neck was stiff from holding her head bowed. But still, she stayed. Her awareness of the world retreated, and she lost herself in the rhythm of prayer, feeling a growing sense of communion with the Divine. Her earthly concerns faded, and a new sense of peace and equanimity filled her.

At least, until Alais poked her in the side to tell her it was time for dinner.

Carenza did her best to hold on to the calm she had found in the chapel as she headed to the great hall behind her sister, but unfortunately, it had unraveled completely by the time she was seated beside her mother. This evening followed the pattern of the previous one, except that this time, her sisters joined. It was another awkward dinner during which she was completely ignored beyond bland niceties. Lord de Broase expounded at length on the bloody tactics he used to keep the peace in his extensive territories. Her stomach churned.

After dinner, her mother signaled a servant to usher in three troubadours to perform. One of them was Gerard. Of course. Alais elbowed her in the ribs, and she sent back a withering look.

"Lord de Broase," her mother announced, "We are honored by your presence this evening." At the mention of the earl's name, Carenza noticed something harden in Gerard's gaze, but a moment later, it was gone, replaced by his usual insouciance. "Here in Winchelsea," her mother continued, "we are great patrons of the arts, and these are but a few of the troubadours that visit our halls. For you, we have invited the very best."

"Thank you, Lady de Vere. You honor me," Lord de Broase replied, grimacing like he was trying to ignore a toothache.

Lady de Vere turned to the troubadours. "Gentlemen, you may commence," she told them and sat to enjoy the performance.

Gerard stood and began to strum his lute. He caught her eye and smiled mischievously. Goodness gracious! Had anyone else noticed? What did he mean by it?

Carenza glanced at Alais, whose eyes had assumed a glassy, dreamy look with the very first chord. She gave her a little kick and got a sour look in return, so she gave her sister an innocent smile. Although this was an agonizing evening for many reasons, at least she could use it as an opportunity to torture Alais. The more she thought about it, the more convinced she was that

Gerard was singing work composed by someone else, at least on the good days. It was even possible it might have been her secret rescuer who was responsible for those words. The bad days were all his, she suspected. Would her rescuer reveal himself in some way?

"I have a song to sing
Of a bird that took wing
and chanced to hear my verse
While I did rehearse.
The secrets of my heart
Were hidden in my art."

Carenza's eyes widened, and she fought to keep her breathing even. She'd never expected the shipwright to be so bold. It had to be him. Who else would speak of a "gentle bird" that chanced to hear his verse? Her face flushed, and the bodice of her gown was suddenly too tight. Would other people notice her reaction? She glanced around surreptitiously at the others sitting around her. No, they were all watching the performance with rapt attention except Earl de Broase, who was picking at his nails.

She was so absorbed in thought that she forgot to pay attention to several stanzas. When she regained the thread, he was wrapping up a verse:

"Come rest beneath my wing
While I beguile your heart."

Oh my. Had she made more of an impression than she thought?

"Another claims your heart,
Yet I composed this verse."

She had told him she was running away from a marriage she

didn't want. Was he trying to win her away from Lord de Broase? He had to know how hopeless that was, though the mere thought made her heart race. Or was he just playing a game? Troubadours always sang of love, and they never meant it. Oh dear, she'd missed another stanza.

"Do not make me rehearse
The reasons why my heart
Is trembling as I sing.
You'll recognize my verse,
Or I have lost the art
Of making words take wing."

A game, then. Or perhaps a dare.

"Caught as you took wing,
You asked why I rehearse.
Now I must use my art
To steal back my heart.
I send this secret verse
To her who makes me sing."

What was she to do with his secret verse? Why was he doing this? What could he possibly gain?

"You've driven me to sing.
I've given you my verse.
Now, give me back my heart."

The song ended. She applauded with everyone else, hoping no one noticed how deeply she was blushing. Fortunately, Gerard didn't show any signs of giving away the game. It truly was a secret communication, delivered in plain sight. It was skillfully done, she had to admit.

"Gerard," she called after him as he turned to sit, "that was an unusual rhyme structure. Very complex. I've never heard anything like it."

"It's called a sestina. It's a French invention." He gave her a conspiratorial smile.

"Well, it was very clever," she said, adding a touch of admonition to her own smile.

"Thank you for your praise, my lady. That is the highest of compliments coming from you." He bowed and took his seat.

Carenza hardly even heard the other performers. One sang an old tune about two horses that was full of obscene double-entendres. The other sang the usual boasts about how he was better than all the other troubadours and therefore more deserving of his lady's love. Carenza was too busy pondering Gerard's song and the puzzling man who wrote it, and she was surprised when everyone stood up, the evening apparently over.

As she started to make her way toward the door, Gerard stepped close and murmured in her ear, "I know a secret troubadour that wants to see you again. Invite him to the castle to perform, and he'll come."

Her heart raced at a furious pace at his words. What should she say? Her mother and Lord de Broase were looking on.

"I can't discuss this now," she whispered quickly. He nodded and turned to joke with another performer. She needed to leave before anyone noticed how ruffled she was.

Limping over to Lord de Broase, she bid him goodnight. Fortunately, there was nothing in his manner to suggest he noticed anything amiss. He was as cold and uncaring as always. Her mother gave her a speculative look but said nothing. Desperate for privacy, she started the long walk to her upstairs bedroom moving as quickly as her injury would allow.

And, just her luck, Alais hung back to walk with her. "I knew it was you, and now I have my proof," she said, offering her arm to Carenza as they climbed the stairs to help her walk faster.

Carenza's heart beat faster still. Alais couldn't possibly suspect the truth, could she?

"I have no idea what you're talking about," Carenza said, gritting her teeth at the pace her sister set.

"I saw you blushing while Gerard sang. He hardly looked at you, but of course he wouldn't if he was trying to hide his true aim," Alais said, wide-eyed and waggling her eyebrows.

Alais was just guessing. She had to be. "You were blushing more. Don't think I didn't see you." Maybe going on the attack would distract her?

Alais sighed. "I can't help it. He's just too pretty. And when he sings, it's like he's singing directly to me."

Carenza smiled and patted Alais' arm, relieved her deflection had worked. "You'll find the right man someday. And I promise he'll be a far better catch than Gerard." She gave her sister a little hug as she turned into her room. "Goodnight, Alais!"

"Goodnight, Carenza," Alais said as she flounced down the hall to her room.

Carenza sighed with relief as she watched her sister go.

Elaine was waiting when Carenza finally closed the door behind her. She could talk to Elaine, who she knew would keep her secrets, just as she kept Elaine's. She slumped onto the bed, unable to stay on her injured ankle a moment longer.

"Oh dear, that looks swollen," Elaine said, taking off Carenza's slipper and propping her foot up on the bed.

"It's the least of my troubles, believe me," she said with a groan. "Elaine, I have a favor to ask. I'm going to write a letter, and I need you to give it to Gerard. He can read it; in fact, he'll have to, but it isn't for him. He'll know who to give it to. Tell him that if there's a response to my letter, he should give it to you, and you'll pass it along. Will you help me?"

"Ooh, secret correspondence. Of course, I'll help! Though my price for entering into this conspiracy is that I want to know everything. You know I'll keep your secrets, but first, I need to know them."

So Carenza told her everything, blushing furiously, while Elaine helped her prepare for bed.

"Gerard's verses aren't his own?" Elaine asked at the end. "That's disappointing, though I suppose I should have realized." She shook her head. "I'll forgive him, though, as long as he keeps whispering sweet words in my ear, and kissing me with those pretty lips…"

"Elaine!"

Elaine rolled her eyes. "I'll help you find your poet, my lady. Maybe he'll teach you about kissing and give you a little joy before you have to marry that awful earl."

Carenza gasped, scandalized by the mere thought.

"And you don't even know his name?"

"No, I don't," she said, the heat of a blush staining her cheeks. "Can you bring the ink, quill, and parchment over here so that I can write in bed? Better bring a tray, too, so I have something to write on."

"I'll retire, then, my lady," Elaine said with a smile, leaving her to compose the most dangerous letter she'd ever written.

CHAPTER EIGHT

"DANIEL! DANIEL! I need to talk to you," Gerard shouted over the din of shipwrights at work. Today, he was dressed in a lurid pattern of green-and-black diamonds that his first patroness, a noble widow from Dover, had commissioned for him. Several of the men Daniel worked with pointed and laughed at Gerard's getup.

Daniel excused himself, hastily pulled on his shirt and tunic, and came running. "What is it, Gerard? Is it de Broase?"

"You need to read this," he said, handing Daniel a scroll. "I suggest you sit down."

They perched on barrels outside the warehouse. Daniel unrolled the parchment. On one side, it said, "For the poet behind the poet." On the other was a poem. Daniel mouthed the words as he read:

"There's a song that I heard
From a strange mockingbird
About meeting by chance
And romance at a glance.
Since you know my name,
You owe me the same."

Daniel smiled as he read the rest of the poem in silence.

When he finished, he looked up at Gerard, who was biting his nails. "I must admit I'm impressed. She copied my rhyme scheme from last night and made it her own. It was well done." After a moment, he added, "She wasn't foolish enough to give this to you herself, was she?"

"No, of course not. Elaine gave it to me, though I can't say I'm happy about her involvement. Now she knows my verses aren't always my own, which is rather embarrassing."

Ah. Daniel hadn't thought about that. It would be disastrous for Gerard's success as a troubadour if word got out that his songs weren't his own. A mere minstrel couldn't earn nearly so much in patronage. But Elaine had reason to keep his secret, as did Carenza. The letter Daniel held in his hands could destroy Carenza's reputation if anyone found out about it, which would be detrimental to them both.

"I had no way to know she'd involve Elaine. For that, I am truly sorry."

Gerard gave him a pointed look. "Fortunately, Elaine has forgiven me. She gave me a kiss and a spank and told me she'd keep my secret so long as I keep this letter discreet. And I don't suppose anyone knows except for Elaine and Carenza. If it goes no further, I can keep performing as a troubadour."

"They have nothing to gain and everything to lose if anyone hears about this letter, so I think you're safe," he said, clapping a reassuring hand on Gerard's shoulder.

"I still think infiltrating the servants might have been the safer way to go."

Daniel ran his hand through his hair.

"You're right. That's probably what I should do. But Carenza is in my head, and I can't stop thinking about her and de Broase and the awful life that awaits her as his bride and I…. I…" He paused and took a deep breath. "I want to give her something that is just for her, something to make her smile before her life turns into a living hell." He sighed.

"Look, I want you to be happy," Gerard said, suddenly serious. "I would love to see you find love again—"

Daniel stiffened. "You know I'll always love Adele." Even now, it hurt to speak her name aloud. The pain of that loss would always be with him.

"I loved my sister too, but it's been six years. It's all right for you to move on." Gerard gave him a pensive look. "Though maybe not to Carenza de Vere."

Daniel laughed mirthlessly. Carenza was out of the question for so many reasons. Even if his heart wasn't broken beyond all healing, she was far beyond the reach of a mere shipwright. And since he had taken an oath never to claim his name and title, that was all he would ever be. Carenza de Vere was not for him, no matter how much she might occupy his thoughts.

Gerard tilted his head and gave him a speculative look. "So now that you've started this foolishness... Are you going to write her back?"

Daniel let out a long, slow breath, unable to form a response. This was a dangerous game he was playing, but having begun, he couldn't bring himself to stop. He probably could get into the castle disguised as a servant with some careful planning, but trading verse with Carenza to win an invitation held so much more appeal.

"That wasn't an answer," Gerard said, narrowing his eyes. "You want to keep this going, don't you? You're going to ignore my simple and sensible solution, and you're going to write her back."

However much Daniel wanted to deny it, Gerard was right. He wanted this. He was already planning and composing. The return letter was half written in his mind. He shouldn't send it. He couldn't send it. And yet...

"Christ's teeth, Daniel," Gerard said, dropping his face to his hands. "And I thought you were the responsible one."

Daniel kept silent, thinking about the delicate curve of Carenza's neck, imagining its silky softness beneath his lips. He shook himself when he realized what he was doing. "I'm sorry. I don't know what's come over me."

"I do. Why can't you just go tup a friendly tavern wench, like a normal man?"

Daniel gritted his teeth and clenched his fists, tamping down the familiar urge to punch his brother-in-law in the face. Gerard leaned back out of reach, as if reading his thoughts.

"Fine," Gerard said, throwing his hands up. "Fine. Do this stupid thing. As you say, no one knows about any of this except her and Elaine. I can vouch for Elaine. She won't tell tales."

Daniel stood up and began pacing. He couldn't stay still. He couldn't sit with all the thoughts boiling inside him—snippets of verse, revenge plots, the sweet scent of almonds and spice, the heat of Carenza pressed against his chest, curled in his arms…

Gerard watched him with a furrowed brow. "I suppose it can't hurt to give her ladyship a few more smiles before we kill her future husband. Come to think of it, seducing de Broase's fiancée is a rather delicious revenge."

"I'm not seducing her for revenge."

"Ah, so you admit you are seducing her."

"No."

Maybe.

He could pretend all he wanted, but deep down, he knew exactly what he wanted to do. He wanted to kindle a flame in her to match the one she'd set within him, use his words to make her crackle and spark. He wanted to haunt her dreams as she had begun to haunt his. It was complete madness, but there was no denying what was in his heart.

"So, you are going to write?"

Daniel gave the tiniest of nods.

"God's blood," Gerard grumbled. "You're a madman. Just promise me one thing."

"What?" This conversation needed to end, and Daniel needed to go back to work before Marcel got angry. Besides, the comforting distraction of working with his hands would stop his mind from straying where it shouldn't.

"For God's sake, don't fall in love with her. That's the last thing we need."

Ignoring the way his heart skipped a beat at Gerard's words, Daniel smiled. "There's little danger of that. She's completely out of my reach." Thank God. Or else the temptation might have been too much.

Gerard arched an eyebrow. "As long as you remember that."

"I gave an oath to forswear my title when I married your sister. I've kept it all these years, haven't I?" What did Gerard think he was going to do—claim his title and court Carenza de Vere? Ridiculous. "I'm a simple shipwright. Nothing is going to change that. She's as far beyond my reach as the moon and the stars."

No need to mention how very close she'd been in his rather torrid dreams last night.

"Good." Gerard clapped him on the shoulder. "Don't forget it. I should be going. I promised Elaine I would take her out for luncheon at the Lute and Tambour. The proprietor offered me a free meal if I entertain his guests tonight. I'll see you anon."

Daniel watched his friend saunter off along Fish Street and turn onto Castle Street. He needed Gerard's warning more than he liked to admit. It wasn't only Carenza's beauty that captivated him but her quick mind and the way she seemed to see into his soul with those dark, sparkling eyes.

Shaking himself, he turned and entered the warehouse, where he was greeted by the sweet smell of wood mixed with the pungent stink of sweaty men. Shedding his shirt and tunic once again, he picked up an axe and went to work, welcoming the singularity of focus that always came when he did physical work.

"Where does that fancy friend of yours get his clothes?" Marcel called out over the din of woodwork from the opposite end of the log Daniel was working on. "You couldn't pay me enough to wear that fool's motley."

Chuckling, Daniel called back, "He's my brother-in-law, unfortunately. He has about as much fashion sense as common sense, but the ladies up at the castle love him."

"Lucky him. Have you seen those de Vere girls? Ripe as summer peaches, they are. Not that I've had more than a passing glance. The baron guards them well, as he should with treasures like that."

At the mention of the de Veres, Daniel's hackles went up. Marcel meant no harm, but it bothered him to hear them spoken of so. "I'm sure it's none of our business what the young ladies look like. What happens at the castle is none of our affair." He said this to remind himself as much as Marcel.

"True. The closest the likes of us would ever get is the ladies at the Bird in Hand. Am I right?" Marcel said with a wink.

Daniel had heard of that brothel, and thank God, he'd never been. They specialized in famous ladies, past and present, including a saucy, redheaded Queen Eleanor. He'd heard rumors they also had a Carenza, an Alais, and an Iselda, but he'd never given them credence. How could the baron allow something so brazen right under his nose?

"I wouldn't know. I've never been."

His axe was dull, and he stepped away to use a whetstone while Marcel continued to do finer work with a plane. Daniel hoped it would put an end to this uncomfortable conversation. It made him altogether too angry to think of the dock workers and sailors swiving Carenza in effigy.

"I forgot. You live like a monk," said Marcel, grinning, when Daniel returned from sharpening his axe. "You never drink to excess. You don't chase the ladies. What do you do for pleasure? There must be something."

Marcel was a good man, but Daniel didn't dare reveal too much of himself. Still, he had to give some account of himself. "I make up songs," he said at last. "It occupies my mind and keeps me out of trouble."

Except when it got him in trouble, like that song he wrote for Carenza. Her letter was tucked neatly into the money pouch on his belt, burning a hole in it. What a hypocrite he was, pretending to stay away from the de Vere daughters and out of the castle's affairs when he was in the midst of flirting with Lady Carenza so that he could kill his uncle, the Earl of Hawkhurst.

"Making up songs, eh? What an odd way for a man to spend his time," said Marcel, scrunching up his face. "But I suppose there's no harm in it. Why don't you sing us something? The men like a good song to work by."

Daniel racked his brain. What had he composed that would suit the moment? His songs were all about courtly love, intended for the halls of nobility, not a shipwright's warehouse. Not a thing came to mind. He would simply have to improvise something.

Banishing all thoughts except words and rhymes, he began:

"One day, a pretty maid walked by.
She winked at me and caught my eye.
When I winked back, I made her sigh.
But my heart belongs to the deep blue sea.
I walked away and left her there
Despite her sweet come-hither stare.
But nothing could bring me to care,
For my heart belongs to the deep blue sea."

The rhythm of the men's axes and chisels shifted to follow his verse, and several shouted out in appreciation. Daniel raised his axe and began to chop in time to the song with the rest of them. As he continued to spin his verse, all his cares seemed to wash away. He could almost forget the letter in his pouch, the arrival of his uncle, and the seductive vision of a skull nestled between soft and tender breasts. The music carried him, and the challenge of composing occupied his restless mind. As long as the song continued, he was merely a shipwright enjoying hard work and camaraderie with his fellow workers.

After more verses than he could count, his voice grew hoarse, and he was forced to bring the song to a conclusion. The men all shouted and called for more. When he refused, they launched into their usual repertoire of tavern songs, and the hours of the day passed with remarkable speed.

Before he knew it, the day's work was done, and the sun was going down. He hung up his axe and put his shirt and tunic back on, forced to leave behind the temporary reprieve that work had offered him.

The moment he stepped onto Fish Street, all his worries returned, first among them how he was going to answer that bold little verse Carenza had sent. Knowing Gerard was occupied for the evening, he made his way up to their attic room, lit a candle, and sat down at his desk. He pulled his crow-feather quill from the clay jar where he kept it, dipped it in his ink pot, and began to write.

CHAPTER NINE

AFTERNOON LIGHT FILTERED in through the stained-glass windows on the north and west sides of the chapel. Candles flickered on the altar, and the smell of incense permeated everything. "My lady," a breathless Elaine whispered as she squeezed into the chapel pew beside Carenza.

"Are you here to pray with me?" Carenza asked. Elaine went to mass on Sundays, but she wasn't overly prone to piety during the week.

"No," Elaine said, checking again that they were alone as she drew a rolled parchment from her sleeve. "I just received this, and I brought it straight to you."

It had been three days since Carenza had sent her secret letter. She had started to think there would be no reply. Now, here it was. She was hesitant to touch it. Touching it meant accepting its existence, accepting that she had invited it, asked for it. She should burn it unread. She should…

No, she wanted to know. She plucked it from Elaine's hand and opened it in a rush.

"Lady, you saw through me
On the day we met,
And I cannot forget
Your sharp wit and beauty.

If you want my name,
I'll tell it if you swear
That this is not a snare
And that it's safe to claim."

That was all. One stanza. No answers. She took a deep, shuddering breath and handed it to Elaine.

Elaine read. "That's it?" she asked, turning the page over, looking for more. "Not very illuminating. He did comment on your wit and beauty. I suppose that's something."

"Barely."

"So, what now? Will you write him back?"

"In time. He made me wait. I can't reply in haste. Can you keep the letter for me? I don't dare take the risk of getting caught with it."

"Of course, my lady." Elaine tucked it away and left Carenza to her contemplation.

Infuriating man. A handful of pretty words to say nothing. Why did he even bother? And what was he hiding? Clearly, there was a reason he didn't dare show his face or share his name. She wanted to march down to Fish Street right then and demand answers. After half an hour of seething instead of praying, she gave up and limped back upstairs to her room, where she pulled out a fresh piece of parchment from her desk drawer and began to compose.

"I won't betray your trust.
Your name is safe with me.
Pray, listen to my plea.
I'll swear what oaths I must."

She needed to know. She hungered to know.

"You said I stole your heart,
And drove you to compose.

But I propose you chose
To pose and play a part."

There was no reason to let him think she had been taken in. She wasn't a fool. And even if there was a seed of truth in his song the other night, it was unwise for either of them to pretend it was anything other than a game. Certainly, she didn't intend to admit in writing that his words moved her, that they left her breathless and restless. No. It was simply a game.

When Elaine came in later to check on her, she handed off the letter with instructions not to deliver it for three days. Three days. That meant she would most likely have to wait six until she received a response. He wouldn't want to seem hasty in his response. Six days of being cooped up in the castle with her parents and Lord de Broase, being paraded out at mealtimes but never invited to speak. Thanks to her ankle, she couldn't go for a ride in the countryside or visit the poor and sick and bring them aid. All she could do was eat and pray and wait.

On the fifth day, she knelt in the chapel pretending to pray but actually composed an extended diatribe on the evils of marriage. Elaine came in and handed her a tiny scroll.

"He's early?" Carenza asked in disbelief.

"So it seems. Eager even, my lady. A whole day early."

"Hmph." Carenza grabbed the note and glanced over each shoulder to ensure privacy.

"Lady, you're too fair

For me to remain strong.

I can't resist for long

When you lay out your snare.

When your last missive came,

You swore not to betray.

I'll trust this once and say

That Daniel is my name."

"Daniel," she whispered, handing it to Elaine. "So now I know his name, but still don't know a thing about how a shipwright ended up a secret troubadour."

"He answered the question you asked. Next time, you'll have to ask a better one." Elaine handed the poem back to her.

"Next time? I should quit now. This is too dangerous. I'm the world's biggest fool for entertaining this nonsense. Elaine, why am I doing this? This isn't who I am. I don't send secret letters to strange men. No good can come of this. I should just stop. Why can't I?"

Elaine took her hand. "Does he make you smile? Do you enjoy what he writes? Do you enjoy writing back?"

Carenza sighed.

"You deserve a bit of joy as much as any other woman. Hang onto it. A little romance is good for the soul, my lady, even if nothing can ever come of it."

"That's not how the priest tells it."

"Never mind the priest. What does he know of a woman's soul?" Elaine crossed herself. "Don't tell him I said that."

After dinner that evening, Carenza sat at her desk, composing yet another response.

"Daniel, where are you from?
Where did you learn your art?
Your verses are too smart.
From what court did you come?
You are a troubadour.
Why hide your gift away
When patronage could pay
You ever so much more?"

The next morning, she gave it to Elaine as she was getting dressed. "I probably asked too many questions. I might scare him away. But I can't help it. I'm so curious. I can't stop thinking about him."

"Just curious, my lady? No other feelings mixed in?" Her maid gave her a playful smile.

"Don't test me."

Two days later, Elaine handed her another scroll as she was getting ready for dinner. "Well, that was quick."

Her maid shrugged. "He's in love."

"No, he's not. This is all a game. Mark my words."

"Well, are you going to read it?"

"Fine." She grabbed the scroll and read the latest missive.

"Lady, you ask too much.

Some secrets I must keep

The cost is far too steep

If I loosen my clutch.

And so, despite your charm,

I can't open the door

And tell you any more

For fear you'll do me harm."

"What do you have to hide, Daniel?" she murmured, handing the note to Elaine.

"Maybe he's secretly a nobleman in disguise, and he'll come riding to the rescue at the last moment to save you from de Broase," Elaine teased.

"Don't be ridiculous. He's a shipwright. I saw him at work. He knew his craft. I'm certain he wasn't pretending." She tapped the scroll against her fingers. "Hmm." She sat down at her desk, pulled out a fresh parchment scroll, and dipped her quill in ink. "Elaine, can you go down to the storeroom and get me a fresh pot of ink? I'm almost out."

Her maid hurried away, and Carenza began to write.

"Sir, you are not the prey.

Admit this is your game

And that I am the game.

All I can do is pray.
You claim that I am dear,
That I've ensnared your heart.
In truth I am the hart
You hunt amongst the deer."

Just as she rolled up the parchment, Alais burst into the room. Carenza jumped in her seat. "Don't you ever knock?"

"What's this?" Alais asked sweetly, plucking the poem from her hand and dancing out of reach.

She gave an angry yelp and jumped up to grab it back, only to have her ankle give way as she put weight on it. She collapsed back into her chair. "Give that back, Alais. It's none of your business."

Alais opened the parchment and read it aloud, her eyes widening with every line. "Oh, Carenza! You are in love with Gerard, aren't you! It's too delicious."

"No!" she yelled, too loudly. "No," she repeated more quietly. "I wasn't writing it to anyone. It was just a silly game I was playing. You know how mother likes to make me challenge the troubadours to rhyming competitions. I was merely practicing my craft so that I'll be ready next time she calls on me."

"Then why are you so upset about me reading it?" Alais eyed her suspiciously. "I think you're hoping Gerard will steal you away before you have to marry Lord de Broase." Carenza blushed bright red, and Alais took it as confirmation. "Don't worry, sister. Your secret is safe with me. I'd much rather see you marry Gerard than that boring earl."

"I have no designs on Gerard. This wasn't written for him."

"Oh, so there's someone else?" Alais looked like she'd just been handed an entire spice cake.

"Of course not. Don't be silly!" Carenza was embarrassed by the shrill note in her voice. "It's just something I wrote for amusement," she said as evenly as she could manage. "Please forget you ever saw it."

To her deep relief, her maid walked in at that moment with the bottle of ink. "Elaine," she exclaimed, giving a significant smile. "I have that practice poem I said I'd give you!" She turned to her sister. "She has taken an interest in verse and wanted to study my approach to give her ideas for her own compositions. Isn't that right?"

Elaine stepped over to Alais and plucked the parchment from her hand. "Oh yes, my lady! You know how much I love poetry." She gave a sweet smile with just a hint of threat behind it. Her sister stepped back and huffed.

"Fine. Keep your secrets. What do I care?" With that, she stormed out of the room, slamming the door behind her.

Carenza sagged in her seat. "What do I do, Elaine? This is a disaster."

"Do?" Elaine answered, patting her shoulder. "Nothing at all! Let Alais think whatever she wants to think. Everyone knows she's prone to fits of fancy when it comes to romance. No one would believe her if she tried to tell on you. And even if they did, I would say you wrote it for me, just like you said. In fact, perhaps we'd best write out another copy so that I can produce this one if asked. We wouldn't want anyone to guess it was sent out."

Carenza nodded and turned immediately to produce a second copy. "Let's wait a week to send this one," she said, handing the copy to Elaine. "If I know Alais, she'll be watching me to see if she can prove her theory, but she's easily bored. I think she'll move on by the end of the week."

The week passed in agonizing slowness. The only good thing that happened was that her ankle began to feel better. She began to walk without a cane and didn't need to keep her ankle wrapped anymore.

On the eighth day after the "Alais incident," as she called it, Elaine found her taking a walk in the garden.

"He answered already? Only one day?" Carenza whispered, feeling suddenly very warm as her maid handed over the letter.

"Lady, your rhymes are clever.
They put my verse to shame.
I'm sure that was your aim.
I've no hope whatsoever.
Your fine mind makes me long
To see you face to face,
Though it is not my place.
I'm undone by your song."

"Face to face," she murmured, her heart beating so loudly, she could hardly think. She turned to Elaine. "Help!" she said with a gulp as she handed over the poem.

Elaine gasped as she read. "Oh my! What do you intend to do?"

Carenza stared into the middle distance.

"If you want to see him," Elaine said, putting a hand on hers, "the safest way would be to invite him to one of your mother's troubadour gatherings. No one would suspect a thing if he's simply one of the group. You needn't speak to him in private unless you wish to."

"Speak to him privately? I couldn't possibly."

"As you wish. But if you did, I would recommend meeting him in the solar after the entertainment ends. The troubadours generally drink together after the performances, so his staying won't be suspect. And no one is anywhere near the solar at that hour. It's very private."

"But it's right next to my parents' room. Won't they hear?"

"The solar has thick walls and a heavy door. It was built for privacy. No one will hear a thing. Besides, your parents like to linger in the great hall on nights when troubadours perform, so they will most likely be far away during your assignation."

"Why do I suspect you've done this before? Perhaps meeting Gerard?"

Elaine just smiled.

"Well, however tried and true your plan may be, I couldn't possibly take the risk. Not to mention that it would be wrong, very wrong. May the Lord forgive me for even thinking about it!" She clutched her rosary and prayed silently.

"At least invite him to come perform. There can't be any harm in that. You can use the occasion to dissuade him from pursuing you further if you are so determined to do the right thing."

Carenza pondered that. Yes, this had been fun, but it was time to end it. There was no possible way their correspondence could continue once she married, which was supposed to happen in a matter of weeks. She would see him one last time and tell him it was over.

"Thank you, Elaine," she said with newfound resolution. "I believe I will do exactly that. This has to end. I may as well tell him in person."

That evening, she sat down at her desk one last time.

"I doubt your love is true

But if you are sincere,

Then come and meet me here.

Come sing, I dare you to.

The singers all compete,

And let their verse take flight.

Come prove the words you write,

Or hide and own defeat."

She slid the parchment beneath her mattress. Pulling out another piece of parchment, she wrote up a formal invitation that he could present to the guards to enter the castle. It was only a game and a hopeless one at that, but this strange man made her feel things.

That was all the more reason it had to end. She couldn't afford to fall prey to love's trap.

Unbidden, a momentary fantasy of his lips against her own,

his arms holding her close, flashed through her mind. She remembered his touch the day they met, the heat of him, the scent of him.

Was this how the sickness started? Was she falling so easily?

It all had to end; there was no question.

CHAPTER TEN

S TARS TWINKLED IN the twilight as Daniel stared out the attic window of the Juggler, filled with exhilaration and, he would admit, some anxiety, pinching the precious invitation in his hand. The cat wound around his feet, rubbing against his leg.

"I gave you a fish. Will you leave me alone? I have things I need to do," he said, nudging it away.

It meowed, and he surrendered, bending down to pet it.

"I got a very important letter today," he told the cat as he scratched its ears. "It could change my life."

He had a way in now. He could free himself of his uncle at long last. John would arrive any minute. This time tomorrow, he might have rid the world of Adele's murderer forever, or perhaps he would have died trying. He wasn't afraid of death. Adele was waiting for him. His only fear was failure. That would be more than he could bear.

The cat yawned and wandered away, leaving him with nothing to do. Long, tense minutes passed as he awaited the sound of Gerard ascending the stairs with John. He fiddled with a small knife, throwing it again and again at a target painted on the wall, never missing the center by more than an inch. Though his swordsmanship left something to be desired, his formal training having ended at age nine, he was confident and deadly with knives.

Four assassins had tried to take him down, three before Adele's death and one since. Every time, he'd bested them, ending them before they could report back and confirm his whereabouts. He loathed killing, but there was no other option. They'd attacked him, and if he didn't dispatch them, they would only bring more. There were moments when he relished the fighting, yet the death at the end always left him feeling ill. But not this time. He would have no remorse about killing his uncle, not after everything the man had done.

The list of his victims always started with Daniel's father, Uncle Raymond's own brother. Then there was Adele, who was murdered to prevent her from producing an heir, and her father, Ferdinand—Gerard's father as well—who'd died defending her. Daniel's mother was done to death by grief, a prisoner in all but name in Hawkhurst. God knows how his sister survived. Someday, he hoped to see her again and reclaim the one member of his family his uncle hadn't killed.

At long last, footsteps sounded on the stairs to the attic, a casual conversation about castle entertainment, an invitation to sing.

"My lord," John said upon seeing him, sweeping into a bow.

"Daniel," he corrected.

"But no one is here, my lord. Why maintain the pretense?"

"Because it isn't a pretense. I gave up my name and title when I married Adele. I'm not going back. I'm not your lord, John."

"As you wish…Daniel."

How many times had they had this conversation, and how many more would they have it again before John would finally believe him?

"I can assure you, good sir, that Daniel is no lord," Gerard said, taking a seat on a crate and inviting John to do the same. "He's more uncouth than me by far. Taught me every swear word I know. And you should hear the crude and filthy verses he composes when I get him drunk." He punctuated his point with a loud burp.

"You keep interesting company…Daniel." John looked at him long and hard, disappointment evident on his wrinkled face.

Daniel looked away, wishing he could make John understand. He'd worked so hard to erase every vestige of who he was from his demeanor. It wasn't a disguise. It was a transformation. He wasn't a noble anymore, whatever John might wish.

"I have a way in." He gave the piece of parchment with his invitation to John.

John laughed. "Still a troubadour, I see. I can't say this is wise, but it certainly is fitting." He handed the parchment back with a serious look. "You realize he'll know it's you as soon as he sees you. Any chance at secrecy will be lost."

"It's a chance I'm willing to take. When he dies, I want him to know it's by my hand."

John nodded.

"Gerard has given me the layout of the castle and told me which room he sleeps in. What's your advice on how best to get to him once I'm in the castle?"

"He'll be less wary before the performance, but it will be difficult to avoid the notice of others. Afterward, everyone will be drunk and tired. He'll be on his guard, but no one else will notice a lone troubadour that disappears early. Leave the great hall as soon as you can manage and tail him until you have him in an isolated spot. He's been ducking into Lord de Vere's solar at odd hours to find a bit of privacy for a quiet conversation. You may find him there. Otherwise, try his room."

Daniel nodded.

"How can I help?" Gerard asked, clapping his hands together and rubbing them.

John looked him up and down and raised a dubious eyebrow. "I recommend you focus on distracting attention after the performance so that Daniel can sneak away."

A broad, drunken smile broke across Gerard's face. "That I can do with aplomb."

"I'll do the same with your uncle's men. A couple barrels of ale to celebrate his lordship's engagement, along with some local entertainment of the feminine variety, should do the trick."

"So it will just be my uncle and that cockroach, Richard, who does all his dirty work. Two against one."

"Can you do it?" John asked, keeping his voice even and casual.

Daniel threw his knife again and hit the target dead center. "Yes," he said, keeping his voice equally calm and casual.

John's mouth quirked into a smile. "It's really Richard you'll have to worry about. Your uncle has never been much of a fighter himself. He's always let others do his fighting for him. You should be able to make quick work of him, provided you can keep him from fleeing."

"Anything I should know about Richard, aside from the fact that he murdered my wife and father-in-law?" he asked, retrieving his knife.

"He's bloodthirsty, quick as lightning, fights dirty. He injured his left shoulder last year, so he's a bit slower on that side. Still, your best chance with him is to take him by surprise and incapacitate him with your first hit."

Daniel sent the knife spinning across the attic once again, hitting the target right next to the mark from the last bullseye. "Understood."

Without warning, John pried a loose piece of wood from a nearby crate and, with a speed that belied his age, jumped up and jabbed at Daniel's throat. Reacting instinctively, Daniel blocked and twisted John's arm up behind his back, swept his feet out from under him, and pinned him to the floor, taking the wood from John's hand and pressing it to his neck.

Gerard, eyes wide with fear and alarm, ran for the knife stuck in the wall, sending John and Daniel into fits of laughter as Daniel released his hold.

John sat up and clapped Daniel on the back. "You'll do fine, lad, just fine."

Gerard held the knife in a trembling hand, looking confused

and ready to do something desperate.

Daniel called, "It's alright, Gerard. He was only testing me. It was just a piece of wood. See?" He held it up in plain view, and Gerard dropped the knife from his nerveless fingers.

"Christ," Gerard grumbled, giving them both a dirty look as he walked past. "I'm going downstairs for a drink."

With Gerard gone, John's laughter died away, and his face was lined with concern once again. "You should plan your escape, my lad. Whether or not you succeed, you'll need to leave Winchelsea, at least for a while, if you are unwilling to declare yourself. If you fail, they'll hunt for you. If you succeed, you'll face the king's justice for killing an earl."

Daniel took a deep breath and closed his eyes. "I'll go to Calais. It won't be safe for me on England's shores anymore."

"I wish you'd reconsider. If you succeed and don't take up your title, Hawkhurst will go to your uncle's eldest, Raymond. He shares more than a name with his father, and Hawkhurst will be the worst for it. If by some chance you fail, you'll be putting Winchelsea in danger as well as yourself. If you took up your title, you'd split your uncle's troops, and Winchelsea might stand a chance. If you don't, I hate to think what will happen here as your uncle takes revenge for the attempt on his life."

Shaking his head, Daniel said, "I swore an oath."

"And those you swore it to are long dead. Do you really believe this is what your wife or her father would have wanted? Ferdinand was my friend before I brought you to his home. We fought together on the Crusade at the siege of Damascus. He was a brave soldier and a good man. I can't believe he would hold you to your oath at a time like this. I didn't know Adele well, but I can't imagine she would expect you to hang back at a moment like this either."

Daniel didn't answer, staring straight ahead into the darkness. He could see Adele in his mind's eye, looking at him with disapproval. He knew exactly what she'd want, and it wasn't this. But could he justify breaking a solemn oath to her just because he imagined she might feel differently if she was still alive? She couldn't release him, and so he couldn't release himself. He had to keep his oath. It was all he had left of her.

"Deny it all you want, Daniel," John said quietly. "You can't change who you are. You'll never find peace running from yourself."

The tense silence extended until it became excruciating. Daniel couldn't speak. If he did, he would say something he would regret, or perhaps give in to the tears welling up behind his eyes. He wasn't sure which. No, he would never find peace until he was dead.

"I should get back to the castle before anyone gets suspicious. Sleep well, Daniel. I'll see you tomorrow."

After John left, Daniel went and laid on his bed, staring up at the ceiling. The cat immediately curled up beside him. He couldn't change who he was, but he loathed being a de Broase with every fiber of his being. Hawkhurst had destroyed his family, turning his uncle into a monster capable of killing his own brother. He longed to be Daniel, the shipwright, Adele's Daniel, plain and simple. But deep down, he knew John was right. A man cannot walk away from his past.

As he drifted off to sleep, he imagined Adele in bed beside him, her comforting arms around him, but as sleep descended, the woman changed. No more blond cascades of hair and mischievous blue eyes. A brown-eyed beauty with ink-black hair and an intelligent gaze that saw right through him took Adele's place. He breathed in her fragrance of almonds and spice as her arms folded around him. Her breasts pressed against his back, her lips leaving a trail of fire down his neck, her hand reaching down to touch—

He awoke, painfully aware of his own aching stiffness beneath the blanket. Carenza. It wasn't love. It couldn't be. He hardly knew the woman. And besides, how could he truly love after Adele? But Carenza stirred something within him, more than lust, though there was plenty of that if he was being honest.

It was her mind. It sparkled and shone in every word she wrote. Every note she sent increased his appreciation of her intelligence and sharpened his loathing for his uncle. The thought of them getting married filled him with bile. Daniel couldn't let it happen. He hadn't been able to save Adele, but perhaps he could save Carenza. Tomorrow, he had to succeed.

Carenza, what are you doing to me?

She'd felt so right in his arms. He'd only held her for a moment, carrying her after she fell, but he could still feel the imprint of her warmth against him when he closed his eyes. He hadn't been that close to a woman since Adele. This had only been a moment's contact, completely innocent as far as Carenza knew, but her touch stirred memories he'd locked away for years.

He turned his thoughts back to Adele, remembering the torrid desperation of their wedding night, the intoxicating feel of her warmth and her shape beneath his hand and against his body. But the memories were too distant and the pain too great. Before long, his thoughts were fixated once again on Carenza. Aching with guilt but helpless to stop, he traced her form in his mind. Her lips brushed against his own, her legs wrapping around him, welcoming him with a heat and fury that nearly made him explode at the mere thought.

Painfully aroused, he lay in bed, wracked with guilt.

Forgive me, Adele. It's been so long. I'm only a man. I don't love her. I only love you.

But as sleep took him at last, the woman who visited him in his dreams once more wasn't Adele.

Chapter Eleven

"Are you ready?" Gerard asked, pulling on a tunic that was royal blue on one side and bright yellow on the other, and tucking a dagger into his boot.

"As ready as I'm going to be." Daniel had declined to borrow one of Gerard's outfits and put on the simple dark green cotte he wore when he married Adele, the only garment he owned aside from his work clothes. He hid a dagger up his sleeve and another in his boot. It was a wonder that Gerard managed to be so successful with women, dressing as he did. He checked his outfit for cat hair one last time. Everything was pristine. "Let's go."

They arrived in the great hall, a vast stone room with a high ceiling, lit by braziers and torch light with an elaborately carved hearth by the head table. The walls were hung with tapestries that he could hardly make out in the dim light. The eastern wall had four tall, thin windows tapering up into gothic arches. The waxing gibbous moon shone through the blurred panes of glass.

Daniel sat with half a dozen other troubadours who had come for the evening's competition. Servants offered them wine and refreshments as they waited for Lord de Vere and the other noble guests to arrive from dinner. The other troubadours were all dressed in their motley best. Daniel sat grim and serious as the others drank and joked. He wasn't here to have fun.

A servant entered and announced the arrival of Lord and

Lady de Vere, Lord de Broase, and fifteen or so other noble guests. They all seated themselves in chairs arranged in a semicircle at the front of the room. Lord de Vere sat beside Lord de Broase. Carenza sat between her mother and two young women who could only be her sisters.

Daniel saw Carenza's eyes pass over the troubadours at the other end of the room, and he felt a jolt as their eyes met. She looked away quickly and smoothed her skirts. Her deep red dress was cut even lower than the one she'd worn that day at the docks. It must have been her mother's choice. It didn't seem like a dress an aspiring nun would choose for herself, though he certainly appreciated the overall effect. She was still wearing her skull rosary, of course, the skull nestled in the delicate curves of her lovely, ripe decolletage.

He turned his gaze to Lord de Broase, who blinked and went wide-eyed on seeing him. A look of pure loathing crossed his uncle's face before he composed himself and returned to the look of bland disinterest he had worn previously. Daniel smiled at the floor. There was no turning back now. He'd taken the risk and let himself be seen. It was almost a relief. He was committed. He was ready.

"My lords and ladies," a servant announced, "the Lord de Vere would like to welcome you all to an evening of song and verse. These talented troubadours will perform songs of love for your pleasure, and Lady Isabella will offer five silver coins to the performer she deems the best."

The servant came over to the troubadours, and they drew lots for the first performance slot. Daniel watched as one by one, each performer took their turn. He was reassured that none of them were better than him. Well, perhaps Gerard had him beat. Yes, Gerard was singing words he wrote, but Gerard had the better voice. Daniel was the last performer to be called. He stood and took his place, looking everywhere but at Carenza.

CARENZA BIT HER lip and grabbed her rosary as Daniel took the floor. He looked elegant in simple green, unlike the parade of rainbow-clad fools that came before him. They'd been corresponding for just under three weeks, and she hardly knew what to do with herself seeing him again in the flesh. He was avoiding her eyes, but as a member of the audience, she was free to stare as openly as she wanted. He raised his lute and played simple chords with a practiced hand. In a deep and rough voice, he began to sing.

"Songbird, take flight
And leave tonight
To a land far away
Where my lady waits for day.
Find her and remind her
How my subtle words entwined her.
Don't let her forget she's in my sway."

She sat spellbound, her lips parted, her eyes wide. His voice filled her, caressed her, and transported her to another world where they were alone, just the two of them. She was helpless, suspended in resonance and beauty. Stanza after stanza spoke of love's cruelty, his lady's indifference, and the pleasures he could promise if only his lady would have pity. She had always approached poetry as a game. Her verse was acerbic, direct. But this was something else altogether. It was sublime, transcendent, filling her very soul with longing.

"Don't leave me in doubt.
You've heard me speak out.
I'm pierced by love's dart.
Don't tear me apart.

Look kindly on me.
Be gentle with me.
I've nothing to give but my heart."

He was speaking to her. It wasn't just a troubadour's pose. He turned his eyes to her on the final notes. She melted beneath his gaze. Didn't he know how impossible this was? Had she led him on? Had she given him false hope? She needed to speak with him, make him understand, even though she wasn't sure she understood herself. She hadn't planned to take up Elaine's offer to help them meet privately, but now that he was here, she knew she had to. Whatever conversation they needed to have, it wasn't one that could be conducted in public.

The audience applauded loudly once the spell was broken. Her mother stood and turned to the gathered audience.

"I believe we have a winner," her mother announced. "Good sir, pray tell, what is your name?"

Daniel glanced at her and then Lord de Broase, who looked livid for some reason, before answering her mother, "My name is Daniel." Carenza's heart threatened to pound out of her chest.

At that moment, he looked positively regal. He claimed his name like a king, not a common shipwright. There was a look of challenge in his eyes as he and Lord de Broase held each other's gazes as if he was vanquishing a formidable enemy rather than merely winning a poetry contest. Who was this man?

"Daniel, thank you for coming today and performing. I hope that you will join us again in the future. We were most impressed with your performance." Her mother held out the small bag of coins.

Daniel dragged his eyes away from Lord de Broase and bowed to Carenza's mother, accepting the leather purse.

"Wait," Lord de Broase said, standing up. "You give out your coin too easily, Lady de Vere. I think this man is an imposter. Does he look like a troubadour to you? Clearly, this man is just some laborer who wanted a peek at courtly life. I think he plagiarized someone else's composition. I strongly recommend against giving him the prize."

Daniel's head snapped up, and he stared at Lord de Broase as though ready to tear out his throat. What could possibly account for such enmity? They couldn't possibly know each other, although looking at their faces, there was a surprising resemblance. If she didn't know better, she might think they were related. She looked to her mother to see what she would do to defray the strange tension in the room.

"Lord de Broase," her mother said, clearing her throat. "I see no cause to doubt this man, but if you are suspicious, we can easily put him to the test to see if the wit behind his verse is truly his own."

"What do you propose?" asked Lord de Broase without taking his eyes off Daniel.

"Your betrothed is quite skilled with verse. I propose a competition. If he can keep up with Carenza, then he's the real thing. Carenza, will you do the honors?" Her mother looked at her expectantly with a proud smile.

Carenza's mouth fell open. Then she closed it and cleared her throat. This was an unexpected turn of events. She'd done this before, of course, but never with so large an audience and certainly not with someone as skilled as Daniel. Taking a deep breath, she stood up and squared her shoulders.

"Master Daniel," she said. He locked eyes with her the moment she said his name. Suddenly, the room was far too hot for comfort. "It seems my mother is proposing a little sparring, if you will indulge us. I set the rules. We'll have six stanzas each, and we'll take turns. I go first. Follow my lead."

Normally, she entered these contests full of confidence. This time, she was filled with nervous excitement. For once, she was going to have a chance to match wits with someone at her level. A delicious challenge.

Daniel raised an eyebrow and then gave her a sly smile. "I accept, my lady. Shall we begin?" He cocked his head sideways, and his smile grew downright wicked.

"Gerard, can you do the honors with the lute?" Carenza asked without taking her eyes off Daniel. Gerard started strumming a quick and familiar rhythm to provide accompaniment to their improvisation.

Carenza took a deep breath, put her hand on her hips, and launched into her opening parry.

"Sir, come and play my game.
Defend your claim to fame.
I'll put your verse to shame.
Come dance with me."

Daniel's grin widened, and he gave her an appreciative nod. Without pause, he offered his riposte, stepping toward her with predatory grace.

"Lady, I'll play your game,
But know I am not tame.
I'll set your heart aflame
If you'll dance with me."

Carenza raised her eyebrows, and her heart beat faster as she narrowed her eyes in a look of challenge. Oh, this was far too much fun.

"Sir, sing me a refrain
Of love you can't attain
Or I'll think your boasts vain.
Romance me."

Daniel pursed his lips and gave her a bold look that swept over every part of her like a flaming caress.

"Lady, love is pain.
My efforts are in vain.
There is nothing to gain
From romance, you see."

Carenza turned her back on him and folded her arms beneath her breasts, needing a reprieve from the heat of his eyes. She looked back at him coyly over her shoulder.

"So all the poets say,
But still they sing all day,
Each one pining away
For a glance of me."

Daniel walked around her and knelt before her in supplication. It was too much. Much too much! Carenza blushed.

"Lady, your sweet face
Makes fools like me give chase
And then forget their place.
But what chance have we?"

Carenza gave a laugh and narrowed her eyes at him. Heavens, he was gorgeous, kneeling there, arms open, chestnut brown eyes full of mischief.

"Why none, as you well know.
I will lead you to woe.
You'll have nothing to show
From romancing me."

Daniel stood and turned to address the audience.

"Friends, listen how she taunts!
Her cruel comeliness haunts,

And her clever tongue daunts."

He stepped toward her again, suddenly right beside her shoulder. She could feel his heat, smell his scent. She took a quick, shuddering breath at his closeness, hoping no one saw how he unnerved her.

"Why toy with me?"

His voice was low and husky. He meant it. He wanted to know. She didn't have an answer, not one that made sense. She did the only thing she could think of and launched an attack to distract from her confusion.

"Because poets are toys
Who make too much noise.
Sir, you are losing poise.
I claim victory."

The audience reacted with "ooh's" and even an "ouch." She'd scored a hit with that one. Daniel widened his eyes in mock outrage.

"My lady, I object.
Do you even suspect
The bewitching effect
You have on me?"

The audience sighed in sympathy. She hadn't won yet, so the only thing to do was pretend she had.

"But surely, we are done,
And it's clear that I've won.
Good sir, you've had your fun.
Now yield to me."

She gave him an arch, commanding look, full of bravado. She

wasn't sure she'd won, but at a minimum, it had to be a draw.

"Lady, the last word's mine,
And I will not resign.
You know I'll make you pine,
When you fall for me."

As he spoke the last line, he winked at her. His impudence was beyond outrageous, and the audience loved it. There was loud applause and several appreciative hoots. Only Lord de Broase stayed still, watching Daniel with cold intensity. Daniel took a bow, and Carenza curtsied. Then Daniel took her hand, knelt before her, and kissed it.

At the soft touch of his lips, everything else faded into the background. Just a brush of contact, skin against skin, and she felt ripples of sensations she'd never felt before. Warmth spread to every part of her. Something stirred within her, something primal, hungry, unfamiliar. It was entirely new and outside of her experience, and it obliterated everything except the soft pressure of his lips touching her hand. Then he released her, and the spell was broken. Once again, they were standing in the familiar hall surrounded by people.

Her mother was standing and clapping. "Well played, Daniel! Well played! Carenza is not an easy foe, and I daresay you took the day. The reward is yours," she said, handing him a small purse. "I'm sure no one can doubt you now."

Lord de Broase sat with his arms and legs crossed and a deep frown fixed his face. Daniel glared at him.

In the hubbub of conversation as the performance ended, Carenza found Elaine. "I have to meet him. Can you arrange it?" she murmured in Elaine's ear.

"Leave it to me, my lady." She winked and disappeared.

CHAPTER TWELVE

HALF AN HOUR later, at Elaine's signal, Carenza ducked away from the great hall where Gerard stood on a chair, juggling apples and singing old favorites to the drunken crowd. She tiptoed upstairs to the solar door and cracked it open. All was dark except for a few embers still burning in the fireplace, and no one was inside. She fully expected it to be empty, given that her family was all downstairs, but given what she was doing, she couldn't be too careful.

Grabbing a flint from a small table by the door, she lit the candles on the candelabra on the main table, bathing the room in soft light. She began pacing as she awaited Daniel's arrival.

Truth be told, she couldn't believe she was doing this. This was a completely unnecessary risk. The man was bound to take it the wrong way and think it was a romantic invitation. But she had to speak to him. She had to explain why it all had to stop. And she still wanted to know who he was. Knowing his name hadn't curbed her curiosity one bit. If anything, she was more puzzled than before, especially after tonight's performance. She had to know.

Yes, his poem this evening had been a masterpiece, cleverly conceived, beautifully written, and passionately performed. Yes, she had felt the need to fan herself while she listened. It didn't mean she was falling prey to romance. She appreciated a fine performance. That was all. And if she had blushed at the fire in his gaze every time it met her own, it was only because she was nervous that he'd finally answered her and come in person.

Voices echoed from the hallway as the door creaked open behind her. It couldn't be him. He would have come alone. She ducked behind her mother's loom and hoped the shadows would hide her.

"Your orders, my lord?" said a voice Carenza didn't recognize.

"My orders haven't changed in seventeen years."

Oh dear. It was Lord de Broase. Carenza shrank further down.

"I want him dead so that Hawkhurst is truly mine at last, beyond any shadow of a doubt," Lord de Broase continued. "Not that it ever should have belonged to my brother. I should have been born first. He was never worthy to rule. So disgustingly weak. Look where his tolerant policies have gotten us." He spat on the floor. "I did the world a favor getting rid of him."

Mother Mary, full of grace, my betrothed killed his own brother? She hardly dared breathe as she crouched just out of their sight.

"That you did, my lord," the stranger said.

"Roger's boy has eluded me for too long. You should have ended him when he was a pup. Did you see the size of him? Now he's a threat, make no mistake. At least you dispatched that little hayseed he married before she could produce an heir."

He's trying to kill his nephew and already killed the woman he married? *Dear Lord, please save me from marrying this murderer.*

"And her father, too. Old codger came at me with a rusty sword to defend her. Most pathetic display I've ever seen."

The man laughed. It was the most chilling thing Carenza had ever heard.

"But you didn't dispatch the boy like I asked, and now look what happened. Everything I've worked for all these years hangs by a thread because you failed. Track him down, and this time, I don't want to hear about another miraculous escape, do you understand?"

Who was this poor nephew? Was there some way to warn him?

"Yes, my lord. And the situation at Hawkhurst with the peasants, sir?"

"I shall have to return."

"Will you wed now or upon your return, my lord?"

"When I return. There's no time to make the necessary arrangements before I leave, and I'm in no hurry for the wedding. She's the least important part of this whole arrangement. I have an heir already. I wouldn't even bother with the marriage if I didn't need her to secure my claim to Winchelsea and keep her father compliant with the demands I plan to make. I'll leave for Hawkhurst tonight."

She gasped and covered her mouth with her hand, praying they hadn't heard her.

There was a pause, heavy with silence, and she knew they had. "There's someone in here, Richard. Find them."

She hunched down, holding her breath, gripping her rosary in desperation.

Dear Lord in heaven, please don't let them find me, please don't let them find me, please don't let them find me....

The man grabbed the back of her dress, hauled her out into the open, and placed a blade at her throat.

"Carenza?" Lord de Broase barked in surprise. "What the hell are you doing in here?"

"I...I..." She couldn't breathe. She couldn't speak. There was a dagger at her throat. How was she supposed to think of something at a time like this?

"Meeting a lover?" Lord de Broase asked. "I shouldn't be surprised after that performance this evening. They said you were practically a nun, but—"

"I left something here," she said in a shaky voice. "My book of prayers. I just came to fetch it. Then I heard voices. I'm not supposed to be wandering around the castle alone this time of night. I thought it might be my father, so I hid."

"A likely story. Well, whatever your reason for being here, I'm afraid you heard some things you shouldn't have." The knife at her throat pressed in, piercing her skin. She let out a small cry.

"Keep quiet," said the stranger called Richard, his voice rasping in her ear.

"Such a pity. I would have enjoyed you warming my bed, but I'm afraid I can't let you live. I'll have to marry one of your sisters instead." He drew a caressing finger down her face, filling her with nausea and disgust. Then he turned away.

"Take care of this," de Broase said as casually as if he was asking for his horses to be brought round. "Make sure it can't be traced back to me. Better yet, see if you can make it look like my nephew did it." Then he left her alone with Richard, shutting the door firmly behind him.

"Well, my lady, it's just you and me," Richard whispered.

She had to do something, and she had to do it now. Perhaps someone would come to the rescue? But it was too late at night, and no one would be in this part of the castle.

Daniel might be coming, but he might have decided it was too dangerous when he heard voices or….

She couldn't wait any longer, or she'd wind up dead.

Bending double, she threw Richard off balance. He lashed out with his blade, giving her a nasty cut on the chest. Grabbing the candelabra, she swung at Richard's head.

The room went dark.

There was a sickening crack as it made contact, and he yowled.

The door opened behind them, and someone collided with Richard.

In the shadows, two men scuffled. She heard thudding and muffled groans from the floor nearby as the fight continued.

As she inched away, supporting herself on the table, her legs shook too much to stand. There was a loud grunt, and the sounds of combat ceased. She wasn't sure who had won. She needed to see better. Where was the flint? Where was the flint?

She lurched to the small table by the door, found the flint, and with shaking hands, worked to light a candle. It took several attempts before she was successful. If not because of her trembling but because her panting breath puffed out the flame before it could catch on the wick. Finally, though, in the pale flickering light, she saw Daniel coming toward her. She swayed and collapsed in his arms.

"You're hurt," Daniel said, his voice tense and hoarse. "What did he do?"

"He had a knife. He tried to kill me." It had been such a near thing. She was shaking all over.

"Thank God you're safe!" He eased her into a chair and knelt before her in the candlelight. "But you're injured. Let me look." He ran a finger lightly beneath the cut across her chest. His finger felt like fire against her skin, and she gasped. "Did I hurt you?"

"No, no…. It's nothing."

He took a cloth from the side table with all the embroidery materials. There was a pitcher and basin on that table as well. He poured a bit of water into the basin and dipped the cloth before coming over to wipe away the blood from her injuries.

"The cut on your chest isn't deep." He turned his attention to the cut on her neck. "This is deeper. It may scar, but you're in no danger." He pressed the cloth to her neck. His face was so close to hers, so close. His hands were holding her so gently. She was trembling beneath his touch. Was it the relief of being saved? Was it shock? Why did she seem to be drawn closer and closer to him? Why did she keep glancing at his lips?

"Thank you for rescuing me," she whispered, trying to resist the magnetic pull of the moment. His eyes locked on hers. That made it worse, much worse. Too late, she realized what was happening, but she didn't stop, couldn't stop.

It was wrong for so many reasons. Setting aside her personal feelings about love, a kiss meant marriage, and this was not a man she could ever marry. This was not a man she should even be seen conversing with. It was impossible, and she should leave now before it was too late.

And then it happened, impossible and inevitable. Their lips touched softly, gently. This lightest of caresses robbed her of the ability to think, judge, and act.

She drew back slightly. Long ago, she'd decided she could live without this, wanted to live without this. And here she was, entirely helpless beneath his spell. No, not helpless. Somehow, beyond all that was rational, she wanted this, invited this. She was a participant, not a passive recipient. She moved infinitesimally closer to him, her lips parted.

His lips found hers again and delved deeper, tugging her lower lip just the slightest bit as if unwilling to release it. She clutched the chair beneath her as sweet hunger, unlike any she had ever known, consumed her. God help her. She wanted more even as she knew she should push him away and leave. This was everything she had sworn she would never do, would never even want. She told her body to move, to get up and leave, but she stayed.

He took her mouth as if tasting a delicious plum, drawing her in with his tongue twisting around hers. A moan escaped her as she responded, leaning into him, tasting him in return.

She reached up to touch him, pull him closer, one around his neck, the other twining around his waist. The heat and power of him overwhelmed her senses. His kiss tugged at her soul.

His hands loosened her hair as his kiss grew more urgent, hungry, and ferocious. She surrendered to his touch, aware in a place far removed from conscious control that she should stop. She must stop. But she didn't.

He did. He leaned away, taking a deep, ragged breath, gently lifting her hands away from him and placing them in her lap, leaving her panting and unsteady. "I'm sorry. I shouldn't have done that."

"Don't," she said, her throat tight and her voice choked.

"Don't apologize. I don't want to hear that you're sorry." She knew he was right. He shouldn't have, but after a very bad night, she didn't think she could bear to have him be sorry for kissing her.

It was her first kiss. She'd never dreamed it would feel like this.

"I came intending to tell you we must stop. It's gone too far. I don't know why you're toying with me—"

"I'm not," she objected. He raised an eyebrow. "I'm not!" Of course, that's what he thought. What else could he think? It was beyond foolish to bring him here.

"And how was I supposed to interpret our little 'dance' earlier?"

"And how is it that you know how to dance so well? I asked you here because I needed to know who you were. You are such a puzzle. It's driving me mad. How does a shipwright who has never been to court come to compose troubadour lyrics?"

"How does an aspiring nun come to compose better than most troubadours?" He gave her a wicked grin, which she did her best to ignore. He wasn't wrong. She had no business composing love poems.

"So, who are you?"

"I am Daniel."

"So you say. How did you come to be who you are, and what was going on between you and Lord de Broase?"

"Those are dangerous questions."

"Tell me," she demanded. "Please," she added, realizing she really had no right to pry. But she had to know! Was it possible he was somehow tied to the nephew Lord de Broase was hunting? Or, perhaps, was he the nephew de Broase was hunting? She thought of the tense look on de Broase's face as soon as he'd spotted Daniel and the resemblance between them. She'd even thought they appeared related. *Was it possible...?*

"I grew up near Hawkhurst, and I was given an education in my youth. My mother was French and loved poetry. I fell on hard times and was forced to find a trade, so I became a shipwright's apprentice. Now, I'm a shipwright. There. You have my story."

Her suspicions sharpened. Why would he be so evasive if he didn't have something to hide? "That's hardly an answer."

"That's all you'll get. Now I have a question for you. Why does de Broase want you dead?"

That brought her up short. The cuts on her chest and neck throbbed as she pondered how to answer. Did she dare reveal how much she'd overheard? She decided she had nothing to lose by telling Daniel.

For once, she didn't have to create a story to avoid being married to a man she didn't want. The fact that he'd ordered her to be killed should be reason enough.

"Lord de Broase and Richard came in while I was waiting for you. There was no time for me to leave, so I hid. They were talking about killing his nephew, who they'd been after for seventeen years."

Daniel gave her a sharp look. "Did they say the nephew's name?"

"No." She watched him for some sign that would confirm her suspicion, but he gave nothing away.

"Then they found you?"

"Yes. They said I'd heard too much, and Lord de Broase told Richard to kill me and blame it on his nephew, then left."

A strange, unreadable expression came over Daniel's face. "I just missed him."

"Yes." What was going on behind those eyes? This man was as much a mystery as he'd ever been. "He said he was leaving tonight for Hawkhurst," she added. "Something to do with trouble with the peasants."

Daniel growled. But why? Surely, Lord de Broase's leaving was cause to celebrate? At least, for her. What cause did Daniel have to celebrate? There was much unexplained.

And there was a body.

"What are we going to do with Richard?" she whispered.

He got up and walked behind her to where the man lay. She couldn't quite bring herself to turn and look. "He's gone. It seems he fell on his own knife somewhere along the way."

Carenza took a deep breath, not sure whether to be relieved or horrified. She wasn't entirely sure about his 'fell on a knife' explanation either. "It's for the best. It's a better death than he deserves after all he's done."

And what did he do to you? she yearned to ask.

"It also makes your story about what happened here easier. No one can say I was here except you and me." He returned to stand in front of her.

"What happens next?" she asked, peering up at him. Had she really kissed this man only moments before? It seemed to have happened hours earlier, maybe even weeks. Months. And yet, she felt like she'd known him forever, even as she didn't know him at all.

A month ago, when she was still at the abbey, things had seemed so simple, and she hadn't appreciated it…she wished she could go back.

"Go to your father. Tell him the truth about de Broase and Richard. Tell him Richard attacked you, you hit him with a candelabra, and he fell on his own knife. All of that is true, so it should be easy. Just don't mention me."

"Of course not." She couldn't possibly mention Daniel. The consequences for both of them were unthinkable. Her reputation would be ruined, but that was unimportant compared to what would happen to him. His life would be forfeit. A shipwright couldn't ruin a noblewoman or kill an earl's servant without the harshest of punishments. Unless he was more than he claimed. "What will you do?"

"It's best if I don't say."

Carenza couldn't hold back any longer. "Are you the true earl of Hawkhurst?"

"No," he said with such force she shrank back. "I'm a commoner," he said more calmly, "a mere shipwright, nothing more.

You saw me at my trade." He wiped his hand down his face. "And you, Carenza de Vere, are altogether too inquisitive. Don't you ever stop?"

"No," she said. "I don't." And why should she stop? Especially now, after they'd shared a kiss—after she'd nearly been murdered by a man Daniel had ultimately killed. She narrowed her eyes and opened her mouth to ask more.

"Do you feel strong enough to stand?" he asked before she could speak. He was definitely changing the subject.

She huffed.

He offered a hand, and she took it. Her legs supported her. With shaky hands, she dusted her skirts and patted her hair. She looked alarming, she was sure, but it was comforting to pat and smooth regardless. It made her feel more mentally composed.

"It seems I do." She began making her way slowly to the door, Daniel at her side. As she came level with Richard, she stopped short and shivered. He put a hand on her arm and squeezed to reassure her. It was all she could do to keep walking instead of letting herself lean into him. Somehow, she put one foot in front of the other and kept going.

When she reached the door, she stopped. She should have opened it and kept walking. She shouldn't have said another word. Instead, she stopped and turned. Daniel was right behind her. So close. Much too close.

"I leave Winchelsea tonight, never to return," he warned.

"Then we won't see each other again." She put her hand on his arm and didn't take it away.

"No."

"And we certainly won't..." She leaned toward him, her lips inches from his.

"...Kiss again?" he finished.

She nodded. And swallowed. He was so close. It was hard to form words.

"No, we won't," he said, leaning toward her as she backed into the closed door, caressing her cheek and tracing her jaw with his finger.

"And this is goodbye forever." She'd never known she was capable of feeling as she did now. Terrifying as it was, she was disappointed that she was going to have to give it up—give him up, and the feelings he created—and say goodbye.

"Forever." He nuzzled her neck and nibbled her ear.

"Kiss me?" The words came out unbidden. She couldn't take them back. She wanted this one last time before she had to give it up—forever. She was certain no one else would ever make her feel this way, not with this intensity. She needed one last, perfect kiss with this man she could not solve, could not rationalize. The man who could keep pace with her verbal jousting, who could melt her with words, or a touch, or his lips…

He paused for a moment to look into her eyes, his gaze scorching her with its heat, and then he devoured her. His lips and hands were everywhere, exploring each curve, pressing, kneading. He was feasting on her, and she was offering herself, arching her back, letting him lift her leg and press his hips into hers. She was powerless against the frenzy of his need and of her own. She would have let him do anything at all.

"I want you so much, Carenza, so very much…" He pulled away from her abruptly and stood panting and wild. "But you have to go. Now." He backed away, hunched and wary. "Go, Carenza. Go now. Go to your father. Please."

And at last, she turned and went, tearing blindly along the hallway and down the stairs until she arrived in the great hall where her family was still gathered.

CHAPTER THIRTEEN

ANIEL TRIED TO catch his breath as the heavy wooden door closed. He wasn't sure how long he had before Carenza reached her father, and he sent men down to see after Richard. He needed to leave quickly and go after de Broase, but she'd left him in such a state. Her gorgeous dishevelment would surely haunt his dreams for the rest of his days. And nights. For a brief moment, she had been his, and now he would never see her again.

She had no idea what she'd done to him. No idea at all. The way she saw to the heart of him, despite his obfuscations... Her insight and intelligence sparkled in every word and made him ache with desire even as her naïve trust held him back.

He was fairly certain she didn't know why she'd invited him tonight. She thought it was excessive, irrational curiosity, and didn't realize she was flirting. Her words roused him, kindled needs within him he had long kept at bay, but she was such an innocent. She planned to be a nun, for heaven's sake.

Considering the heat of her response to him, he couldn't imagine a woman less suited to be a nun. The man who married her would be very lucky indeed. And he hated that man with unbridled fury. At least he could now be sure it wouldn't be his uncle, not after tonight.

Daniel used that burst of sudden fury to launch himself into motion, opening the door and checking the hall before he made his way stealthily to his uncle's chamber. He heard voices raising the alarm downstairs. Slipping through the door to his uncle's chamber, knife held high, he prepared to end this once and for all. But as he crept silently over to the bed in the pitch-black room, he didn't hear a thing, no breathing, no rustling beneath the sheets. Reaching out ever so slowly, he felt along the bed and discovered it was empty. His uncle wasn't there.

As he turned to leave, there was a noise at the door. He hid behind it as it opened and pinned the man who came through it to the wall, knife at his throat. "Daniel, it's John. Richard is dead. Your uncle is about to leave for Hawkhurst. I must join him. Go now, or you'll miss him."

Recognizing the voice, he lowered his weapon. "Thank you, my friend."

Daniel ran down the stairs, calling to mind the map of the castle he'd memorized, and followed the servants' hallway out to the stables, avoiding the commotion in the great hall. As he exited the castle, hooves clattered on the cobblestones of Castle Street, and he knew he was too late. His uncle was gone. Moments later, he saw John on his horse, galloping to catch up. If only he'd had his own horse at the ready.

Cursing to himself, he ran after them until he lost them in the distance. Unwilling to give up, he made his way to the Juggler. Running in the chill night air brought him back to himself. The rage died down, replaced by cold determination. Gerard would have everything packed and ready by now for their journey to France. But there was no way he was fleeing again.

Unbidden, a vivid memory of the feeling of Carenza's lips swept over him, wiping away his plans. He'd never wanted a woman like he wanted her. Even with Adele, beautiful, sweet Adele, it hadn't been like this.

Adele. It had been so long. More than six years now. He touched the rings that hung on a long chain beneath his shirt, their wedding rings, and his father's signet ring, and said a little prayer. Eternal rest grant unto her, O Lord, and let Your perpetual light shine upon her. Amen. Adele was gone. She had been gone a long time, but he still couldn't let go.

"She moves me, Adele," he said softly to the night sky. "But my love is a curse. I can't let what happened to you happen to someone else. What do I do?"

The night sky failed to provide an answer as he tore down Castle Street.

Gerard was waiting for him when he arrived at the Juggler.

"Daniel, your boat is ready, and everything is packed," Gerard said with the most serious face Daniel had ever seen on him since the day they'd lost their family.

"I'm not going. I need my horse to go after my uncle," Daniel said quietly.

"By yourself?" Gerard wasn't thinking of joining him, was he?

"Don't you dare try to come with me. You get on that boat like we planned and head for Calais. I'll come join you once I've dealt with my uncle."

"I'm not going to Calais," Gerard admitted. "I'm done running."

Daniel took a deep breath. "That may not save you. You know what happened to Adele, to your father."

Gerard gave him a level stare. "As if I could forget how that bastard murdered my sister and my father. Maybe if I stay, I'll be able to slip something in his drink and have my revenge."

"You're joking." He studied his friend, incredulous, but suddenly not so sure it was a joke. Gerard put on his most innocent face, which somehow fooled everyone by fooling no one.

"Of course, I'm joking," Gerard said with a nervous laugh. "You think I'm competent enough to turn assassin? Look, I like it here. I'm happy here. I have a good life. Lady de Vere pays me well to be her songbird. And I'm willing to take the risk to stay. And then there's Elaine."

"Elaine? I thought you and she were just..."

"We were just. But when you and I started making plans to

leave, I realized it was something more. She's a good and sweet woman, and I don't want to leave her. I'm in love, Daniel. I mean, truly in love, not as a flirtation. Tonight, after the performance, I told her how I feel. I asked her to marry me, and she said yes. So, you see, I can't go." Gerard lapsed into silence.

Daniel stared at his friend. Gerard looked different—older, more serious. And even, sober. Perhaps Gerard had finally grown up.

"Congratulations! I had no idea. Your father would be so proud." He gave Gerard a squeeze on his shoulder.

Gerard looked sheepishly at the ground and then back up. "I had to settle down sometime. I can't run forever. I'm sorry, Daniel. You've been a brother to me. I will always wish you well in everything you do. I hope our paths cross again someday."

"What about the poetry? How will you manage without me?"

"You think I've learned nothing all these years? I can hold my own, though perhaps never as well as I would with your help. I've been performing my own work more and more of late. Don't think I don't appreciate your assistance. I'd never have gotten this far without you, but it's time for me to stand on my own."

Daniel nodded and smiled. When had this happened? How had he not noticed Gerard becoming a man who could stand on his own? It was a wrench to say goodbye, to leave just when he was becoming the man Daniel had always hoped he could be.

"I'm not your father. I'm not your blood brother. But for what it's worth, I'm proud. You're my family, and I love you. I'll miss you, my friend. Take care of yourself. Take care of your wife. Stay safe."

"I'll miss you too. Be safe and stay alive. Maybe even find love again. Heaven knows you deserve a little happiness in your life. Adele would want you to be happy."

Daniel was silent. What could he say? Happiness was not in his future. It couldn't be. Not until he was rid of his uncle one way or another. He pulled Gerard into one last hug.

"And take care of Sir Percival, will you?"

Gerard drew back and stared. "Sir Percival?"

"The cat."

"You named the cat Sir Percival?"

Daniel's ears heated, and he shrugged.

"Fine. I'll take care of the cat, but I am not calling it by name. Everyone will think I've gone round the bend."

Daniel clapped Gerard on the shoulder in thanks.

"I need to go now, or I'll lose de Broase."

He mounted his horse and tore down the cobblestone streets without a backward glance.

MINUTES LATER, HE arrived at the southern gate, which was closed for the night. He told the guards he needed to leave on an urgent trip to Hastings for medicine for his sick mother, and they let him through.

Soon, he was out in the countryside, Winchelsea castle dwindling in the distance. The night was clear, and the moon and stars scintillated in the heavens. The celestial view filled him with sadness and longing.

There was a particular star on Orion's belt that he'd long ago decided was Adele's home in the heavens. Alone in the night, he whispered to her.

"I'm chasing my uncle again, Adele. And I had to say goodbye to Gerard. He's staying put this time. He says he found happiness. I believe him. I just hope it doesn't get him killed. I know I promised you I'd take care of your brother, but I can't keep dragging him around like a fugitive forever. Will you forgive me for leaving him?"

Daniel rode on in silence. The night air was still, without a breeze, but around him, the darkness was alive. An owl hooted in the distance. Some nocturnal creature rustled in the bushes by the road. Crickets chirped.

The natural world seemed to be speaking to him if only he had the power to understand.

"And there's something else. I feel awkward talking to you about this, but…tonight, with Carenza, I had feelings…. I had feelings that I hadn't felt in a long time. I care about her, Adele, more than I would like to admit. And I left her in danger."

He listened to the soft thud of his horse's hooves on the dirt of the ancient Roman road, a steady rhythm chasing him through the night.

And then he heard an additional set of hooves coming toward him at a trot.

He pulled off the road, dismounted, and waited, hidden in the trees. It was probably one of his uncle's men, come to finish him off. He crouched and waited, knives in hand.

As the rider became clearer, though, Daniel recognized the man's profile. He stepped forward and called out, "John? What are you doing?"

John halted his horse and dismounted.

"Your uncle sent me after you. He's ordered me to finish the job Richard failed at. I can't go back while you live."

Oh no. Poor John!

"Take me into your service, and together, we can end him," John said, kneeling before him.

"I'll accept your aid and friendship but not your fealty. I'm no lord."

"You may change your mind when I tell you the rest," John said, rising.

"The rest?"

"Your uncle thinks Lord de Vere is weak. Since he lacks an heir, Winchelsea goes to whoever can stake the strongest claim. And your uncle is very angry at the de Veres for letting you in the castle and you, for killing Richard. He now plans to return to poison Lord de Vere, as he did your father, and force Lady Carenza into marrying him to solidify his claim to Winchelsea."

"But he just tried to kill her."

"He's decided he wants her alive. For now. He thinks Lady Carenza is in league with you, possibly deceiving him with you, and he blames you both for Richard's death. Once they are wed, and Winchelsea is his, he plans to exact his revenge on her as well."

Daniel closed his eyes. This wasn't supposed to happen. The whole point of killing Richard had been to make Carenza safer.

"You'll never succeed at getting to him now that he's on his guard, even with my help," John continued. "You need to declare yourself and confront him openly if you're going to have any hope of saving both Lord de Vere and Lady Carenza."

"I can't," Daniel said, deadly quiet. He clenched his fists unconsciously until his nails dug into his palms. "I'm not taking up that name, especially not after what my uncle did to Adele and her father. The name 'de Broase' is tainted beyond repair."

"Ferdinand was my friend, too. Don't use his memory as an excuse not to—"

"I made an oath when I married Adele!"

"So I've heard," John roared, his eyes full of an anger that Daniel recognized but had never felt directed at him. The last time John had looked this furious was the day Daniel's father had been killed. "He asked you to take that oath for Adele's protection, and from what he told me, the idea was yours, not his. Ferdinand would never expect you to keep the oath if reclaiming your name could help you avenge his and Adele's deaths. You owe it to them to turn around and fight with every weapon at your disposal."

Daniel watched John with fury and disbelief, unable to respond. Adele was dead because of that name and title.

"As one of Ferdinand's oldest friends, I can tell you he would want you to let go of the oath and do what's right. But if that's not enough to convince you, take a moment and think about what Adele would want. Be honest with yourself. What would she tell you if she could speak to you from heaven right now?"

What would Adele say? Dare I even ask? He'd clung to the

oath all these years because it was simple, clear-cut. Adele was anything but. And yet he knew the truth as he closed his eyes, bracing against a realization that had been a long time coming. Even before John caught up to him and hurled harsh words at him, he'd been thinking these very thoughts.

"Adele would want me to do whatever it took to defend Carenza and her father," he said slowly, staring at the ground, unable to meet John's eyes. "She would want me to let go of the oath, take up my name and title, and bring down my uncle."

He turned to John and saw softness and sympathy in the old man's eyes.

"I suppose it was always going to come down to this," Daniel said hesitantly. "He's never going to stop trying to kill me. I can die pointlessly trying to take him down alone, or I can stand up and fight with knights at my back. I know the odds are against me. I can defend myself, but I'm no knight. But it will be worth it if I can do some good. I couldn't save Adele, but perhaps I can save Carenza."

Carenza. That was why he truly needed Adele's forgiveness and permission. Carenza was utterly unreachable for Master Daniel, the shipwright, but Daniel, Earl of Hawkhurst, could court her, marry her even. If he took up his title, he knew he wouldn't be able to resist. In fact, he would have a moral obligation to offer his hand after that kiss they shared.

Forgive me, Adele. You've been gone for six years. I'm so lonely, and you're not here. He stared up at the stars—at her home in Orion's belt—for a long moment. Without warning, a sudden, warm, and gentle breeze rustled through the leaves overhead and brushed his face before it stilled, and the night was still once more. Suddenly, he knew. He felt lighter, hopeful for the first time in years. Thank you, Adele.

Nodding to John, he said, "I can't go after him in Hawkhurst. As you said, he's too well-defended. And I can't go back to Winchelsea and expect the baron to believe I'm anything more than a troubadour."

"My lord, if I might make a suggestion?"

No matter what he'd told John, it still set his teeth on edge to be called "my lord," but he held back and accepted it without objection. "Yes, of course. What do you recommend?"

"Ashford, my lord. I think it's time you paid a visit to your sister."

"Do we have time for that?"

"I think the trouble with the peasants will keep your uncle occupied for at least a few weeks. He won't want to leave Hawkhurst until it's dealt with. And it is high time you visited your sister."

He smiled. Maggie. Dear God, but it would be good to see her. Now that his uncle knew he was alive, he doubted visiting her would cause her any more danger than already existed. "Ashford it is."

Together, they turned their horses and headed north.

CHAPTER FOURTEEN

AFTER TWO DAYS of riding night and day on back roads, keeping a low profile, and getting barely any sleep, Daniel and John arrived in Ashford midmorning and went in search of a place to stay. The bustling market town offered a range of accommodations. John chose a modest establishment with a thatched roof and freshly painted wattle and daub walls called "Traveler's Rest."

The friendly innkeeper led them through a bustling common room filled with merchants and other travelers breaking their fast with fragrant bread and hard wedges of cheese. The room the innkeeper led them to was considerably larger than his attic garrot back in Winchelsea. Fresh rushes and herbs were strewn on the floor, and the beds were covered in thick woolen blankets. It was the most luxury Daniel had enjoyed in years, certainly an improvement on the last two nights on the hard ground. It looked like heaven after their journey.

As soon as the door closed behind the innkeeper, Daniel availed himself of the washbasin to rid himself of the grime of the road. He changed into his simple, green wool cotte with black wool hose. His dusty and well-worn boots would have to do. They were all he had.

Ready as he could make himself, Daniel ventured out into Ashford's bustling streets. The turrets of the earl's castle were plainly visible above the thatched and tiled roofs that lined the town's stone-paved streets. He wound his way past carriages, carts, and merchant stalls until he arrived at the castle gates.

Taking a deep breath, he straightened his back and approached one of the uniformed guards.

"I have an urgent message for the Lady Magdalena from her family. I was instructed to deliver it into her hands." Thanks to his father's signet ring, he was able to show the de Broase seal stamped in wax on the false letter he had in his hand. It seemed the surest way to be allowed a quiet word with his sister. No one would dare question correspondence from House de Broase. To his deep relief, it worked. The guards escorted him to a small receiving room just off the entrance.

Daniel stood and waited in the opulent space. It had a narrow window, just wide enough for an archer to shoot out of in case of a siege. The noon sun shone brightly, and no lantern was necessary to see the rich brocade cushions on the richly carved and highly polished wooden chairs, which he didn't dare sit on. How had he ever thought such luxuries were normal? And yet he'd spent his childhood in a similar castle, completely oblivious to how different his life was from everyone else's.

After a few minutes, a woman came in, dressed in saffron silk and wearing a ruby necklace. Her face was achingly familiar, even after all these years. How could he have stayed away for so long? She was the only family he had left. Why hadn't he come sooner? He could have disguised himself, somehow. Found a way into the castle that didn't require him to use his father's signet ring or reveal that he was still alive.

He only hoped she would recognize him as his uncle had. If she didn't, he would try again tomorrow with John's help, but they agreed that it would be better if Daniel met her on his own the first time.

Turning an imperious face to him, she demanded, "Well? Where's the message?"

She didn't recognize him. He struggled to keep his face even and conceal his disappointment. It was hardly surprising. They'd been so young when they were separated, and of course, he hadn't had a beard back then.

"Maggie, it's me. Daniel."

She froze, then recoiled. "How dare you! My brother died seventeen years ago. I'm calling the guards." She turned to go, and he caught her arm. "Unhand me this instant," she demanded.

But he refused to let go. "Wait, Maggie. It's me. I can prove it. Here's our father's signet ring," he said, pulling out the chain around his neck that carried it. "And look, I still have a scar from that time when I was eight, and you hit me too hard with a toy sword after I broke your doll." He showed a small, puckered scar on his left collarbone. "You used to call me Bitsy because I was so much smaller than you when I was little, but you kept calling me that long after I outgrew you. Do you believe me yet?"

Lady Magdalena gave him a long, searching stare. Her eyes grew moist, and she placed her hand on her heart.

Daniel released her arm. Had he gotten through?

"Bitsy? Can it truly be you?" Her voice was soft, hopeful.

"I swear to you, Maggie. It's me." Tears gathered in his own eyes, and he blinked them away. Saints above, it was good to see her!

"But how?"

Daniel sighed, drinking her in and wishing he wasn't on an urgent mission. How lovely it would be if they could simply sit and be together as a family.

"How long do you have?"

"For you? All the time in the world." She clutched him into a hug, tears streaming down her face. "I always hoped Uncle Raymond was lying. I didn't dare believe it, but I always hoped. You must tell me everything. I want seventeen years of agonizing detail. Don't you dare leave anything out!"

She sat down on a brocade settee across from him and invited him to sit in the highbacked chair behind him. Then she popped up again.

"Where are my manners? You must be hungry. You were always hungry. Let me have refreshments brought. Oh! And I need to cancel everything. Just a moment. Don't go anywhere."

She ran out of the room, leaving Daniel laughing over the whirlwind that was his sister. Some things never changed. Other things changed a great deal. When he'd last seen her, she had been a wide-eyed, gullible chatterbox, quick to anger but also quick to forgive. Now she was very much her ladyship, the countess, commanding and impatient. She looked different, too. How could she not? The eyes and nose were the same, but she was no longer the human twig he remembered. She had filled out and even become pleasantly plump. It had given her an air of gravity and presence that she never had in her youth.

Moments later, she returned in a whirl of skirts and shut the door. "They'll be bringing refreshments shortly. Now. Tell me everything."

So, he did. Starting with his flight from Hawkhurst the night after their father was murdered, he told her about how John hid him away on Ferdinand's farm. He told her everything about Adele and learning to be a shipwright. When he shed tears telling of Adele and Ferdinand's deaths, Maggie reached out and placed her hand gently on his. That soft connection almost broke him. For so many years, the only two people he could confide in were Gerard and John. But even they could never understand like Maggie always could.

Pulling himself together, he dashed away his tears and continued to his life in Winchelsea and the recent events that had led him to seek her out. Fury coursed through his veins as he described the latest perfidy of their uncle.

"He tried to murder his own fiancée?" Maggie said with a gasp as he reached the end of his tale. "That's a new low, even for him."

"If I had found him that night, I would have killed him, especially after what he did to Lady Carenza—"

"Yes, about her," she said. "Are you in love with her, Daniel?"

He'd carefully left out anything that might hint that he cared about Carenza in more than an abstract way. How did she see through him so easily?

"In love?" he asked to buy time.

"You said a lot of things about honor and revenge, but somehow, I don't think that's the whole story. You could have gone after Uncle Raymond any time once you were big and strong enough to defend yourself. But you didn't. It wasn't until Lady Carenza de Vere stumbled into your warehouse that you felt inspired to take action. I think there's more to this than you're telling me." Maggie looked at him expectantly.

"Lady Carenza is a beautiful and virtuous woman whose intelligence is unmatched—"

Maggie made a tsk sound.

"Except perhaps by you, my dear sister." He gave her a hopeful smile, and she gave him an appreciative nod. "But she's far beyond my reach. I'm only a shipwright, Maggie."

"Pshh," Maggie said, waving her hand. "You're Earl Daniel de Broase. A princess isn't beyond your reach."

"If she was within my reach, I'd ask for her hand in marriage, but I'm not an earl. At least not yet."

He looked up at her. It was time to make his request. It was what he came for. He only hoped she wouldn't throw him out on his ear.

"I was hoping you might help me change that," he said. "Not enter into open conflict with Uncle Raymond. I wouldn't ask that of you. But I have thoughts on how I could reclaim my name, defend the de Veres, and end Uncle Raymond's reign of terror. And yes, maybe even win Carenza de Vere. But I'll need some financial assistance if you're willing, and perhaps your powers of persuasion. I promise I'll pay the money back if I'm successful." And he had to succeed. There was no other option. "Will you help me?"

She gave him a broad smile. "I thought you'd never ask. Let's go find my husband." Grabbing his hand, she pulled him up and dragged him unceremoniously out of the room, through the cavernous, vaulted entrance hall, and up the grand stairs into what must be the count's solar.

An elegant man with chin-length blond hair, wearing a deep-blue velvet cotte with a scalloped skirt, sat at a perfectly polished writing desk, scribbling away on a sheaf of parchment. A servant stood stiffly beside the desk with a satchel full of scrolls. Daniel thought of his sad little desk back home and the secondhand parchment he scraped and reused. Even standing beside his sister, he couldn't help but feel awkward and out of place.

The earl turned and smiled warmly, and his blue eyes twinkled with affection when he saw Maggie. "Hello, my love. Thank God you came. My correspondence today is deadly dull, but Brimsley here insists that I must respond to each and every letter I've received. If you hadn't interrupted, he would have had me at it for hours."

Brimsley cleared his throat and said in deep, mournful tones, "I only wish to be of service, my lord."

"And so you are, my good man." The earl winked at him, then turned back to Maggie before appraising Daniel, who was standing by her side. "Who is this you've brought with you?"

Maggie clutched Daniel's hand, grinning widely.

The earl's eyebrows raised all the way up his forehead.

"You'll never believe it, but..." She paused. Maggie always knew how to make the most of a dramatic moment. "This is my brother, Daniel."

The earl frowned and crossed his arms, looking Daniel up and down. "Your brother."

"Yes."

"The one who died when you were a child."

"The very one."

The earl stepped closer, eyeing their clasped hands with a deeply furrowed brow. Daniel tried to pull away, but Maggie held fast. Of course, the earl didn't believe it. Why would he? He was probably thinking of all the ways he could eviscerate this imposter for daring to touch his wife.

"Maggie, I'd like you to step away from him," he said in a low, quiet voice that brooked no dissent.

"No, Alfric. I won't. Not until you believe me."

Maggie stared her husband down.

Once again, Daniel tried to pull his hand away, but Maggie was having none of it.

"He has our father's signet ring and a scar on his collarbone exactly where my brother did. And he knows things only my brother would know. Look at his face, Alfric. Doesn't he look like a de Broase?"

The earl stared at him in silence for a seemingly endless moment. Daniel could hardly breathe. Slowly, the earl's scowl turned quizzical.

"I suppose…" The earl looked back and forth between Daniel and Maggie. "I suppose he might be a de Broase. It's hard to tell behind all that scruff. He does look somewhat like your uncle."

Daniel failed to hide his wince.

A smile broke across the earl's face, and he laughed aloud. "Don't worry, Daniel. I'm not fond of your uncle either."

Maggie's eyes widened. "Does that mean you believe him?"

The earl let out a long sigh, then looked back and forth between the two of them.

"What was the nickname Maggie had for you when you were a boy?"

This again. Well, if this was what it took to prove his identity, so be it. "Bitsy," he admitted through gritted teeth.

The earl chuckled and shook his head. "Welcome back to the family, Lord Bitsy de Broase."

Daniel grimaced, his face hot with embarrassment. "Thank you, my lord."

It was done. For better or worse, Daniel was a de Broase once more. He shoved down the surge of loathing that welled up at the thought. This was what he had to do to save Winchelsea, to save Carenza. It would all be worth it if he could end his uncle's reign of terror.

CHAPTER FIFTEEN

"WE NEED TO send a messenger to the king to let him know Raymond de Broase is not the rightful earl and that he's plotting against me. He'll sort this mess out," Carenza's father said as they were winding up breakfast.

A hunk of buttered bread and an apple sat untouched on Carenza's plate. Her stomach churned at the thought of food.

"The earl may have left without a word," her father continued, "but I suspect he will be back. He must know we know his secret, and I'm sure he isn't happy about what happened to Richard. My dear, I think you should stay with the sisters for a bit."

"Your father is right," her mother said. "You should go to the abbey until this is resolved." Under her breath, she added, "I could murder that man."

Carenza stared at her. There was hurt and fury in Lady Isabella's eyes. Her mother was actually angry on her behalf for once, though she couldn't forget that her mother tried to make her marry de Broase in the first place.

"If you want to be a nun, we'll support you," her father said. "I can't force you to marry, not after this. We'll find some other way to keep Winchelsea fed."

Carenza blinked back tears. She'd cried and cried these last two days. She couldn't seem to stop. "I'll go to the abbey if that's what you think is best, Father."

Her father squeezed her hand.

"I'll go pack."

The enormity of her father's words slowly sank in as she climbed the stairs to her room. After all this time, her parents were finally agreeing to her chosen vocation. It was everything she'd wanted, and yet, she felt cold and numb. Her hands trembled as she pulled out the simple black dresses she wore at the abbey and laid them on the bed for Elaine to pack. Each breath was labored as she tried not to succumb to the darkness welling up within her. She felt as if she was shipwrecked just like her brother, being pulled under by the relentless tug of currents far more powerful than she.

Two nights ago, when everything had happened, she had been propelled by a surge of emotion that left her shaking but also gave her preternatural clarity and focus. Her heart had felt like it was going to beat out of her chest; her stomach had been clenched. But her mind somehow floated above it all, observing every minute detail while somehow detached from events, both good and bad.

After she'd finished telling a carefully composed tale to her father, though, the detachment had collapsed. Everything came rushing in at once—the horror of the events with Lord de Broase and Richard, the passion, heartbreak, and guilt of what happened with Daniel. She'd foundered in a raging sea with no land in sight. The tears had started then, and she'd been unable to stop them since.

Now, her prayers had been answered, and she was released from the obligation to marry, preparing to depart for the abbey. Wasn't this what she wanted? Wasn't this what she'd prayed for every day since Lord de Broase had asked for her hand?

Elaine came in and found her standing in the middle of the room, trembling with the effort to hold back tears. How long Carenza had stood there like that, she could not say.

"There, there, my lady. There, there." Elaine guided her to

the bed and helped her sit. "I'll send down to the kitchen for something to revive your spirits."

Elaine disappeared out the door.

Closing her eyes, Carenza clasped her rosary and began to pray. What else could she do but throw herself on God's mercy? She was too lost and confused to chart her own course. The dream of becoming a nun had been her sole focus for so long, but faced with the chance to fulfill it, all she wanted was to return to the warm embrace of the man she'd never see again—a man she hardly knew.

The door creaked open, and Elaine returned with a ceramic cup filled with some herbal concoction that Carenza drank without question, ignoring the way it burned as it poured down her throat. It certainly contained spirits of some sort. Perhaps that would deaden the pain, at least for a little while.

Embracing oblivion as warm tendrils eased her mind's torment, she returned to her prayers as Elaine bustled around her room, packing her things.

Several hours later, she and Elaine sat on a bench at the dock while footmen loaded their luggage onto the ferry. She watched the warehouse where Daniel worked, hoping against hope to grab a glimpse of him, even though Gerard had told Elaine he was gone. When they boarded the boat, and she turned her gaze from Winchelsea, the tears started again despite her best efforts to hold them back.

Elaine put an arm around her, pulling her close. "There, there, my lady. Shh. There, there."

"I don't even know why I'm crying, Elaine. I just can't seem to stop."

Surrendering to Elaine's warm embrace, and heedless of the sideways looks from the ferryman, Carenza gave in and sobbed. There was no holding it back. The tide had overtaken her.

At the abbey, Elaine helped her settle into her usual room, a bare cell just like those of the sisters, with a narrow straw pallet, a small, arched window, a writing desk, and a crucifix. She curled up on the bed and stared at the wall, and she stayed that way all afternoon. Just before dinner time, the abbess came in, short and round and gray-haired with an air of presence and authority that could rival a king's. Carenza couldn't remember the abbess ever visiting her in her room before. She tried to make herself sit up but only managed to roll over. Further movement felt impossible.

"Mistress Elaine told me what happened, Carenza, but if you're up to it, I'd like to hear it from you." The abbess' eyes were kind, but her voice was commanding.

Carenza lay staring at the wall next to the abbess. She couldn't manage eye contact at the moment. After a long breath, she began, "My intended husband Lord de Broase tried to have me killed. I shouldn't have been in the solar. I should never have been there. But he found me and then left me with his man, who—" She stopped, resisting the urge to vomit. "His man held a knife to my throat, and he was about to…". She could taste bile in her throat and swallowed hard. "I fought. I hit him with a candelabra. I bit him. I stomped on his foot. And then…" And then Daniel arrived. "And then he fell on his knife."

"And then what happened?"

And then I kissed a man who would never marry me. I kissed him twice. I felt things I had never imagined, improper things, impossible things. He set me on fire, and I wanted to burn. I would have let him have me, but he stopped. He left. And now he's gone, and I'll never see him again.

"Then I went to my father. The man was dead. Lord de Broase left abruptly, without a word."

"Is that everything, my child?" It was as if the abbess knew she was lying, but how could she?

"Yes."

The abbess sighed. "Oh, Carenza. You poor thing! You must take strength from your faith in this moment of darkness. 'Yea, though I walk through the valley of the shadow of death, I will fear no evil, for thou art with me.' Never forget that your Heavenly Father is with you and that He gave the life of his only

Son so that you might be forgiven for your sins. If the Almighty can forgive you, then you must also forgive yourself, my child."

"I shouldn't have been in the solar."

"Perhaps it is unwise to wander the castle at night unaccompanied, but it's hardly a sin."

"No, you don't understand, I shouldn't have—" Carenza stopped.

"What don't I understand, child?" The abbess sat patiently and waited, as if she knew there was more to the story than Carenza was letting on.

"Mother, I had feelings for a man." She hadn't meant to say it. She wished she could take it back. It just came out. The urge to confess was too strong.

"And you were going to meet him?"

Carenza nodded, tears streaming down her face. She couldn't bring herself to speak.

"Oh, child. I assume the man in question was not your fiancé?"

Carenza shook her head.

"Suppose you try telling me what happened again, the whole story this time."

"I was going to meet him in the solar, but Lord de Broase came in with his man, and I hid. What I told you about Lord de Broase and the man who tried to kill me was true. And then he came in. I don't know which of us killed Richard. It was dark. We couldn't see. And then…. And then I kissed him. It was complete madness. I don't know what came over me. I was so scared and so relieved, and he was so close. I should never have met him in the first place. I should never have gone to the solar. None of this would have happened if…"

"I don't believe one minute this all started with the solar, child. What were you thinking, meeting a man like that? I would never have thought it of you!"

"I wasn't thinking at all. I don't understand what came over me."

The abbess sighed and shook her head. "And where is this man now?"

"Gone." He was gone forever. She would never see him again. That hurt more than everything else combined. Tears filled her eyes once more.

"That's probably for the best." The abbess lapsed into silence. "You know, I always suspected you might not be cut out for the life of a nun. I always thought you'd likely be happier with a husband and children. You were so certain you didn't want that, but I wonder what you think now."

After a long pause, where she tried—again—to remember how much she'd wanted to be a nun and then thought about how she'd felt in Daniel's arms, Carenza murmured, "I don't know."

"I'll have dinner brought to your room tonight, but I would like for you to join us for prayers and meals starting tomorrow. And you should go to confession as soon as you feel strong enough to rise."

"I will."

"Good. Now eat some food, say your prayers, and get a good night's sleep. You've been through an ordeal, but in time, you will recover. Although it's hard to imagine now, you may come out of this a better and stronger person. Just follow God's path, and He will lead you to grace."

After the abbess left, the tears finally stopped. Carenza didn't feel peaceful or collected, but the pain had eased. The numbness that settled in was preferable to feeling like an open wound, bleeding unstaunched.

As she waited for dinner, she knelt on the cool stone floor of her cell and prayed to forget what she could never have.

CHAPTER SIXTEEN

DANIEL OPENED HIS eyes to a sea of green. What in heaven's name…? He blinked. Curtains. He was surrounded by curtains. Green damask curtains, to be specific. And his body rested on something so soft, it defied belief. The sensation was unexpected but also familiar to some distant corner of his mind. A featherbed?

Any minute, his mother was going to walk in and chide him for sleeping too late. "Rise and shine, my little slugabed," she would say in a singsong, gently shaking his shoulder as he tried to burrow beneath the covers. "Time for breakfast, my sweet. Shall I sing the wake-up song?"

Not the wake-up song. Anything but the wake-up song. Except that he wanted to hear her voice more than anything in the world.

As if he had conjured it, a female voice floated in from a distance. "Monks are singing, church bells ringing. Time to wake and eat some cake. Sun is shining. No more whining. Mama's here, so get up, dear."

Had it all been a terrible dream? Was he home at Hawkhurst with his family, a child once again?

He pulled a hand out from under the covers and examined it. No, he was certainly a man and not a boy. Those enormous, calloused hands couldn't possibly belong to little Daniel de

Broase.

De Broase.

He rubbed his eyes with the heels of his hands, and everything came rushing back. This was Ashford Castle. He'd been here for a week, though every morning, he'd awoken with the same sense of bafflement. The voice he heard in the distance was his sister, not his mother. And Daniel was a de Broase once more.

Groaning, he forced himself to sit up. He was wearing a long, fine linen nightshirt. It tangled awkwardly around his bulk. For seventeen years, he'd been content to sleep in his braies, but Maggie and his new manservant, Godfrey, had insisted he needed to dress like an earl even in his sleep. Ridiculous.

There was a soft knock at the door.

"Yes," he grumbled.

The door cracked open. "It's Godfrey, my lord. Her ladyship asked me to wake you. We leave in two hours."

Leaving? Daniel shook his groggy head back and forth to shake out the cobwebs. Ah yes. Today was the day they were departing for Winchelsea.

Godfrey's frowning visage peeked through the crack in the door, not a hair out of place on his balding head. The man clearly knew far more about how an earl was supposed to behave than Daniel did, much to Daniel's irritation.

"I'll be ready," Daniel said, waving Godfrey away.

"Of course, you will, my lord. I'll have you packed and ready in no time."

Walking in despite Daniel's dismissal, Godfrey went to the trunk at the foot of his bed and began pulling out clothing for the day.

"I can pick my own clothes." Until a few days ago, he'd had so little there wasn't really anything to pick from.

"Yes, my lord. May I recommend these riding breeches and this cotte for travel?" Godfrey indicated the finely tailored outfit laid out on the bed.

Of the various excessively extravagant outfits Daniel now

possessed, this was indeed the most practical for travel. Reluctantly, he dragged himself out of the exceedingly comfortable bed.

"Thank you, Godfrey. I'll take it from here."

"Of course, my lord."

Sweeping around Daniel, Godfrey began to lift the hem of Daniel's nightshirt.

"What are you doing, man?" Daniel demanded, flinching away.

"My job, my lord. Her ladyship instructed me to have you ready within the next half hour, and there is precious little time."

Eyes widening, Daniel hastily stepped around the bed, away from Godfrey.

"Time for what? If you would just leave, I would be ready in five minutes." It was ridiculous for a grown man to hide behind a bedpost, but that was exactly what Daniel was doing.

"Ready for a roadside tavern, perhaps, but not to ride with the earl's retinue on a formal visit. You will be on view, my lord. People far and wide will see you riding with the earl. You must look like you belong there."

Just when Daniel thought this couldn't get any worse, his sister sang out, "Bitsy, are you ready yet?" from the other side of the door. "You had better not be giving Godfrey a hard time again. If I hear you've given him the least bit of trouble, I'll tweak your ears. Don't think I won't just because I'm a lady now."

Damn it all. Fine. He would cooperate. "I'll be ready shortly, Maggie," he called out.

He narrowed his eyes at Godfrey. "I will wear the outfit you picked, and you can do what you must to my hair and beard and whatever other parts of my face you feel the need to poke and prod. But I draw the line at dressing myself. Have I made myself clear?"

A hint of a smile twitched on Godfrey's lips. "Perfectly clear, my lord."

"Good."

Daniel hurriedly stripped off his nightshirt and donned the

outfit laid out on the bed. Unfortunately, the sleeves involved some sort of elaborate lacing that he couldn't for the life of him figure out how to tie.

"Allow me, my lord?" Godfrey asked, not bothering to hide the triumphant note in his voice.

Squeezing his eyes closed, Daniel thrust his arm out to the side, and moments later, it was done.

"Now, my lord, about your beard…"

IT WAS MID-MORNING when Daniel descended the main stair to be inspected by his sister. Godfrey trailed behind like an unwelcome shadow.

Maggie circled Daniel twice and then looked up at him, grinning. "Magnificent. You look every inch an earl. I knew you could do it, Godfrey. I'm sure he didn't make it easy for you." Her voice echoed in the rafters of the enormous entry hall.

Godfrey puffed with pride.

The earl came striding toward them and stopped short, blinking. "Is that you, Daniel? By God, you are a changed man. The family resemblance is clear as day now. For a moment there, I almost thought you were your uncle."

Daniel closed his eyes and gritted his teeth, willing himself not to react. Was there anything he feared more than becoming his uncle?

"No, not Uncle Raymond," Maggie said, placing a gentle hand on Daniel's arm. "Father. You look exactly like Father."

Opening his eyes, he saw Maggie gazing up at him, blinking away a tear. Daniel took her hand and squeezed it. "May he rest in peace," he murmured for her ears alone.

She nodded and sniffed, then assembled her face into a smile. "It's time for us to go. Is everything ready?" she asked, turning to her husband.

"Yes, my love. Our traveling party is gathered in the court-yard."

"And you've kissed the children goodbye?"

"Of course, and you?"

"Yes. But are you sure we can't bring them with us?"

The earl sighed and shook his head. "We discussed this. It's much safer for them to stay here with their Auntie Mathilda than to go traipsing off across the countryside with us. There could be brigands."

"And we're bringing twenty armed men with us. Surely, no one would dare attack us."

The earl took Maggie's hands in his. "Dearest, we settled this. The children are staying here."

She gave him a resigned little nod.

"Besides," the earl continued, "when was the last time we had a bit of time to ourselves, just the two of us?"

The earl's mischievous grin made her blush.

Daniel looked away. He liked the earl a great deal. Clearly, the man was besotted with his sister, but Daniel would just as soon not watch them making doe eyes at each other. It reminded him too much of all he had lost with Adele.

His heart squeezed painfully, and he tried to refocus his thoughts on revenge against his uncle, but his unruly mind took another path entirely. He was back in the solar at Winchelsea with Carenza, her warm body pressed against his, her sweet lips driving him to distraction. The blinding heat of their embrace seared him, even in recollection.

No.

Daniel was not marrying Carenza for pleasure and certainly not for love. It was for her safety. He could never allow his uncle to harm her while he had the means to prevent it. Most likely, he would need to send her away after they wed to keep her out of Uncle Raymond's reach. While he was duty-bound to offer his hand after that kiss they shared, especially now that he was an earl, he needed to guard against attachment. He didn't want to break her heart.

His own heart was already too damaged to repair. He might now bear the title and wear the trappings of an earl, but beneath it all, he was just as unworthy of her as when he was a simple shipwright. And he couldn't shake the conviction that his love was a curse that doomed those he cared for, no matter how irrational he knew it was. Even now, he was looking over his shoulder at every opportunity, afraid that his uncle would come for Maggie because he made contact.

But how would Carenza see him? Would she realize how unsuitable he was for her, or would she accept?

He wouldn't put it past her to turn him down, despite his fancy clothes and impressive title. It would almost be a relief if she did. He knew Adele would want him to go on with his life, but something still hung on to the memory of what was and fears that history might repeat itself.

But was there a chance he could find love again with Carenza?

Absolutely not. What was he thinking? He was not destined for love and contentment, not while his uncle lived. Carenza was in danger, and it was all Daniel's fault. How foolish of him to show himself to his uncle at Winchelsea. He had been so hell-bent on revenge that he had ignored the dangers to others from his actions.

It was time to right that wrong.

"Bitsy, are you wool-gathering?" His sister's hand on his arm brought him out of his reverie. "It's time to go."

Daniel straightened his cotte and squared his shoulders.

"I'm ready."

Following Maggie and the earl out into the front courtyard, he held his head high. While he didn't care about appearances the way Maggie did, he remembered his father's lessons about how to command men.

Arrayed before him were the soldiers who would fight by his side. He needed their respect and obedience. They could not see him doubt himself for one moment, or the battle would be lost before it began.

These soldiers were a motley bunch, but one did not expect polish from a band of mercenaries. Daniel had interviewed each of them personally over the last week and rejected any that he found wanting. John had joined him, providing a second opinion about which to hire and which to send on their way. Still, Daniel was grateful that a group of the earl's knights would be joining them on the journey to Winchelsea. He believed he had chosen his men well, but one could never be too cautious with mercenaries.

John sat on his horse at the head of the group. "My lord, we are ready to depart as soon as you are."

This was it, the moment when he stepped into his father's shoes and truly became Earl de Broase.

Daniel mounted the destrier beside John as Maggie and the earl climbed into a carriage at the back of the entourage.

Turning back to his men, he bellowed, "Onward to Winchelsea."

As one, they spurred their horses and set out on their quest.

CHAPTER SEVENTEEN

C ARENZA'S QUILL CAME to an abrupt stop on the parchment as she read the next Bible verse she was to copy.

"Let him kiss me with the kisses of his mouth: for thy love is better than wine," it said.

Was it mere coincidence that she was copying the Song of Solomon, or was this some kind of test from the abbess?

Sister Grace looked up from the tall, angled writing desk beside Carenza with a questioning look.

She quietly cleared her throat and returned her attention to the page.

For a week, Carenza had gone through the motions of daily life at the abbey, singing the hours, tending the kitchen garden, and copying texts from the library, which were growing faint with age. She went to confession, said her Hail Marys, and even managed to eat some of the food at mealtimes.

But Daniel was ever-present in her mind, distracting, taunting, beguiling as she attempted to maintain composure. At the memory of his lips, warmth bloomed in places nuns weren't supposed to think about. That warmth was accompanied by a terrible ache at the thought of never seeing him again, of never again feeling the sensations he had awakened within her. Never again would his clever verse tug at her heart and seduce her mind. Never again would his body set hers aflame. He was gone, never to return.

Her eyes returned to the page before her and caught on the verse, "A bundle of myrrh is my well-beloved unto me; he shall lie all night betwixt my breasts."

Carenza stood abruptly, nearly knocking over her stool.

"Sister Francis, I'm feeling unwell. May I be excused to go rest?"

"Yes, dear, you may go."

Hurrying out of the brightly lit scriptorium and away from the four nuns diligently scratching away with their quills, Carenza practically ran through the dim stone halls of the abbey, past paintings and statues of saints, until she reached the quiet safety of her modest cell.

Kneeling by the side of her bed, she folded her hands in a prayer for relief from this madness. This could not continue. A life with Daniel simply wasn't possible. Even if he might be the true earl of Hawkhurst, he'd made it clear he had chosen life as a commoner, and Carenza de Vere would never be allowed to wed a shipwright.

She prayed for his safety and prayed to forget him. What else could she do?

Yet even as she prayed, she sensed that the abbess was right. Perhaps life at the abbey was not for her after all. Something had shifted.

All these years, she'd avoided love and romance, and now she had fallen prey to its lure. As she suspected, no good had come of it. There was nothing to be done. Even if he had stayed, nothing could ever come of it. But now that she had some inkling of what it could be like to be with a man she cared about, she wasn't sure she could give up on the possibility, even if it terrified her. Perhaps love was worth the risk for the right man. For now, though, there was nothing to do but wait and pray. And live.

Dear Lord in heaven, let me remember death that I may take joy in life and the promise of eternity in Your presence. Amen.

The bell rang for Nones, and Carenza forced herself to stand

and walk calmly to the chapel to mark the hour. Arriving late, she squeezed in at the end of the back pew, which was filled with novices. The pungent smoke of incense focused her churning thoughts, and the familiar chants brought her heart solace as she slipped into the familiar pattern of call and response. Colored light spilled in through the tall stained-glass windows lining either side of the chapel.

Just as she was starting to lose herself in the ritual, a low whisper caught her ear.

"Carenza, is that you?"

Glancing at the woman at her side, she did a double take. Big blue eyes and a familiar heart-shaped face peeked out from beneath a wimple. "Genevieve? But how?"

Sister Theresa, sitting in the next row, shushed them, and they both bowed their heads in silence.

How had Genevieve, Carenza's childhood friend, come to be here? What happened to her husband? The last Carenza knew, Genevieve was married to Benedict of Hythe.

A thousand questions tumbled through Carenza's mind as she struggled to come up with a plausible explanation. Afternoon prayers could not finish soon enough. Carenza needed to know everything.

The songs droned on and on, and Carenza clenched her hands together to avoid fidgeting. She should be focused on the Father, Son, and Holy Spirit, but instead, it was all she could do to keep from dragging her friend out to the cloister right that moment for a quiet chat about everything that had happened since they'd last met.

At long last, the singing came to an end. It was time to return to their work as everyone rose and left the chapel. But Carenza grabbed her friend's elbow and led her out to the arched stone walkway that formed a cloister around the central courtyard filled with vegetables and herbs for the abbey.

Thankfully, they were alone.

"Genevieve, what happened? How are you here?" Carenza

asked in a low voice. They might be alone, but one could never be too careful.

"Oh, Carenza. It's so good to see you." Genevieve dashed away a tear, and Carenza folded her friend into a hug. "I know this is where you always wanted to be. I once wanted it too, but I confess I'm here because I have no other options."

"What happened?" Didn't her friend have responsibilities back in Hythe? A family to raise?

The trickle of tears turned into a sob. "Benedict…" Genevieve closed her eyes and shook her head. Taking a deep breath, she tried again. "Benedict died. A fever took him."

"Oh no. My poor, sweet Genevieve. I'm so sorry for your loss."

Carenza let her trembling friend weep on her shoulder for as long as she needed. When the tears began to abate, Genevieve sniffed and straightened.

They walked in silence, holding hands, as Genevieve regained her composure. Squeezing her friend's hand, Carenza asked the question that had been troubling her most.

"Don't you have a family to raise back in Hythe?"

Genevieve shook her head. "I'm afraid not. You see, Benedict and I were never able to conceive. We tried for years, but every time I missed my courses, one or two months later, I would bleed again and lose the babe. After two years of this, the midwife declared me barren. The last time I saw you was right after I received that terrible news. I know I must have seemed out of sorts."

Facts rearranged themselves in Carenza's head. All this time, she'd believed Genevieve was unhappy in love, that she had taken ill with love's fever and been left heartbroken. But this was something else entirely.

"How did Benedict take the news?" Had he been angry? Had he shunned her? He must have been furious to learn he wouldn't have an heir.

"He was as sweet as he could be, and that just broke my heart even more. Not only did I deprive him of an heir but of his dream of being a father. He loved children. I couldn't stand to see the sadness in his eyes every time he looked out at the servants' children playing in the kitchen garden. But he never blamed me for it. He never tried to come up with some flimsy excuse to annul the marriage, as so many lords do in such situations. He was content to let his uncle inherit. But I never expected to lose Benedict so soon." At these last words, Genevieve choked up again.

"Of course not," Carenza said, patting her hand.

Listening to her friend, Carenza's troubles receded. How could she remain distressed about her mere heartbreak when her friend was grieving such a loss?

"When his uncle came to Hythe, he sent me here. There was no chance of marrying me off now that everyone knows I'm barren. Not that I was inclined to remarry anyway, with the loss of Benedict so fresh... So, you see, there was really only one option."

"Oh, you poor dear." Carenza stopped and took both of her friend's hands, looking her in the eyes. "I'm so sorry. I promise it isn't all bad here. The library is excellent, and the peace and quiet might do you good after what you've been through."

Genevieve smiled ruefully. "I'll do my best to be content. But what about you? I know you always wanted to be a nun, but I thought your parents said you had to marry."

It was just like Genevieve to think of others in her moment of distress.

"They did. But recent events convinced them otherwise. I don't want to burden you with my troubles. You have a heavy enough load to carry as it is."

"Nonsense. I want to know. Tell me everything. I could use a distraction from my woes."

Everything. But that would mean talking about... Did she dare confess her indiscretion to her friend? Genevieve had always kept her secrets before. If there was anyone she could trust...

"Let's walk in the garden," Carenza said, pulling her friend out into the courtyard. The clouds had parted, and the afternoon sun was shining down. Herbal scents filled the air as they walked along the narrow stone paths.

"My parents wanted me to marry Earl Raymond de Broase of Hawkhurst."

Her friend stopped short. "Oh dear. I've heard about him, and none of it was good."

Carenza sat on a stone garden bench and invited Genevieve to do the same.

"He's worse than you've heard," Carenza whispered in her friend's ear. "He was plotting murder, and I overheard it. When he discovered my presence, he tried to have me killed."

Genevieve clutched Carenza's hand with a fierce grip. "No!"

"Yes! I just barely managed to fight off his man by hitting him over the head with a candelabra." Carenza paused and swallowed. The horrifying crunch of metal against skull replayed in her head for the thousandth time, making her wince. "The earl stole away in the middle of the night after that. Threats have reached our ears that he may come back to finish what he started, so my parents sent me here."

Genevieve's eyes were wide, and she clutched Carenza's arm.

"By the holy rood, thank heavens you're safe. I don't know what I would have done in your shoes. How terrifying!"

Carenza's skin still crawled with the vivid sensation of Richard manhandling her and holding a blade to her neck. In the moment, she wasn't brave. Her reaction was more impulse than intention. She had to get away any way she could, and she lashed out with the closest thing at hand.

"But that's not the only thing I have to confess," Carenza said slowly. "The only reason I overheard the earl was that I had snuck away for a secret assignation."

Genevieve sat up straight. "What!"

"There was a troubadour—"

"A trouba—?"

"Yes, a troubadour." Carenza's cheeks flamed with heat. But her friend's gaze held no judgment, only amusement.

"I suppose I should have known. You and your poetry obsession."

Oh, this was so humiliating to confess. But she needed to be honest with her friend.

"I always thought love was a malady that addled people's wits, and now I know for certain that's the case because his verse…" Carenza closed her eyes. She couldn't watch her friend's reaction to this, or she would die of embarrassment. "His words set me on fire, and when he rescued me from the earl's man—"

"After you hit the man in the head."

"Yes, after I hit him in the head. But he was still alive and grasping at me. I honestly don't know which of us killed the earl's man. But once the scuffle was over, I lost my head completely and kissed the troubadour."

There. She'd said it. Opening her eyes, she peeked at her friend.

Genevieve threw her head back and laughed out loud.

"Shh. The nuns will come looking," Carenza warned.

"Bah! Let them come. I haven't laughed like this since Benedict passed. Thank you so much, Carenza. I really needed that." As her laughter subsided, she looked Carenza in the eye, smiling. "So what are you going to do about this troubadour you kissed?"

"Shh! Not so loud!" Carenza hid her face in her hands, then balled her fists and put her hands down again. She would not hide from this. Not with Genevieve. "There's nothing I can do," she whispered. "I've been praying to forget him and for God to heal me of this mad lovesickness. But it has made me question things."

"Oh?"

"I've been wondering if perhaps life at the abbey isn't for me after all. How can I dedicate myself to this life when I know that I'm so susceptible to… to…"

"Men?" Her friend gave her a wry smile. "Believe me, there is nothing more wonderful than surrendering to love with the right man—someone who honors and respects you and doesn't try to trample your will. Someone who sparks your affections and proves himself worthy. Is your man worthy?"

"My troubadour?"

Genevieve nodded.

"I don't know about worthy, but he is absolutely delicious."

Carenza clapped her hands over her mouth. How could she say such a thing?

Genevieve's laughter rang out once again, and moments later, there was the sound of feet shuffling on paving stones.

The abbess leaned out of one of the porticos.

"Don't you two ladies have somewhere to be?"

Carenza stood abruptly. "Abbess, I'm so sorry. It's just been so long since I last saw Genevieve."

The abbess looked from one to the other. Her eyes were shrewd and piercing, but her mouth was turned up in a smile. "Yes, that's why I didn't interrupt you sooner. You could both use a friend, I daresay. But cackling like that, you're disturbing the peace. I think it's about time you came inside and went back to your assigned tasks."

"Yes, Mother," they both murmured and scurried off in opposite directions after exchanging a brief hug and a promise to talk again later.

Carenza sat down at her desk in the scriptorium under the censorious gaze of Sister Theresa and began copying again. There was so much to ponder. What did she want when the situation with Earl de Broase was resolved? Was it better to live a life of quiet contemplation, knowing her temperament might be less suited than she originally thought? Or was it better to seek out companionship, someone who would not trample her will like Genevieve said? If Daniel moved her like that, could someone else perhaps do so as well?

No. It was impossible to imagine feeling the way she did about Daniel with anyone else. It was like a sickness, and it would pass. It was best to stay her course and see through her original intent. Better to be a nun than to give in to the madness of which she'd only had a small taste.

CHAPTER EIGHTEEN

WITH CONSIDERABLE TREPIDATION, Daniel stepped down from the carriage and followed his sister and brother-in-law into the castle at Winchelsea, followed by John. He'd only been inside once before, and that night had turned his life upside down. This visit would likely do the same again, given his plans.

Daniel shrugged restlessly in his new clothes. The richly embroidered cotte cost more than he made in a year as a shipwright. But Maggie had insisted it was necessary, as well as the more pointed trim of his beard and a prohibition on haircuts. She and his new manservant, Godfrey, had very particular views on proper grooming for a nobleman. Since he needed Maggie to support him with his vengeance, he had acquiesced. He just wished the cotte was a bit less constraining.

The dozen knights he'd hired came to a halt behind them, followed by eight Ashford knights.

At the entrance, his sister's footman informed the de Vere guard that the earl and countess of Ashford wished to pay their respects to Lord and Lady de Vere. He watched the man blanch and then scurry inside to announce their unexpected arrival. Moments later, they were escorted into a large receiving room where Lady de Vere was waiting.

She made a deep curtsy and spoke. "Your Excellencies, to what do we owe this unexpected honor?"

"It is a pleasure to make your acquaintance, Lady de Vere," Maggie said, bowing her head in acknowledgment.

Maggie's husband, the earl, also offered a slight nod and mumbled, "A pleasure, my lady."

"We apologize for dropping in on you unexpectedly like this," Maggie said, "but my brother has urgent business to discuss with you. I believe you've met my brother, Earl Daniel de Broase, as well as his man John, who was previously in my uncle's service?"

Daniel stepped forward, and Lady de Vere froze, recognizing him but taking several seconds to place him. She opened and closed her mouth several times before she remembered herself and offered a hurried curtsy. "Then what Carenza said is true. You are the true earl of Hawkhurst."

Daniel didn't trust himself to speak.

"Yes. My uncle Raymond is a usurper," Maggie chimed in. "He murdered my father, and he tried and failed to murder Daniel, who has been in hiding from the man for seventeen years. My husband and I would like to see Daniel restored to his rightful place. To that end, we provided him with the funds to hire knights to reclaim his birthright. We heard from John that my uncle is plotting against your husband. My brother wishes to offer his aid and assistance."

"Very generous, my lady," replied a breathless Lady de Vere. "My husband should join us. Yes, I believe he is essential to this conversation. If you will excuse me one moment, I will go and find him."

"Of course, Lady de Vere," Maggie said. When the door closed behind her, Maggie turned to Daniel. "I do believe it worked. She believes you are the true earl. I knew she wouldn't dare contradict an earl and countess, especially with John here for added proof. Congratulations, Earl Bitsy!" She gave him a hug. "And thank you, Alfric, for supporting Daniel's claim." She gave her husband a kiss on the cheek. "You really are the best of husbands."

The earl leaned toward Daniel. "Beware of marrying a woman you love. You never know what madness she'll talk you into." The earl didn't seem at all displeased despite his warning. He seemed to think this was all a delightful, madcap adventure and a welcome break from the monotony of governing. "Though I can't say I'll be sorry to see your uncle go. He's been a thorn in my side for years despite our alliance."

Moments later, Lord and Lady de Vere entered, followed by servants who laid out wine and refreshments. Greetings were repeated with Lord de Vere, who must have been forewarned, evincing less surprise than his wife, and they settled down to business.

"My Lord de Broase," Lord de Vere began, "my wife told me of your generous offer. I confess we very much need the aid. We only have a few knights in our service compared with your uncle, and without help, we wouldn't be able to keep him at bay when he returns. But may I ask why you're doing this?"

Daniel sat forward, cleared his throat, and did his best to appear lordly. "Lord de Vere, I have lived here in Winchelsea in secret for three years now. I have great affection for this place. I do not wish to see my uncle bring suffering to the good and kind people of your town. I came to the castle disguised as a troubadour two weeks ago in the hopes that I might confront him alone. I was unsuccessful, however, and I went to see my sister in hopes that she could aid me."

"Hmm," said Lord de Vere. "I wondered what was between you and him that night. It was clear that there was some hostility between you. It all makes more sense now."

"My lord, if I may, there is one more reason I have returned to Winchelsea," Daniel said. He was surprised that the subject he was about to broach, the request he was about to make, made his heart pound and nerves jangle so much more than asking for aid to overthrow his uncle from the title that rightfully belonged to him. "With your permission, I would like to ask for the hand of Lady Carenza in marriage. Her beauty, intelligence, and virtue are beyond compare, and I promise to cherish, honor, and defend her as she deserves." He was careful not to say the word "love," but hopefully, no one would notice that.

Lady de Vere gasped. Lord de Vere's jaw dropped. Maggie lifted her glass to Daniel. Alfric kept his attention on the plate of bread, cheese, and cured meats he was wolfing down. John stood in the shadows against the wall, grinning ear to ear.

"My...my lord," Lord de Vere said when he recovered himself, "Carenza wishes to be a nun. Recent unfortunate events made us decide to accede to her wishes." Daniel clenched his jaw, thinking about the recent unfortunate events. If it had been his daughter, he would have let her become a nun, too. "We can invite her back from the abbey, and you may ask her. But if she denies you..." He tapered off.

"Of course, my lord. I would never want her to marry against her will. My offer of aid stands regardless of her answer. All I seek is permission to ask the question."

"You have it, my lord. I will send for her at once. It will be several hours before she gets here. Perhaps in the meantime, we could discuss defenses. And Isabella, perhaps you'd like to show the countess around the castle grounds?"

Lady de Vere and Maggie both looked nonplussed at being dismissed, but from the commiserating smiles they gave each other, Daniel suspected they would enjoy themselves a great deal more than the men.

Lord de Vere called for more food, and the next hour was absorbed in discussions of how best to defend the keep. His uncle would almost certainly send assassins to do his dirty work. They had to improve security. And if the assassins failed, they had no doubt that Lord de Broase would attempt to enter by force. Though Alfric was technically staying out of this conflict, aside from funding Daniel, he was an avid strategist who couldn't resist diving into the planning with them. Besides, he loathed Raymond de Broase almost as much as Daniel did. John, of course, was immensely helpful, given his long tenure as a senior officer of the guard for House de Broase.

Lord de Vere's expertise was primarily naval, and he had a detailed plan for how he would secure the port on the off-chance Earl Raymond tried to approach by sea. Daniel had very little to contribute, never having engaged in this sort of endeavor, but he listened attentively and asked questions to ensure he had a thorough understanding of what was being proposed.

"Daniel, what do you think of repositioning these two knights over to here?" the earl asked, moving a bread crust that they were using as a marker.

"What would be the advantage, in your opinion?"

"From this position on the walls, they'd be able to see anyone approaching from the west, Earl Raymond's most likely direction of approach. What do you think, Martin, John?"

Lord de Vere stroked his mustache. "That could work. That could work. Perhaps if we move this knight here," he said, nudging a chess piece.

"And I'll station three knights here," John said, arranging a piece of string around the rook from a chess set.

"Hmm," the earl mused. "Yes, that solves a number of problems. And then we could move this over here…"

"Remind me what that coin was again, Alfric?" Daniel asked.

"An archer," said the earl.

"Right," said Daniel. "And Lord de Vere—"

"Call me Martin."

"Martin, can you remind me how far an archer can shoot from here?"

The door opened, and in walked Carenza. Daniel's heart skipped a beat. She was dressed in simple black linen like a nun but with no wimple. Her hair was tied back in a loose bun, but strands had blown free in the sea breeze and now framed her face. As always, she wore her rosary with the skull. Her eyes were full of concern, and her soft lips formed a fetching frown.

"Father, I came as quickly as I could. What—?" She saw Daniel and froze. Her expression was unreadable. "How?" she asked, staring into his eyes with piercing intensity.

"Carenza, this is the Earl Daniel de Broase," Martin said.

"Here?" said Carenza, disbelief written on every feature.

"And this is his brother-in-law, the Earl of Ashford," Martin continued. Carenza reflexively curtsied, and the earl offered an amused nod. "And you have met John before. He's now in Lord Daniel's service. Lord Daniel has offered us aid in our defense against his uncle." Martin cleared his throat. "And he has asked for your hand in marriage."

"What?" She stared at Daniel, who walked over to her, took her hand, and knelt before her.

His heart beat like thunder in his ears. Heat rose and suffused his face. Time seemed to slow as he looked up into her penetrating eyes. She was so vital and alive, and the way she looked down at him pierced his armor as if it were cloth. For a moment, his defenses fell, and all he could do was bask in her gaze, leaning toward the light and beauty within her. His voice abandoned him utterly.

Then she blinked and furrowed her brow, the most adorable look of consternation on her face.

Returning to himself, he smiled and said in a hoarse voice, "Carenza de Vere, will you do me the honor of becoming my wife?"

"What?" Her eyes widened; she wet her lips with the tip of her tongue.

Daniel's breath caught at the sight. He shook himself and ran his thumb over the back of her hand. Her skin was warm and smooth under his calloused thumb, reminding him of their differences. He needed to remember he was here to keep her safe, nothing more. "Will you marry me?"

"How?"

He was a bit pleased with himself for reducing her to monosyllables.

"Lord de Vere, might I take a walk with your daughter? I believe she has questions for me." He stood then but did not let go of Carenza's hand.

Carenza nodded. Her father shrugged. She declared, "We'll walk in the garden. Elaine will join as chaperone," and proceeded to actually drag him from the room.

Elaine was right outside. Her eyes widened at the sight of Daniel.

"We're taking a walk in the garden," Carenza said as she reached for Elaine with her other hand and pulled her along with Daniel—not that he dragged his feet. As they stepped out into the small, enclosed garden, she released Elaine, who fled to a safe distance, just close enough for propriety.

No sooner had the door to the garden closed than Carenza wheeled on Daniel. "You're here. You told me you were leaving forever, and you're here." She jabbed a finger into his chest. Her eyes held all the suspicion and wariness of an inquisitor, a beautiful, fierce inquisitor on whose judgment all of his happiness depended. "And you're an earl now? You go from being a simple shipwright to…this?" She gestured at his outfit. "And you expect me to welcome you back with open arms?"

She narrowed her eyes to angry slits and put her hands on her hips.

She was magnificent. Daniel had seen her frightened, and bright with poetic fervor, but here, with her eyes flashing and her color high, she was an overwhelmingly beautiful woman. He reminded himself that he didn't intend to fall in love with her, so her beauty wasn't something he should admire—and he certainly shouldn't give in to the desire she kindled. Not that he had much hope of holding himself back. It was all he could do to refrain from claiming her lips right then. But he promised her an explanation, so with difficulty, he tamped down the impulse and forced himself to answer.

"My Uncle Raymond killed my father when I was nine. He intended to have me killed, too, but John hid me on a farm near Dover. With time, I embraced life as a commoner. I had no interest in becoming an earl. I was sent to the port to apprentice to a local shipwright. Eventually, I completed my apprenticeship and married the farmer's daughter."

"You were married? No, wait. Your uncle spoke of her. He had her killed, did he not?" she asked carefully.

Usually, speaking of Adele tore open the old wound, but Carenza's sympathetic gaze was a balm. With her, telling his tale lightened his burden of pain.

He nodded. "Adele died six years ago. Uncle Raymond sent Richard to kill her. Somehow, he found out about our marriage, and he didn't want to take the chance that we would have children that could further weaken his claim to the succession. He murdered her and her father, and he burned down the farm."

Carenza shivered despite the day's heat. He assumed she was thinking of her own near miss with Uncle Raymond. The sight tugged at his soul. His uncle could never be allowed to touch her. There was nothing Daniel wouldn't do to prevent history from repeating.

"I was away when it happened. I was only able to rescue Gerard."

"What does Gerard have to do with any of this?"

"He's Adele's little brother, my brother-in-law. I couldn't just leave him after my uncle killed his family. He wasn't much older than I had been when I fled to the farm."

"Why didn't you try to fight your uncle back then?"

He had pondered that very question for six years. He still wasn't sure he had a satisfactory explanation. He stared down at his hands. "I didn't want to become my uncle. Everything about that life filled me with loathing. It still does. I didn't want to be a de Broase. I still don't. I don't want to hold power over men. I just want to do an honest day's work and live my life." He looked up at Carenza, her eyes assessing and wary. "I was content as a commoner. I only wanted peace. If he'd only left me and my wife alone, I never would have troubled him." Daniel shook his head.

"Then why are you coming forward now?"

"I couldn't leave you at his mercy, not after what he did to

Adele. That night I came to perform, I planned to confront him, but I couldn't find him after the performance. I heard a commotion in the solar. And, well, you know what happened."

Carenza swallowed. "I thought I'd never see you again. Why did you come back?"

For you, he almost said, but he caught himself in time. He was marrying her for her safety, and he planned to send her away somewhere out of reach when his uncle returned. He had to be careful with her heart and his own.

"That night, I set out to chase him down by myself. I thought it was best to go it alone, but all I could think about was how I'd left you undefended if I failed and he came to take his revenge. I couldn't let him hurt you, not if I had the means to save you."

Carenza's eyes had softened just a touch, but wariness remained. How could he make her see? How could he make her agree?

"How do I know this isn't just a troubadour's tale spun to take me in? What proof can you offer?" He almost had her. She was relenting if she was asking for proof.

"My sister, Magdalena, is now the Countess of Ashford. She can confirm everything I've told you, as can John and Gerard." He took a deep breath. "Marry me, Carenza. Please say you'll marry me."

She took a long look at him, and he could barely breathe. He'd told her everything. He longed for her to say yes. He needed her to say yes, but she stood aloof, eyes still uncertain. Taking her hand, he brought it to his lips. It was like taking a drink of strong wine. Even this tiny taste of her left him intoxicated and thirsty for more. He looked up into her eyes, and they shone with a tangle of emotions he couldn't begin to identify. Turning her hand over, he kissed her palm, unable to relinquish her without another taste.

Gasping, she leaned into him as if hypnotized. Suddenly, her hands clasped him with fierce strength. She pulled him toward her with an eagerness and hunger that matched his own and kissed him. Her kiss felt almost vengeful. Her lips pulled and tugged at his. Her tongue drove him to the brink of insanity. And he wanted nothing more than to continue, to fan this flame and let it consume them both. He was losing control. He had to stop.

"Marry me, Carenza," he whispered in her ear. "Please, marry me so that we can be together. I need you. I need all of you. Please stop torturing me, Carenza!"

Pulling away, she looked up at him, fire in her eyes. "Only if you promise my will is my own. I can be a partner to a man, but I cannot submit to one."

For a moment, he wanted to laugh, but he saw she was deadly earnest.

"I promise your will is your own. I do not want a submissive wife."

She looked at him long and hard.

At last, she said, "Fine, I'll marry you."

"You will? Really?" Daniel felt untethered from reality. Had she said yes? Was it possible?

She smiled and nodded.

He pulled her into another kiss, no less frenzied than the last. She would be his. Soon. Entirely his for the rest of his life.

Or at least until his uncle returned. And then…

No, that was a problem for another time. At this moment, Carenza was his. All his.

"But I have another question," she said, pulling away and leaving them both panting. Of course, she did. She always had questions. He had to hold back a laugh. "Why do you want to marry me?"

"Why do I want to…? Carenza!"

"Why? Why do you want to marry me? I think I deserve to know."

"Because I can't stop thinking about you. Because you drive me wild with desire." This was true, at least. He couldn't love her, but he couldn't help but desire her.

She folded her arms and narrowed her eyes. "So it's only

because you lust for me?"

"That's not fair." It was a little fair. Oh, how he lusted for her.

"No? Then why?" She tapped her foot expectantly.

He had to answer carefully. She couldn't know the depth of his feelings for her. At least not until his uncle was defeated. His love had been a death sentence to too many already.

"Because I think we could make each other very, very happy. Because you are beautiful and intelligent and virtuous, and I can't imagine a more excellent wife for me. You're the only woman who has ever been able to exchange verse with me! But beyond that, it's because I want to keep you safe from my uncle. Because I need you in my life."

"Hmm."

"Hmm? What does 'hmm' mean?"

"I suppose your answer is acceptable." She had the same look she'd worn during their poetry battle, as if she were assessing an opponent and plotting her next attack.

"And how about you? Why are you willing to marry me?" Daniel countered before she had a chance to continue her interrogation.

She narrowed her eyes and examined his face. "Because I—" she started and then stopped. "Because you're still a puzzle, and I haven't solved you yet."

"Hmm." He desperately wished he knew what she had started to say first. She was holding something back. He was certain of it.

"And I like it when you kiss me."

He arched an eyebrow. "Oh, so it's only lust then?"

She smiled and kissed him again, and he was lost, drowning in her warmth, her fervor, the sweet, delicious taste of her. It was more than he could bear. He was losing control. He let himself taste her neck and cupped her breast through her modest frock. It felt like heaven in his hand. He wanted more.

Just then, they were interrupted by a delicate "ahem" from Elaine. He had forgotten her presence. Shuddering, they pulled apart and tried to compose themselves.

"I think the weather might turn. Perhaps we ought to go back inside," Elaine said to an apple tree that was magically absorbing all her attention. "We wouldn't want anyone to…ah…get wet."

He chuckled. "No wonder Gerard wants to marry you, Mistress Elaine. You're made for each other."

"What? Elaine, are you getting married? Why didn't you tell me?" Carenza ran over to give Elaine a hug.

Elaine glared at Daniel. "I was going to tell you, my lady, but you were so distressed, I thought I had best wait. And then someone had to go and open his big mouth."

"Oh dear! Daniel, I don't think I can marry someone Elaine disapproves of." She gave him a look of mock disapproval.

So he bent his knee to Elaine. "Mistress Elaine, will you give me your blessing to marry Lady Carenza?"

"After what I just saw, I might have to cause you bodily harm if you didn't marry her. You make her happy, Lord Songbird, or you'll have me to answer to."

CHAPTER NINETEEN

THE WEDDING WAS to be in one week. It was a bit faster than was strictly proper, but they wanted everything settled quickly in case Lord de Broase showed up to make trouble. The earl and countess agreed to stay through the wedding, but they wanted to be far from Winchelsea before Uncle Raymond showed his face.

Carenza had a million details to take care of and almost no time to contemplate what was happening, but every time she had a moment to breathe, she found she was plagued by a ridiculous and pointless question: Was this love?

It made no difference. She knew that marriage wasn't about love. It was a practical arrangement. It was a legal contract, a matter of alliances and properties and dowries. It was a means of ensuring succession. She was lucky to be marrying a man she liked, and even, someone to whom she was attracted. She knew most other women of her status weren't nearly so lucky.

Daniel would be kind to her, she was certain. But would he respect her? Would he allow her to study and write and pursue her interests freely?

She had no experience of these things, having never had feelings for anyone else. She'd never been in the least bit tempted. Until Daniel, she had taken that as a sign that she should take holy orders. She hadn't wanted marriage and didn't seek love.

Love was nothing but a topic for verbal jousting with her mother's troubadours, and the pleasure she took in poetry was competitive, not romantic. Until Daniel.

With him, the game became something more. She'd refused to put a name to it when they first met. Such feelings were unthinkable between two of such different stations. Until the day he proposed, she dismissed her feelings as a sickness that she would simply have to wait out until it went away. But now that they were to marry, she was both hopeful and concerned the feeling wouldn't go away.

When he'd asked to marry her, he'd carefully avoided the word "love." She'd nearly blurted it out but caught herself at the last moment. It was too dangerous to say it out loud. What would it accomplish? Perhaps if she never said it, she could keep her emotions in check and avoid the pain love would inevitably bring.

Every day since they'd become betrothed, he'd spent an hour walking in the garden with her, with Elaine as chaperone, and Carenza peppered him with questions on every topic but the one that preoccupied her the most.

"Where will we live after we marry?" she asked the day after he proposed.

"Well, I imagine we'll live here in Winchelsea until things resolve themselves with my uncle."

"And after that?"

"After that?" He looked pained at that question. "I suppose we'll figure that out when it comes." He gave her a sad smile. Why did the thought of victory make him sad?

"Have you and my father settled on a dowry?" He stiffened. "What's wrong?" she asked, furrowing her brow. "Are you dissatisfied with it?"

He let out a long, slow breath. "I don't like being paid to marry you. No one gave me money or land when I married Adele. I know it's how these things work for nobility and that it would be insulting for me not to accept a dowry from your father. I mainly accepted it to make sure you'd have something if anything happens to me. So, my lady, I am certain it's not up to me to be satisfied or not. What is important is if it's enough to satisfy you."

He peered down at her with one eyebrow tilted. "But in answer to your question, he's giving me a hundred silver pieces and a manor house with the surrounding lands. Ownership of the property will rest with you. I insisted on that. I am limited to the right of usage only for as long as I live. And, as I stated, if something were to happen to me, you would hold the land and also receive whatever remains unspent of the dowry and the funds my sister and her husband, the earl, gave me. Rest assured, you'll be well cared for."

She thought of her brother and touched the skull on her rosary. Life was fraught with frailty, and death was always near at hand. But was that not all the more reason to live life to its fullest while one could? Her betrothed's cold calculations—even if they were for her benefit—left her chilled. "It seems you've given rather more thought to your death than to our future together."

His laugh sounded forced. "Of course not, Carenza. I hope we will spend many happy years together." He smiled, but his eyes were still filled with sadness. But then he kissed her, and everything else was forgotten.

The next day, she asked, "What is Hawkhurst like? I imagine we'll end up living there after your victory. I've never been."

He took several deep breaths before responding. "I hardly remember. I was nine the last time I saw it. But it doesn't matter. I don't plan to live there, no matter what happens. I hate the place. I don't ever want to go back. When I defeat my uncle, I'd much rather let my cousin keep Hawkhurst and settle some-where near Winchelsea so that you can stay close to your family." And then—once again—he kissed her. She recalled very little conversation that particular day.

The following day, she asked, "Will you be inviting anyone besides the earl and countess, John, and Gerard to the wedding feast?"

Daniel looked pained and shook his head. "No."

"That can't possibly be everyone you know."

"I've told you my history," he said harshly. "Surely you don't think I would risk people's lives by befriending them."

"Oh." She could not manage to say more. She should have known, but somehow, the magnitude of his loneliness and isolation hadn't sunk in until that moment. "Your last wedding must have been very small." The words tumbled out before she could stop them.

"Actually, it wasn't," he said with a sad smile. "We were married on May Day, and the whole village was celebrating. Adele loved big festivals—all the music and dancing and merrymaking. Everyone in the village loved her. And I did, too."

Her stomach clenched. He loved Adele. He said the words, just not to her.

"What was Adele like?" It was a terrible question for her to ask. She knew it would pain him to answer and pain her to hear it, but she couldn't help herself. She needed to know.

"Hmm?" He'd been staring off at the sea, lost in his own thoughts.

"Adele. What was she like?"

He looked Carenza in the eye, and she winced at the raw pain she saw there. "Adele was kind and good and innocent, and she's gone." The tone in his voice told her that was all he would say. Sometimes, his words were like stained glass, revealing light and shadows but obscuring any view of what lay behind. Someday, she hoped he would tell her more, but for the moment, she kept silent. He wrapped his arms around her and held her close.

And then he tilted up her chin with his finger and kissed her, and she melted in his embrace.

The following day, she was determined to steer clear of his past or any topic that was likely to drag him into melancholy. "Do you know how to swim, Daniel?"

"Swim?" he asked, as if she had inquired if he knew how to

fly. "No. I can build a boat and sail a boat. But I'm no fish."

She smiled at him. "I'll have to teach you. It's a very pleasant way to spend a summer afternoon. Besides, it can save your life if your boat ever fails you."

"You can swim?" he asked in astonishment. "Are you secretly a sea witch? It would explain so many things. You certainly look the part with your skull." He touched her chest, tracing a finger lightly around where the skull rested. Carenza thought her knees might give way beneath her. He put an arm around her to hold her steady as he continued tracing along her neckline, sending shivers to parts of her body she generally avoided thinking about.

"Yes, I can…I can swim," she said, unable to focus on words while distracted by such delicious sensations. "My brother taught me when we were children." Daniel nuzzled her neck. "Daniel, what are you doing?"

"I'm building anticipation."

"For what?" she whispered.

"Our wedding night." He grinned. "Just three more days to wait." He nibbled on her ear. "You were telling me about how you are a sea witch who can float in the water without drowning?"

"Our wedding night?" She took a deep breath, trying to calm herself. Try though she might not to worry, she found it hard to reconcile what her mother had told her about procreation with the feelings she had when she was with Daniel. Nothing about the act her mother described sounded appealing in any way.

"What's wrong, Carenza?" he asked, straightening, and giving her some room to breathe. "Are you nervous about our wedding night?"

She blushed. "My mother explained what would happen. I'm prepared to do my duty. I confess it doesn't sound very pleasant, though."

With a twinkle in his eye, he took her hand and leaned close. "What did she tell you?"

In a barely audible whisper, she confessed, "She said that a man presses something in a hole between a woman's legs and leaves a sticky liquid there. She also said that something inside a woman tears, and she bleeds the first time." She winced as she finished.

Daniel burst out laughing. "Oh, Carenza!" he gasped. "Oh dear, sweet, brave Carenza! You poor thing! I can't imagine a worse description. No wonder you're terrified." He pulled her into his arms, shaking with laughter.

"So it's not true? She was very specific. She said the sticky liquid and the blood were important." She looked so hopeful that Daniel laughed even harder. Relief that it wasn't as horrible as her mother had made it sound moved through her, though she was also annoyed he appeared to be laughing at her. So she gave him the fiercest scowl she could muster.

"You, of all people, know what a difference words can make." Still shaking with mirth, he cupped her face with his hand. "I cannot imagine a less enticing way to describe what should be a consummation of pleasure, passion, and joy for us both. Might as well call a fine wine 'rotten grape juice' or silk a 'tangle of insect string.' She really did choose the absolute worst possible wording."

"And what words would you use?"

He glanced over at Elaine, who was studiously observing a mother bird and her chicks nested in a pear tree. "I don't think even Elaine would allow me to speak to you on such a topic before we're wed."

"Please tell me," she said in a low voice. "I need to know."

"You always need to know everything, don't you?" The look he gave her was one of pride, not condescension.

"Yes, I do." There was no use pretending otherwise. She was who she was. He should know who he was marrying.

"Here's what I will do. On our wedding night, before we begin, I promise to tell you in my own words what will happen, and I promise to answer your questions. Will that satisfy you?"

"I'm never satisfied. Haven't you figured that out yet?"

He gave her a wicked grin. "Never? We'll have to see about that."

And then he kissed her, and she surrendered to his sweet caresses. Until Elaine interrupted them, at any rate.

Two days before the wedding, the last time she would see him before the ceremony, Carenza had more questions than ever, but she held back.

"I'm ready for my daily interrogation, my lady," Daniel said, kissing her hand as he joined her. He placed her hand in the crook of his arm as they wandered through the garden.

She smiled. "Today, I think you should ask the questions. We know so little of each other. Surely, there must be something you want to know."

"Hmm." He scratched his beard. "Why did you want to be a nun?"

She laughed. "According to the abbess, I wanted it for the wrong reasons. I wanted to be free to spend my life in study, contemplation, and devotion. I was never tempted by romance, at least not before you. I found the idea of marriage rather frightening. I didn't particularly want to become a strange man's property. And as we've discussed, my mother's description of wifely responsibilities was a bit distressing."

"But you're not afraid to marry me."

"Mostly no." She was surprised by her own answer. It was a fresh realization.

"Why?"

"I suppose because you've promised not to treat me like chattel and to allow me my own free will. I think you'll be gentle and kind to me. You've promised not to stand in my way if I want to spend the time in study and contemplation. With you, I believe, it may be possible to live the life I craved and enjoy the pleasures of marriage and family at the same time. Even before you came back, I had decided against taking holy orders."

"Oh?"

"Before I met you, I had no sense of what I was giving up. But now…" She tapered off, uncertain how to complete the sentence without confessing to feelings she didn't want to speak aloud.

"Now?"

She took a deep breath, trying to form an answer that didn't include the word "love." He hadn't said it to her. It was better all-around if they avoided the topic.

"When I was at the abbey after you left, I realized that the joys of marriage and family were something I cared about and that I wasn't willing to give up on them after all."

"Oh, I see. You mean you didn't want to give up this?"

And then he kissed her, filling her with a sweet ache that made her head spin. As always, it seemed. She wondered briefly if her wifely responsibilities included kisses like this. It didn't matter, she decided—as long as he always kissed her like this, she supposed, she'd endure having him putting a sticky liquid into her mysterious, unknown hole.

The night before the wedding, as she was getting ready for bed, Carenza finally broke down and asked Elaine the question that had been troubling her. "Elaine, I know that it's ridiculous to worry about this, but how do you know if you're in love?"

"You can't be serious, my lady! The way that man kisses you, it's a wonder the whole garden hasn't gone up in flames!"

"Well, yes, but sometimes I think he's doing it to distract me, or possibly himself. Whenever I try to talk with him about the past or the future, his eyes grow sad, and then the next thing I know, his lips are on mine, and everything I planned to say or ask is gone from my head."

Elaine sighed and shook her head.

"The thing is," Carenza said, "I'm worried I might be in love with him, but I don't know if he's in love with me. But I have no experience with this. I don't know what to think of any of it. Not that it matters. I just don't like it when I don't understand."

Elaine cleared her throat. "No, you don't, my lady."

"Well, what do you think?"

If anyone could tell her the truth, it was Elaine. There were no secrets between the two of them, and Elaine had the good fortune to find love twice, first with Sir Luke and now with Gerard.

"I don't know how you know you're in love. I figure it's likely different for everyone."

"But…"

"Be patient, I wasn't done. I think that if you think you're in love, you probably are. You certainly have all the symptoms."

As she feared, she was lovesick.

"Symptoms?"

"For heaven's sake, my lady. You're the one that's a poet. What do all the troubadours say?"

It was hard to relate any supposed symptoms to herself. She shook her head. "But…"

"As for him," Elaine continued doggedly, "you'll have to wait and see. Either he'll say it, or he'll show it. To my mind, he's already shown it, but if you need to hear the words, you just have to wait. They'll come eventually."

Carenza's heart leapt at the possibility that he might love her. Foolish heart.

"I know you don't like uncertainty, my lady, but there's no rushing it. You'll know when you know."

Clutching her rosary, Carenza huffed. Dear Lord in heaven, let me remember death that I may take joy in life and the promise of eternity in Your presence. Amen. And please grant me patience. Now, if possible. Please. Amen.

"I'm going to wish you goodnight, my lady, before you ask me any more questions." Elaine left before she could even say goodnight in return.

Carenza stared at the ceiling, fingering her rosary until the wee hours of the morning and wondering about the nature of love between a man and a woman.

CHAPTER TWENTY

FOR DANIEL, THE wedding was a blur, punctuated by indelible moments that he knew he would remember as long as he lived. Today, he was happy, and he was making Carenza happy. The sacrifices to come would all be worth it for this brief period of bliss. And perhaps, if he was very lucky, he would defeat his uncle and bring her home to Winchelsea again. They could live near her family, as moving to Hawkhurst was unthinkable.

The truth was that after a lifetime under threat from his uncle, he hardly dared imagine life after victory. Everything had narrowed to a single point, and until he'd ended the threat, he couldn't see beyond it. But Daniel was finished running from his birthright. Today, he would stand forth as himself. Today was for freedom. Today was for joy. Today was for Carenza in her beautiful blue dress, holding white lilies, her eyes filled with fervor.

He didn't think she loved him; at least, he hoped she didn't. Nearly everyone he loved and who had the misfortune to love him had died. He was determined not to let Carenza share that fate. He would keep his love hidden to avoid risking her heart. But he would make every effort to give her the happiness she deserved, to give her joy, pleasure, adoration, and freedom.

That morning, Godfrey dressed him in the finest outfit his sister had procured for him. It was a heavy, green brocade tunic with elaborate botanical patterns woven in. It was belted at the waist and fell in heavy folds to his knees. He wore fine, brown linen hose underneath and was shod in leather slippers with pointed toes. He felt a bit foolish, but Godfrey insisted he was magnificent.

His sister and the earl kept him company all morning, reassuring him he was a fine match for Carenza every time he started to worry that this was all a terrible mistake. Though he was desperate to marry her, he couldn't quite convince himself he was worthy. Thankfully, Maggie refused to let him succumb to his doubts, and before he knew it, they were leading him to the steps of the church, where the ceremony would be performed, and depositing him up front with the priest. Crowds of townsfolks gathered in the street to watch the spectacle.

When he saw Carenza walking toward him on her father's arm, the world fell away. She was radiant in a simple, demure, twilight-blue silk gown in the bliaut style with lacing on the sides that made the fabric follow her curves. The wide, scooped neck, fitted sleeves, and floor-length hemline were adorned with a gold embroidered trim. A delicate gold belt draped around her hips, making a V in front with the end dangling down into the generous folds of her skirt. Her ink-black hair peeked out from beneath a delicate white veil, held in place by a gold circlet on her head. Warmth and intelligence sparkled in her eyes as her lush, dusky-pink lips curved into a tremulous smile at the sight of him.

He could hardly breathe as her father led her up the steps and placed her hand in his own. There was a bashfulness in her gaze that he'd never seen before, and her hand shook as he took it. He drank her in, unable to look away from the vision before him. She was a dream made flesh, moonlight incarnate, pulsing and glowing with a light all her own. The priest had to clear his throat to get Daniel's attention.

He could hardly hear the words of the marriage rites, as every sense, every nerve in his body was attuned to her. Every breath, every movement, every glance from her made his heart swell.

She seemed to thrum with life and vitality beside him. Beyond hope, she was his, and he was hers. It was almost too much to bear.

"Do you, Earl Daniel de Broase, take Lady Carenza de Vere to be your wife?" he heard the priest ask him, the words penetrating his awareness.

"I do," he said, his voice rough with emotion.

"Do you, Lady Carenza de Vere, take Earl Daniel de Broase to be your husband?"

"I do." Her voice was clear and fervent.

The priest asked them to repeat their vows after him, and he dutifully spoke the words.

"Carenza, I take you to be my wife, to have and to hold from this day forward. I promise you fidelity and loyalty of my body. I will keep you for better or worse, for richer or poorer, in sickness and in health, until death do us part." *And if death parts us, you can be free to do whatever you wish, my beautiful, vibrant Carenza.*

"Daniel, I take you to be my husband, to have and to hold from this day forward. I promise you fidelity and loyalty of my body. I will keep you for better or worse, for richer or poorer, in sickness and in health, until death do us part."

Yes, have me, hold me, Carenza. I'm at your mercy.

They exchanged rings, and the priest declared them husband and wife, and they entered the church to take their first communion together as a couple. When it was done, they walked down the church steps together in a daze. They feasted with their guests back at the castle and laughed and danced in the great hall. He had no idea what he ate or drank. He couldn't recall any specific conversations except for the odd, strained congratulations from Gerard, who left the banquet early. He lost himself in the joy of having Carenza by his side, oblivious to everything else. And then it was done.

At last, they were alone together in a bedchamber that had been prepared for them. Though it was a generous room, the large canopy bed draped in deep blue seemed to dominate it, promising pleasures to come. The floors were strewn with fresh rushes and herbs, releasing a sweet fragrance with each footstep. A large tapestry hung on one wall depicting a woman seated in a garden as a man played a lute beside her. A fire burned in the simple stone hearth to take the chill off the spring evening.

Daniel could hardly believe he was here. He had been holding back from being with a woman for so long. It had been six years. And with Carenza, he had been good and patient. Tonight, at last, he could go beyond mere words and teasing kisses. He could touch, and taste and feel.

And beyond all hope, the woman before him—his wife, he thought with deep satisfaction—was the most passionate woman he had ever encountered. Their kisses were like summer storms, overtaking them with thunderous intensity, drenching them in need, and crackling with a white-hot heat that left them scorched. Until tonight, he always stopped short, always made sure she walked away before he lost all control. But tonight, he didn't have to. Tonight, he would let the storm take him, riding it to its completion.

Carenza stood before him, casting nervous glances at the imposing canopy bed, smiling shyly in her cascading blue silk dress. He had no doubt that once he kindled her passion, she would lose herself in the moment and respond with all the intensity and abandon of their previous encounters. But first, he had to put her at ease. He needed to take this slowly and give at least as much pleasure as he took, careful to put her needs before his own.

He pulled her to him and kissed her slowly and gently, savoring her taste and breathing in the sweet and spicy fragrance of the scented oil she wore. She leaned into him, her tension giving way to hunger at his touch, as he knew it would. Continuing his languorous kisses, he carefully removed her veil and began plucking out the gold pins that secured the braided coil of her hair. Tiny, white cherry blossoms he hadn't noticed before because they'd been hidden by her veil, fell to the floor as he unwound the braid and freed her glorious mane. When it was undone at last, he buried his face in its silken warmth, breathing deeply.

"I've never seen your hair down," he said, standing back for a moment to look at the skein the color of midnight that now cascaded over her shoulder, "It's like you've stolen the night sky and spun it into silk."

"Oh. Thank you," she said, suddenly shy again.

He caressed her cheek. Her discomfort manifested in a thousand tiny tells—the way she couldn't meet his eye, the nervous twitch of her lips in her wavering smile, the fiddly movement of her fingers at her side, the subtle tremor in her breathing. He took off his heavy brocade cotte and laid it over a chair so that he could feel each subtle movement she made as he embraced her again and kissed his way down her slender neck.

It was time to have mercy and give her what she wanted.

"I'd promised to tell you—in my own words—what will happen now and give you a chance to ask questions."

Her smile broadened, and her shoulders relaxed. "Yes, you did. I'm glad to hear you intend to keep your promise."

"Did you think I would forget?"

"Not when I'm here to remind you," she said with a teasing look. "Well?"

"Well then," he said slowly, stroking her hair, "I will start by tantalizing you with kisses and caresses, melting your worries, kindling your passion until you are trembling and moaning in my arms." As he spoke, he ran a finger lightly along her jaw, down her neck, and down her front between her breasts. He heard a small gasp and felt her body soften at his touch. Good. Very good.

"Then I will unwrap you, reveal you, bare you to my touch so that I can caress your secret places and taste the tender flesh that you keep hidden from the world." He tugged at the pleasantly low neckline of her dress, letting it snap back against her skin. Then he grazed her breast with his thumb and, with his other hand, clasped a perfect buttock, pulling her hips against his. He was already aroused, and the feeling of her pressed against him made him groan with need.

"I will arouse you until you cannot speak, except to beg for more," he murmured in her ear, nibbling on her earlobe. "I will stroke your body into a frenzy of need and desire. I will open you, unfold you—" he lowered his mouth to her neck as he spoke— "feed your hunger until it consumes you, and you need me like you need air to breathe." His own hot breath whispered against her skin. She moaned and sank against him, arching to seek the kiss he withheld.

"Then, and only then," he whispered in her ear, "will I complete our union, and you'll ask me to do it. At your invitation, I will enter you, fill you, and in doing so, bring you to the very pinnacle of ecstasy. There will be a moment's pain for you, but I will also give you pleasure unlike any you have ever known. We will complete each other and become one, move as one, until our passions release us, united body, mind, and soul." She was panting in his arms, looking up at him with eyes glazed, all resistance dissolved. "Questions?"

"Just one."

"Yes?"

"What do I do? You told me what you would do, but I still don't understand what I'm supposed to do."

Daniel couldn't help but smile. Oh, Carenza. "You should do whatever you feel inspired to do. You can move your body however you want. You can touch me, kiss me, embrace me, stroke me, tickle me…"

"Tickle you?" Her eyes went wide.

"If you wish." He grinned and winked.

"But I don't know where you're ticklish, or even if you're ticklish!" She was giggling now. He didn't think he'd ever heard her giggle before. It was a delightful sound.

"Ah, but won't it be fun to find out?" He took her hands in his and brushed each one with his lips. "Now. Are you ready?"

She took a deep breath, closed her eyes for a moment, and gave a brief nod.

With a hungry groan, he enveloped her in his arms and tasted her mouth. He poured years of denied hunger and frustrated desire into that kiss. Lips and mouth delved and twisted and tantalized, and her mouth was so sweet, her response so filled with naïve enthusiasm.

She answered his desire with her own, and the bonfire between them grew at an almost alarming rate. He wanted her, needed her. And he wasn't sure he would have the strength to hold back and give her the pleasure he'd promised if she kept kissing him like this. He pulled back for a moment to take a breath. "Oh, Carenza, you have no idea what you do to me. No idea at all."

Shifting, he moved his attention to her neck and shoulder where she couldn't enflame him with her lips and tongue in quite the same way. He needed to regain a modicum of control to execute the seduction he had promised—to romance her, tantalize her, make her squirm, and sigh. And for that, he needed to keep his head, at least for now.

He executed a delicate calligraphy on her neck with the tip of his tongue, and her nails dug into his back as she made a soft, breathy sound that drove him wild. His concentration and control slipped even further despite his best efforts.

Time to unwrap her. He traced his fingers down to the ties at the sides of her dress that held her bodice tight. With quick tugs, he untied each bow, and the tight fabric across her breasts loosened, giving him new access. Sliding the wide neck of the dress and linen shift down over one shoulder, he reached beneath the fabric to touch one breast, teasing the taut nipple with his fingers, before he lowered his mouth to the plump, full flesh.

"Oh!" she gasped and slid her fingers into his hair, gripping tightly.

He caressed and squeezed and nudged until he lifted her breast above the neckline, leaving it open to the full fury of his passion. Her back arched as he nibbled and licked, and her arms dropped to her sides, finally giving him respite from her tantalizing touch.

"Daniel!" Carenza yelped. "What are you…what are you…?" She was having difficulty forming words under his tender assault. Good, he thought. That's as it should be. "What are you doing?" she finally finished.

Of course, she had to ask. She needed to know. She needed him to put it in words. "I'm tasting your secrets. I'm worshipping your shape. I'm kindling the fire inside you until you burn beneath my touch."

A wicked, mischievous thought occurred to him. "Why? Is it too much? Do you want me to stop?" He pulled back. She gasped in shock. Stepping away was extremely difficult, given his current state of arousal, and it would be absolute torment if she said "yes." But he wanted her invitation to continue, wanted her to admit she needed this as much as he did.

She stared at him. It took her a moment to form words. "No, please don't stop. Please."

He smiled, relieved his gamble had worked, and reached out his hand to tease her exposed nipple with his fingers. "What do you want me to do, Carenza? Tell me."

Her mouth fell open. She closed it. It fell open again. "I…I…" Her breath was rough and uneven. He didn't really expect an answer. He was trying his hardest to render her completely inarticulate. But something made him ask. Maybe it was the sheer pleasure of seeing her at a loss for words.

But she put her lips next to his ear and answered in a husky voice, "I want to feel your bare skin against my own. I want to feel your weight against me. I want to touch you, feel you. I want to learn what pleases you and torture you with pleasure the way you're torturing me right now."

He let out a long, inarticulate noise halfway between a moan and a whimper. Reaching beneath his fine linen shirt, she caressed his chest and back, using her nails to scratch ever so lightly, sending shivers of sensation to his very core. Then she pulled the shirt off, letting it flutter to the ground. Then she unfastened her golden belt and pulled her gown over her head, leaving her only in her low-cut linen shift. He found himself growling as he reached beneath the hem of her shift, running his hands up her calves, then her thighs until he found her hips. He paused for a moment there so that he could reach around and savor the soft curves of her bare, rounded buttocks. Then he slid his hands up her sides and pulled the fabric over her head.

She stood before him fully revealed at last, and it took his breath away. She was a triumphant goddess, fire in her dark eyes, her mouth open with desire, her lips red and plump from their kissing. Her breasts were fuller than he'd imagined, her hips rounder and more womanly. Her modest dresses had hidden the perfection of her form, and now that she was revealed to him, he could almost weep at the sight.

"'Beautiful body in the colors of youth, what suffering you make me endure,'" he quoted, unable to come up with words of his own for once.

"Ventadorn?" She smiled. Of course, she recognized it.

He nodded, then swept her off her feet and laid her down on the bed. Her hair cascaded around her head, framing her from head to hips as she lay bare and exposed before him. She was simply the most beguiling thing he'd ever seen.

"Your turn," she commanded, biting her lip in anticipation. Leave it to Carenza to turn things around on him. He swiftly removed his hose and ornate slippers to join her in bed. She gasped at the sight of him, fully revealed. Her eyes went wide, and she furrowed her brow.

"What happened…? How…? I didn't know a man's flesh did that. Not that I've ever seen a naked man before. But I've seen little boys bathing in the river, and they don't look like that. Does it hurt?"

Daniel smiled at her endearing innocence. She was worried for him, genuinely worried! "It doesn't hurt. It feels very, very good. This is what happens when a man is filled with desire, and I desire you so very much, Carenza."

"It feels good? It looks…uncomfortable." She brushed his shaft very lightly with one finger, and he jerked and moaned at her touch. Her eyes widened further, and she raised her eyebrows. "Interesting!"

"Would you like to know how it feels when you touch me there?"

She nodded cautiously.

He reached between her legs to touch her. While she gasped in surprise, she didn't shrink away. She was hot and wet, nearly ready for him, but he'd promised she would invite him to take her. It was time to drive her wild and make her beg. Finding the small nub of pulsing flesh, he sought, he began circling his finger slowly and delicately, making her shake and gyrate beneath his subtle torture.

"That's what it feels like when you touch me there," he murmured, quickening the pace of his fingers. He slid a finger inside her, and her back arched off the bed. He slid in another finger. She was slippery and tight, and he could feel the pulsation of what was building within her.

"Daniel, something is happening. I need…. I need…" Her voice trailed off, and a wail of pleasure replaced words until she could gasp, "Please… now…"

"Now," he agreed, spreading her legs and sliding into her at last. "It will hurt for a moment." He intended to go slowly, but she arched to meet him, and before he knew it, he was pressing against her maidenhead. He kissed her lips, unleashing a torrent of passion from her, and he broke through, helpless to stop. She emitted a small squeak as her last barrier broke but then wrapped her legs around him to pull him close. "Carenza? How does it feel?"

Instead of answering, she pulled him down into another kiss, moving her hips against his, and they fell into a rhythmic motion that grew wilder by the second. The pulsation within her grew and grew until her whole body went tense, and she cried out beneath him. She trembled as the wave subsided, leaving Daniel frenzied and far beyond conscious control. With a cry, he let his own wave of pleasure overtake him, obliterating everything, at long last finding fruition after so many years.

As he rolled to his side, barely conscious after the power of his release, he closed his eyes. It had never been like this. He didn't know it could be like this. It shook his very soul.

When he could move again, he pulled her to him so that the length of her was spooned against him. She fit him so well, perfectly curled in his arms. He breathed in her scent and felt the beating of her heart beneath his hand. He felt at peace in a way he hadn't in years—a moment of pure bliss.

"So, my poetess," he asked as the power of speech returned, "What words would you use to describe this?"

Carenza laughed. "Someday, if you're lucky, I'll tell you. For now, let's just say I'm happy I decided to marry you instead of becoming a nun."

She snuggled closer, and he held her, so warm and alive and lovely. He'd missed this part, the tenderness and intimacy of the moments after the storm subsided. Burying his face in her hair, he realized with a start that he hadn't thought about Adele once since he'd seen Carenza walking toward him on her father's arm.

CHAPTER TWENTY-ONE

CARENZA SNUGGLED AGAINST her husband, her body still humming after the revelatory experience of their coupling. Never in her wildest imaginings had she suspected her body could feel so much. Had she always possessed this capacity for ecstasy, waiting only for a lover to unlock it, or was it part of the transmutation of marriage where two become one, a blessing only accessible to those who had been joined before God? She felt blown apart and reassembled into something new, every part of her warm, tingling, and wildly alive. Surely, this had to be part of the strange and holy alchemy of marriage.

This morning, her mother hinted there could be joy and pleasure from joining, that perhaps she had attempted to scare her with the blood and sticky liquid talk. Then she heard a noise at the door and caught Alais trying to eavesdrop. Her mother seemed relieved by the excuse to cut their talk short. But nothing her mother said prepared her for this.

Daniel dozed next to her, his breath warming the back of her neck and his arm wrapped around her. Their joining seemed to have robbed him of consciousness, whereas she felt like she was fully awake and alive for the first time in her life. And she was hungry for more. How often could they do this thing? Would it feel like that every time? She found herself squirming in his embrace, pressing against him, craving more contact even with the length of his front against the length of her back.

It wouldn't be kind to wake him up, so she tried to relax her body and drift off to sleep. But it was no use. There could be no rest with the delicious ache she felt at his touch, and he was touching her everywhere right now. She would simply have to distract herself until exhaustion took her. He asked her what words she would use to describe this. Perhaps composing would do the trick.

You had the key to me, my love

Unlocking joys I'd never known.

With words and whispers, you alone

Could give me pleasures undreamt of.

Before you touched me, I was lost

Each verse a kiss that sparked a flame.

"Each verse a kiss that sparked a flame," she whispered to herself, trying to think of what should come next.

"Hmm?" Daniel murmured into her neck. He shifted in his sleep, and the hand that had been limp on her abdomen began moving up until it reached her breast. Finding her nipple, he began teasing it, rolling it back and forth until it was hard and sensitive beneath his touch.

She gasped at the sudden wave of sensation, then felt something twitch at the base of her back and press against her and realized his arousal must be coming back to life. The aching hunger within her intensified, and she moved against him, a subtle shifting of her hips to create delicious friction.

He made a rumbling noise and nuzzled her neck as his hand traced a lazy trail down from her breast to the center of her heat between her legs. Once again, he found the sensitive place she'd never known existed and began to stroke. Unable to contain herself, she writhed against him, needing more of the tantalizing feeling that was too much and not enough all at the same time. A breathy noise she was certain she'd never made before came from her throat, and much to her embarrassment, she felt heat and moisture where his fingers were touching her.

"Mmm. So warm and wet," he whispered in her ear before nibbling on it.

"Is that a good thing? Am I supposed to be wet? I was worried."

"It's a very good thing. It means what I'm doing gives you pleasure."

"Yes, it does." Oh, so much pleasure, more than she ever thought possible. How had she gone her whole life without knowing? "Just now, when you were asleep, I was wondering how often we could do this and whether it would feel as good as it did the first time. I was also wondering if my body always had the capacity for these feelings or if it's a special blessing that comes with marriage."

He shifted so that he could look at her in the firelight from the hearth. There was an impish smile on his face. He sank a finger into her and increased the speed of his strokes. "Always so many questions, wife. But I love that about you, so I will answer them while I make you come."

"Come?"

"The little death. The pleasure that builds and builds until it becomes too much, and it bursts within you, robbing you of sense and leaving only sensation. I want to watch you lose control as I touch you, taste you." She clenched and pulsed around his finger at his words. "Oh my. So close already?"

He slid another finger in and sucked a nipple into his mouth, and the sensation intensified even further until it was unbearable. A powerful wave overtook her and flooded her senses, tossing her in its wake until, at last, it subsided, leaving her spent.

"My God, Carenza," he said, watching her in awe.

"You shouldn't blaspheme," she teased, biting her lip.

"Sometimes there are no other words." He found her lips and kissed her into delirium as he spread her legs and nudged against her entrance.

"You didn't answer my questions," she reminded him, torn between satisfying her curiosity and surrendering to the euphoria that was about to fill her.

He stilled, poised above her.

"You are relentless."

"And yet you still married me," she said with a grin.

He kissed the tip of her nose. "And I'm so very glad I did. What was your first question?"

"How often can we do this?"

He chuckled and began moving against her without entering, sliding against her most sensitive places, making her gasp. "Excellent question. I need time to recover after making love to you, but I don't need to be inside you to give you pleasure, as we just proved. And I intend to give you as much pleasure as you can stand."

The tip of him teasing her, hot and demanding, as her sensitive flesh throbbed in response. Still a bit sore from their earlier encounter, she was all the more sensitive for it. There was nothing she wanted more than to feel him filling her and moving within her.

"I accept your challenge," she whispered in his ear before tracing it with her tongue, making him moan as she moved against him, intensifying the friction. "Will it always feel this good?"

"I certainly hope so. I have every intention of driving you wild on a regular basis." He placed himself at her entrance and began to slide slowly and inexorably into her, filling her and sending ripples to every corner of her body.

He pulled back slightly and thrust into her so that he was fully sheathed, and she lost the ability to speak, kissing his neck and shoulders to show him what she could not say. He was also beyond words, eyes squeezed closed and lips parted as he struggled to catch his breath. Yes, this was just as good, perhaps better.

He paused within her, and she stretched and adjusted to his

presence. In this brief respite, she couldn't stop herself from asking, "And my body? Do I feel this because I'm married, or was this always within me?"

"Carenza," he groaned through gritted teeth.

"Please. I need to know."

With great effort, he lifted his head to look at her, his eyes full of the barely contained madness of desire.

"Always within you," he whispered, thrusting again and sending a bolt of lightning up through the top of her skull. Breathing heavily, he pulled almost all the way out, leaving her feeling empty and hollow. He swallowed hard, struggling to catch his breath, and added in a more even voice, "Though the pleasure is greater with someone you care for." He stroked her cheek. "Touch alone does not create feelings this intense. Attraction and affection are needed for the deep pleasure we share."

Attraction and affection, but not love? She should be relieved, but somehow she wasn't.

He pressed into her again and filled the aching emptiness, and she forgot what they were discussing. It couldn't have been that important. All that mattered was that he continued what he was doing, sating her burgeoning need. She wrapped her legs around him and matched each thrust with a counterthrust, undulating beneath him, deepening the sensation and quickening the pace. He was right. This was just as good as the first time but different. The mindless yearning that struck her dumb was more familiar now. The languorous bliss was something she could nudge to a higher peak as she learned her body's responses.

She shuddered with a pulsation that she now knew was a sign her own release was coming, and she felt an answering throb from him. They were almost there, almost.... They strained against each other and with each other, prolonging the torturous tug of the moment before, and then...

She was weightless, floating on a summer sea, a thousand glowing blue specks carried by a wave, churning, flying, crashing before coming to rest in the soft, warm sand. One with the tide, she let the wave rock her until it subsided, lapping gently at the edges of her awareness. The light within pulsed and winked out as she returned to her own body and to the man collapsing beside her, peace and contentment permeating her whole being.

"Daniel," she asked, curling up against him and resting her head on his chest.

With eyes still closed, he mumbled, "More questions?"

"No. At least not yet."

His chest rumbled as he chuckled.

"You were right," she said. "It was better this time. I didn't think that was possible, but it was."

She kissed his chest, and he tightened his arm around her. This time, his warmth and her contentment combined to make her drift off into a deep slumber.

⫸⫷

IN THE MIDDLE of the night, when the embers of the fire had burned low, a violent jerk from Daniel awakened Carenza. His head thrashed from side to side, and his arm crushed her against him. She tried to extricate herself, but he only gripped tighter, now with bruising force.

"Daniel, you're hurting me," she said as she tried to shake him awake with her free hand.

With a sharp intake of breath, his eyes flew open, but he seemed to still be in the grips of his dream. "Carenza, you're safe," he said, holding her tighter still and kissing her head as if he'd just saved her from mortal peril.

"Let me go. You're hurting me," she said, trying to wriggle away from his wild-eyed embrace. Awareness returned to him as the horrors from his dream receded. He released her and pushed himself away, running his hand over his face.

"I'm so sorry. I didn't mean to hurt you. Did I bruise you? Let me see." He sat up to light a candle on the table beside the bed and lifted it as he gently ran his fingers over her side where he'd been gripping her.

"You didn't bruise me, Daniel. I'm fine."

"I'm so sorry." He put down the candle and buried his face in his hands. "I should have known this would happen. I'll sleep on the floor. I'll ask them for a cot tomorrow."

"No." She sat up and wrapped her arms around him, caressing his face. "Stay. Please. It was just a bad dream."

He shook his head. "I'll hurt you again. It's only a matter of time. I have a lot of bad dreams."

"Wait," she said, refusing to relinquish him. "Tell me what you were dreaming." She leaned her forehead against his, and he met her gaze with the saddest eyes she'd ever seen. "Please. I'm your wife."

He closed his eyes and nodded.

"Lay back down with me?"

"No, I—"

"Just for now while you tell me about the dream."

He acquiesced, and they lay down facing each other, legs tangled together.

"I have these dreams almost every night," he said, weaving his fingers through hers and kissing the back of her hand. "It starts with my uncle killing my father. I see my father's face after his death, cold and still. Then there's the long, terrifying ride from Hawkhurst to the farm near Dover, chased by my uncle's assassins. At the farm, I meet Ferdinand, Adele, and Gerard. The dream turns hopeful.

"In a blink, years pass, and I see Adele on our wedding day, only to have it replaced by the horror of the burnt farm and…and…her body. I bury her and Ferdinand, and everything goes black. It used to end there, but now it keeps going. I see you and feel your lips against my own from the night we first kissed. And then my uncle, he… he…". He stopped and swallowed. "You were dead, and I couldn't save you. I was too late."

"It's all right. I'm here. I'm safe," she whispered as she held and caressed him.

"But not from me. I'm so sorry I hurt you." He started to pull away again.

"Shh. You didn't mean to. You were asleep." She hooked her leg over his hip to keep him from escaping. "I want you to stay." She kissed his forehead, then his cheek, as she rubbed his back in slow circles. "Please stay."

He opened his mouth to object, and she covered it with a kiss. He tried to pull away, and she leaned in further, dipping her tongue between his lips and drawing him out. He moaned into her mouth, and she felt him twitch to life against her thigh. There was no way she was going to let him sleep on the floor on their wedding night.

She didn't know much about how to seduce a man, but she was determined to use all the wiles she possessed to keep him with her. It wasn't his fault he held her too tight, and she was afraid if he left, he'd never come back. He belonged in her bed. Our bed, she mentally corrected herself. There had to be a way to convince him to stay. Thinking back to earlier in the evening, she remembered how he reacted when she touched him. Maybe if she touched him again, she could make him forget or at least give him comfort.

Reaching down, she grasped him with a firm hand. His eyes went wide, and he made a strange choking sound. The hot flesh she held grew and twitched at her touch.

"Carenza, what are you doing?"

"Convincing you to stay." With her other hand, she traced a circle around his tip. He jerked, but she held fast. Her own desire was awakening as she traced her fingers up and down the length of him, then teased the tip again, spreading the tiny bead of moisture that had formed there across the velvety flesh, making him pant and thrust into her hand. On impulse, she drew him forward and rubbed him against her own moist flesh, using him to pleasure herself in ways she'd only just learned were possible.

"Carenza, you're going to be the death of me," he whimpered.

"Death can come at any time, and life should not be wasted," she whispered as she placed him at her entrance and slid down onto him. There was a power in being the instigator, and she liked it. She moved beside him, her breasts skimming against his chest, and he followed her pace and rhythm, but she craved more.

As if he intuited what she needed, he rolled to his back and helped her sit astride him. It was delicious and new. But when he thrust up into her, she cried out and collapsed against his chest.

"Did I hurt you?" he asked, instantly apologetic and concerned.

"No," she panted. "It was just…so much. It took me by surprise." Pushing herself upright against his chest, she began to move her hips. His hands supported her and helped to guide her as together they found their rhythm. It was a heady thing to be in control, and it sharpened her pleasure to see him writhe beneath her. Each time he pressed into her, she felt a burst of ecstasy as he filled her more completely than she ever thought possible, touching secret places she had never known.

Everything she thought she knew about herself was lost as they explored her depths together, unknown geographies made of heat and light, virgin territory made known only through pressure and touch from within. Her maidenhead had merely been the portal, not innocence lost, but a beginning of new knowledge. There was so much to feel and learn, and she was voracious, as she always was with a mystery unexplored. She stretched toward the unknown as pleasure overflowed its banks and brought her floating and shuddering back to the man she loved, lying beneath her, losing himself within her. Daniel.

As she had hoped, he drifted off after his release, all thoughts of sleeping on the floor lost in sweet oblivion. She curled against him once again and listened to his heartbeat, thinking she was in grave danger of falling deeply, irrevocably in love.

CHAPTER TWENTY-TWO

CARENZA'S BREATHING WAS deep and even as Daniel extracted himself from her embrace. He'd let her think he was asleep, and for a moment, he had been. This woman was so much more than he'd ever dreamed, and her fierce love left him utterly spent. His body had surrendered, but his mind would not let him be. As he drifted off, the old nightmares began anew. Fortunately, he jerked awake before he became so lost that he hurt her again.

Easing out of her embrace, he slid out of the enormous featherbed and stood up, rubbing the sleep from his eyes. If he was at home in his attic, he would write the demons away, scribbling with his quill until the poison drained. There was a desk in the corner but no quill or ink. The pale moonlight and the dying embers of the fire hardly offered enough light to write by, and he didn't dare light a candle for fear of waking her.

What had he gotten himself into? Now, not only was he Lord de Broase, but he had a wife. And what a wife! With her, the past fell away, and he let himself be the man she wanted him to be— an adoring husband, a passionate lover, a sparring partner for her wit. It was as if the last seventeen years hadn't happened.

But they had. The shadow of his past hung over them even here on the joyous occasion of their wedding night. His uncle was coming—the man who burned everything to the ground and left him with ashes. The shadow of death loomed over them even in the confines of their wedding chamber. Not even here were they safe.

Carenza shifted in her sleep, her luminous face peaceful and content. No shadow hung over her dreams.

His heart ached at the sight of her. He had to fight the urge to clutch her to him and never let go. But he would have to let go, and far too soon. He'd made all the arrangements with his father-in-law. In a matter of days, she would board a ship to Aquitaine with her mother and sisters, and there they would stay until it was safe to return. Until Uncle Raymond was dead.

Daniel's hands curled into fists at the thought.

No. He wasn't going to think about his uncle on his wedding night. Parchment and a quill. That was what he needed.

He dressed hastily in his discarded wedding clothes, careful not to make a sound. Opening the heavy wooden door ever so slowly, he stepped into the hallway. Everything was silent. No one stirred. Candles burned low in sconces at each end of the hall, offering some meager light as he crept to the main staircase.

Moonlight from narrow windows high up lit his descent. In case of attack, archers would stand on the walkway beneath those windows and use them as arrow slits. From there, they had a clear shot to the outer courtyard where they could rain havoc on any attackers. Winchelsea Castle was strong, thank God. His uncle would not find it an easy target, especially now that they were prepared for his arrival.

And here he was, thinking of his uncle again on his wedding night. Battle strategy and defensive positions were the last thing he should be thinking of, with his wife of a few hours sleeping upstairs.

Something stirred near the great hall as he made his way down the last few stairs. A lifetime of over-caution made him halt and hide in the shadows. Who could be stirring at this hour? Could it be that his uncle sent an assassin disguised among the wedding guests to take him down when he was at his most vulnerable?

Daniel shook himself. That would be ridiculous. His overactive imagination was making too much of a few bumps in the night.

The shadow of a man approached.

"Daniel, is that you?"

It was John's voice. Daniel heaved a sigh of relief.

"Yes, John. I'm afraid it is."

"Don't tell me you've left that beautiful creature you married all alone upstairs. It's your wedding night, my boy…I mean…my lord. Why are you lurking down here?"

Why indeed? If only he had an answer for why nightmares chased him from sleep every night or why he couldn't see a shadow in the darkness without assuming treachery.

"Nightmares," he said at last. "I didn't want to wake Carenza."

"Ah," said John, all too understanding. "Come with me. I'm off to the kitchens to see if they can make me a cup of warm milk with honey. That puts me to sleep every time. We should get one for you, too."

Daniel smiled. "That sounds perfect. And what has you up at this hour, my friend? Why aren't you asleep in the great hall with the other guests?"

John chuckled. "I could blame it on Sir Benedict's snoring, but in truth, it's simply old age. I've found as I've grown older, sleep has grown more elusive. Rare is the night when I can manage to sleep until dawn."

"We have that in common, then."

They walked on in companionable silence until they reached the kitchen. A young woman wearing a mob cap and apron was stoking a fire in a large, plain hearth that lit the room in a warm orange glow. Various cast iron pots were suspended by chains over the fire, still bubbling with the remnants of last night's feast. Herbs, onions, and game hung from the rafters above them. The fires for the enormous ovens were dark.

"My lord," said the young woman, dropping the poker she

was using with a clatter. "You startled me. I didn't expect anyone to be up at this hour. What can I do for you?"

"Could you make us some warm milk and honey and let us sit by the fire for a bit?" John asked, smiling kindly at her.

"Of course. Right away." She scurried off to get some milk.

Daniel and John seated themselves on a roughhewn wood bench by the fire.

"So, how does it feel to be married, my lord?" John smiled expectantly.

If only there was a simple answer to that question. Daniel should have been elated, blissful, madly in love, with not a care in the world. And he was, except for that last bit. Somehow, marrying had made all his cares seem heavier rather than lighter.

"I'm terrified," he said before he could stop himself. "She's so beautiful and intelligent and full of life. I could never live with myself if anything ever happened to her."

John patted Daniel's knee. It was such a fatherly gesture that it made Daniel's heartache all the more. How different this day would have been if his father had survived! But John was here, as much of a father as anyone still living.

"I thought I knew fear," Daniel continued. "But nothing I ever felt on my own behalf equals what I fear for her. With Adele, I was full of hope. My fears were vague. I never imagined my uncle would take out his hatred for me on my new bride. But now I know the horror and grief of loss. I know what Uncle Raymond is capable of. And I fear for Carenza more than I could ever fear for myself."

"Ah, you're in love," John said, smiling sadly.

Daniel stiffened. "Please don't say those words aloud. When has my love ever brought anything but suffering and death? I don't dare love for fear of cursing my beloved with my ill fortune."

The kitchen maid returned with a small pot of milk and hung it over the fire. She shuffled off to another part of the kitchen and busied herself washing dishes.

"My lord, you are not cursed. Don't take upon yourself the sins of your uncle. He alone is responsible for his actions."

"And I am responsible for ending him." Daniel clenched and unclenched his fist in a steady rhythm. "I will stop him before he can harm another soul. He will not have her. He cannot. I will hunt him to the ends of the earth before I ever let him come anywhere near her."

John patted his knee again. "Soon. Very soon. But not tonight. Tonight, you should be with your wife, celebrating life and love while you can. Revenge can wait."

Hanging his head, Daniel nodded. He knew John was right, but the foreboding in his heart would not give him peace, would not let him enjoy untainted bliss even on a night like this.

The milk bubbled in the pot, and the kitchen maid came over and poured it into two ceramic cups, adding honey and stirring it in. Then, she handed a cup to each of the men.

Daniel accepted it with a grateful nod and took a sip. It took him back to his childhood. His mother used to give him warm milk with honey at night before bedtime. Something sweet to give him sweet dreams, she always said. The warmth trickled through him, relaxing his clenched muscles, and as the full weight of his exhaustion fell upon him, he stifled a yawn.

"Works like a charm, doesn't it?" John said with a sideways grin.

Daniel smiled back despite himself. "I don't think I've drunk milk and honey since I was in the nursery."

"Let it do its magic, my lord, and go back upstairs to your wife. The fight with your uncle will be upon us before we know it. You deserve a little peace and happiness first. Don't let worries about tomorrow rob you of the joys of today."

Daniel's eyelids drooped as he drank down the milk, savoring the memories it brought as much as the delicious taste and smell. "I think you're right. It's time I return to my wife."

John patted his knee again. "You do that."

Standing, Daniel gave in to an enormous yawn. Perhaps he

was finally exhausted enough to rest.

"Thank you, John." Daniel squeezed the older man's shoulder. "Let's meet an hour after dawn to discuss defenses. For now, I'm off to bed."

Groggy and blinking, Daniel wound his way back through the castle and up the stone staircase to his bedroom. He closed the door silently behind him and stoked the embers of the fire, adding another log to fend off the early morning chill that was creeping in.

Carenza stirred, and he froze. She looked so peaceful and content in sleep. And so soft and vulnerable. The need to touch her and fold her in his arms overwhelmed him.

Stripping off his clothes as quickly as he could, he climbed carefully into bed beside her, spooning her curled form. The last dregs of the nightmare dissipated with the warmth and comfort of holding her close. He kissed the creamy skin of her shoulder and buried his face in her hair, breathing deeply. With her, he was safe. He was home.

He could never tell her how much he felt for her. No matter what John said, he would not risk subjecting her to the curse of his love. The only way to lift that curse was to rid himself of his uncle. But until then, he would show her every way he could, short of saying the words.

She snuggled closer against him, and he gave at last into the sweet delirium of the moment, all thoughts of revenge banished at last. There was only the two of them in all the world. Everything else dropped away. Whatever the morning might bring, tonight, he was all hers.

CHAPTER TWENTY-THREE

CARENZA TOYED WITH the apple tart on her breakfast plate, trying to decide if she was hungry as Elaine changed the bed linens, carrying away the evidence of last night's activities. Well, not just last night. Also, this morning. Her husband woke up hungry for her, despite having taken her three times the night before. He might have made it twice before breakfast if he hadn't agreed to meet with her father and John about defenses. No, she wasn't really hungry for food, she decided, though she made herself eat an egg for the sake of maintaining her strength and stamina.

"Well, my lady, aren't you the blushing bride this morning! I take it you two enjoyed yourselves?" Elaine asked as she put new sheets on the bed.

Carenza grinned sheepishly.

"Your mother will be pleased," Elaine said, nodding at the soiled sheet.

"What? You don't mean she actually plans to check them."

Elaine raised her eyebrows and nodded. "And preserve them, in case there should ever be questions."

"Blood and sticky liquid," she mumbled.

Elaine paused and raised her head. "What's that?"

"Tell her I have done my duty, Elaine," Carenza said aloud.

"Ha! Duty indeed. And I suppose he's also just doing his duty, ensuring the succession?"

Carenza erupted in uncontrollable giggles. "Oh yes!" she said, gasping for air. "Very concerned with the succession."

The giggles infected Elaine. "Oh, I'm sure. Repeated efforts, by the looks of it! Such a dutiful husband!"

Carenza could hardly breathe from laughing so hard.

Alais burst through the door. "What are you two laughing about?"

"Alais! You can't just barge in here without knocking. What if my husband was with me?" Carenza wished she had something to throw at her sister.

"I knew he wasn't. I saw him downstairs with Father," said Alais, helping herself to bread and butter from Carenza's plate.

"Why are you in here?"

Alais leaned across the table conspiratorially. "I wanted to know if what Mother told us is true."

"About the blood and sticky liquid?" Carenza asked, raising an eyebrow. Elaine clapped a hand over her mouth, shaking helplessly in silent laughter.

Alais nodded, eyes wide with anticipation.

Carenza narrowed her eyes and studied her sister. Last night, she'd been outraged by her mother's description. For years, that description had filled her with fear and disgust, and now she knew exactly how misleading it was. But then she tried to imagine what she could say to Alais at this moment that would be accurate without planting a temptation to sin before marriage. Suddenly, she understood her mother's strategy all too well. When Alais was ready to marry, Carenza would speak to her before her wedding night, but until then…

She composed her face into a somber expression and looked Alais in the eye. "It's all true, Alais, including the blood and sticky liquid."

Elaine had to sit down on the bed, her shoulders shaking with the laughter she was holding in for her sister's sake. She knew the strategy as well.

"No," Alais challenged in horrified disbelief.

"Oh yes! If you don't believe me, I can prove it." It took all her resolve to keep a straight face.

"No, you can't!"

"Oh yes, I can. Elaine, show her the sheet." She narrowed her eyes and turned to Elaine with great solemnity.

Elaine held up the soiled sheet, visibly biting her lips closed to keep from exploding.

Alais gave a little scream and went running out of the room.

The moment she was gone, Carenza and Elaine both lost all control. It was several minutes before they could breathe or speak.

"Your mother is a diabolical genius," Elaine said, wiping her eyes.

"Yes. She is." Carenza had always been sure of this, but rarely did she have cause to appreciate it. It was strange to think that she was out from under her mother's thumb. Already, she felt she appreciated her mother more with the benefit of a little distance.

"Speaking of your mother, I had better hurry up with these sheets, or she'll have my hide." Elaine scurried out of the room with her bundle, and Carenza was left alone to puzzle out what she was going to do with herself during her first day as a married woman.

She went to the window of the unfamiliar bedroom and looked out. Below was a courtyard where the knights trained and practiced. Her husband was down there with John, practicing forms with a battle axe. She wondered why he hadn't opted for a sword. She would have to ask him later.

He was fluid and precise in his movements, just as he had been that day by the dock shaping a wood plank, and there was no denying that he was a graceful man despite his strength and size. There was a confidence and certainty to his movements, just as there was in his poetry. And just as there was in his lovemaking, she thought with a blush. Even though she was a bit sore, she wondered how long she was going to have to wait today before she could have him back, and they could ruin some more sheets together.

She puttered around for several hours, trying to pray, then trying to write, then giving up and setting out in search of her husband. She found him coming in from the practice yard, glistening with sweat. The raw muscular power of him took her breath away. Her throat went dry, and she bit her lip.

"Carenza," he said, smiling. "I was about to come find you. I had an idea for this afternoon. How would you feel about going sailing? I have a little boat of my own, just big enough for two. I thought it might be nice to get out of the castle for a bit."

"That sounds lovely! I haven't done that since…" She paused. She hadn't been sailing since she'd lost her brother, God rest his soul. Her smile dropped, and her hand moved to her necklace.

His brow furrowed, and he touched her arm. "Is something wrong? We can do something else if you'd prefer."

She shook her head and forced a carefree smile back on her face. "Of course not. I'd love to go sailing."

She could do this. There was no reason to fear the water. She'd practically lived on it growing up. And wouldn't it be better to remember Charles by living life fully than by avoiding what used to be one of her favorite things to do?

Soon, they were down by the dock with a basket of food and blankets, and she was climbing into Daniel's boat. It was named "Adele," she noted with a pang. Even so, she took a deep breath, resolving once again not to resent his love for his first wife.

"I made this to prove my skill at the end of my apprenticeship. I carved every board and sealed every seam myself. I even sewed the canvas for the sail. I've worked on ships that were much bigger and grander, but this is my pride and joy."

The quality of the craftsmanship was exquisite. She could hardly see where the boards met, and every surface was perfectly polished as if it had never been used, even though the boat must be six years old, from what he said. She ran her hand along the perfect column of the mast, appreciating the curve of the wood beneath her touch.

"She's a beauty," she said with a smile as they cast off. "Clearly the work of a master."

He smiled broadly at her compliment, reddening just a touch, if she wasn't imagining things.

"Do you go out sailing often?" she asked as the sail caught the stiff ocean breeze, and they tacked out into the harbor.

"Not as much as I would like, but I try to get out as often as I can. I feel very free out here, like I've left all my cares behind. My uncle can't find me out here," he said with a laugh.

Her smile faded. "No, no one can find you out here," she said with a sad sigh. As soon as she said the words, she wished she could take them back. This was not a conversation for their first day of marriage. Today was supposed to be happy and joyous.

"What is it, Carenza?" His voice was low and soft.

She looked out at the horizon. There was no avoiding this story now. He was going to learn of her grief eventually, one way or another. "My brother was lost at sea. He was on a ship headed back from Ireland. They were sailing through the Channel along the southern coast. Then, it simply disappeared. Eventually, the ship was declared lost, and everyone aboard dead. It was hard to accept without proof. I held out hope far longer than I should have, but Charles is gone." She touched the skull on her rosary and closed her eyes. It still stung as if it happened yesterday.

Daniel took her hand and kissed it. "I'm sorry for your loss."

She took a deep breath and let it out slowly. "I haven't done this since I lost him—going out for a sail for fun. We used to sail over to that tiny islet over there," she said, pointing it out, "It's called Dolphin Island. We used to spend the day swimming and eating oysters. Mother hated it when we disappeared for the day like that, but she never tried to stop us. She said no one would marry me if I didn't keep out of the sun and stop behaving like a sea witch."

"Ah, so you are a sea witch. Good to know," he said, his eyes twinkling with merriment.

"Oh yes," she agreed, more than happy to change the subject. "How do you think I lured you into my trap?" She gave him a seductive look.

"Aha! So you admit you ensorcelled me," he said, tugging her hand and pulling her over into his lap so that he could nuzzle her neck.

"Mm," was all the response she could manage as his hand wandered and his lips on her neck distracted her, filling her with hunger.

"I'm suddenly regretting that we're stuck in a tiny boat," he muttered. "I'd better find us a place to land." He adjusted course and headed for Dolphin Island. "And, my siren," he whispered in her ear, "perhaps you should sit back over there for a bit so that I don't capsize us in a fit of passion."

Reluctantly, she returned to her seat across from him, her body humming with desire. "I think I'd best stick to dry topics so as not to make your predicament any more uncomfortable," she said, boldly observing the evidence of his ardor and attempting to distract herself. "I saw you practicing with an axe this morning. Why an axe and not a sword?"

He laughed. "Because I've used an axe every day for well over a decade, and I haven't had a lesson in swordsmanship since I was nine. I need every advantage I can get in the coming fight."

"I'm certain you're going to win. God couldn't possibly let such an evil man go unpunished."

He busied himself with minor adjustments to the sail and tiller, not meeting her eyes. "I'm not a knight. I've never fought in a battle or even so much as a tournament. My uncle's men are experienced veterans of many campaigns, and he has more knights than we do, even with the ones I was able to hire. Victory is far from certain. But one way or another, I'll do whatever I must to ensure you're out of his reach. I'll keep you safe, no matter what it takes."

She frowned. "What do you mean, you'll keep me out of his reach? You're not planning to send me away, are you?"

He looked her in the eye, and her breath caught. "I have to," he said. "He's going to kill you. I have to take you out of his reach. I can't let him do to you what he did to Adele."

"What does Adele have to do with anything?" Her throat tightened as if his dead wife's ghost wrapped her hands around her neck.

"I owe it to her memory to make sure he can't touch you. It's the whole reason I married you."

She clutched the side of the boat and widened her eyes, her heart breaking into a million jagged pieces. "So you're telling me you married me out of duty to Adele's memory?"

"No, that isn't it at all. I married you because I needed to keep you safe." He said it as if it was the most logical thing in the world, as if he wasn't tearing her heart out with every word.

She pulled her head back and stared at him, hot fury welling up and coursing through her veins as the pain of his words sank deeper. "Safe? You married me to keep me safe? Is that all? Do you care for me at all?"

"Carenza," he said, not meeting her eyes.

She leaned in, needing him to look at her. "Well?"

"You must understand, my love is a curse. Everyone I love dies. I don't want to see you die too."

His words hit her like a punch. She couldn't breathe, think, or speak. She needed to get out of this boat, away from him. There was no way she could stay trapped here with him even another minute. She wanted to leap out of the boat. And suddenly, she remembered that she could.

She kicked off her shoes, tugged off her dress, then dove into the water in her shift. The islet wasn't far. She'd swum that distance before with no trouble. Letting the cold waves wash over her, she lost herself in the effort of propelling herself forward. She didn't have to think or feel, just move.

Daniel yelled after her, and she looked back over her shoulder to see him trying to maneuver the boat toward her. The wind was suddenly uncooperative, dying down to nothing, and he was forced to switch to rowing. He caught up to her quickly once he took up the oars.

"Carenza, I'm sorry. Please get back in the boat," he pleaded, stretching out his arm to help her up.

She refused. "I'll meet you on the beach." And she swam away. She didn't know what she would say to him when she got there, but she knew she needed time. Her heart pounded as she tried to calm the raging storm within her. She'd as good as confessed her love for him, and all he could tell her was that he wanted to keep her safe.

But then, why did it matter so much that he loved her? Hadn't she known when they married that he wasn't in love with her? Did she even want love? It only led to misery and sacrifice.

Besides, people of their station didn't marry for love. And he was still a better husband than any of her other suitors would have been. He was considerate and kind and passionate, at least so far. He'd promised not to trample on her free will and cared enough to die in her defense. That was something, wasn't it?

No. No, it wasn't. What she really wanted was for him to want to live and spend a long, happy life with her. But that was apparently too much to ask. He was too eager to send her away. He didn't properly appreciate the chance at happiness he'd been given.

But maybe it didn't depend on him? Or, not only on him. Maybe she could figure out a way to help him get through the clash with his uncle, and then maybe they could have the future she wanted. All she had to do was find a way to evade his attempt to send her away.

DANIEL PULLED THE boat onto the beach, laid out a blanket, and sat to watch Carenza making her way to the shore while he tried to sort out his feelings. She swam like a dolphin. It was a miraculous sight. He'd never seen a woman swim before. It was mesmerizing.

He shook himself and tried to focus on what to do now. Clearly, he'd underestimated her feelings for him. He'd thought she'd married him out of a mix of curiosity, desire, and practicality. But apparently, there was more. He would have to apologize.

No, he would have to grovel.

She reached the shallows and stood up in the waves like Venus emerging from seafoam. Her thin shift was transparent and plastered to her skin by the water. She walked up the beach to him with a look of unshakeable determination, the sun glistening off her wet hair and skin. He noticed she still wore her rosary, the skull hanging between her breasts. In her current state, she looked every inch the siren, the sea witch, come to drag him down to the depths with her.

She came and sat beside him, then leaned back on her elbows to bask in the sun, closing her eyes. He wanted to touch her. He wanted to drown himself in her. But first, he had to make things right.

"I'm sorry, Carenza. I should never have dismissed your feelings. It's not fair to you. Please forgive me."

She raised her head to look at him. There was pity in her eyes but also pain. Was there something specific she hoped to see in him? He wasn't sure if she saw it. She closed her eyes again and turned her face back toward the sun. She was otherworldly beside him, distant and aloof and furious but so beautiful, so vibrant. He wanted to touch her, taste her, bring her back to him, make her see.

Tentatively, gently, he leaned to touch his lips to hers. She tasted of sea salt. She didn't kiss him back. He backed away and looked at her face. A tear trickled down from the corner of one of her closed eyes. He brushed it away, murmuring, "Carenza, please forgive me. I'm so sorry. Please. Give me a chance to make it right. How can I make it right? Tell me. Please."

She opened her eyes, welling with tears, and looked at him

with an expression filled with pain and determination.

"Let me stay," she said in a gruff voice and closed her eyes again.

He sat up and lowered his face to his hands. He couldn't do that, and so he couldn't make it right. He'd talked it over with her father and made the arrangements.

Shaking his head, he said, "When de Broase arrives, you and your mother and sisters are setting sail for Aquitaine until it is safe to return, if that day ever comes." Her obvious outrage didn't make him any less determined to go through with the plan. He needed her to be safe. She couldn't die because of him.

"Carenza, we're together right now. Are we going to waste the time we have in anger?"

She opened her eyes again and gave him a withering look. Then she lifted her rosary from where it nestled between her breasts, kissed the skull, stood up, went over to the boat, and pulled her dress on over her still-damp shift. "I want to go back to the castle. I have work to do."

He had no choice but to acquiesce. He gathered up the blanket, pushed the boat back into the water, and they sailed back in silence.

They arrived back at the castle, and Lord de Vere was waiting for them. "The man I sent to watch Hawkhurst has returned. Your uncle is two days out, and he has half again as many fighters as we do. The earl and countess are preparing to leave to ensure they are well away before your uncle arrives. You should say your goodbyes."

Carenza grabbed his hand and squeezed it. "I'll go with you. I'd like to say goodbye to them, too," she said.

"When you're done," Lord de Vere said to Daniel, "we should speak. There's much to do. I'll be in my study." He turned and left them alone.

"Two days," said Daniel. "Carenza, please forgive me. We have so little time."

She yanked him into a small receiving room and shut the

door, and she kissed him as if the world was ending. They collapsed onto the floor and fumbled at each other's clothing, and within moments, he was inside of her. He needed her with a ferocity that shocked him. He wasn't gentle or slow. They coupled with desperate fury. It was over in minutes.

"I'm still mad at you," she said as she patted down her skirts and tied her long hair into a knot at the nape of her neck.

He sighed. "I know." He didn't expect her to forgive him easily. In fact, he was fairly certain he'd regret what he said for the rest of his life. He couldn't take the words back now that they'd been spoken. All he could do was try to make it right.

Except that he couldn't. He wouldn't lie to her and tell her what she wanted to hear. All he could do was hope that she would relent on her own as she had just now. They had so little time left. "Thank you for taking pity on me."

"That wasn't pity." She glared at him. No, it wasn't pity. It was something else entirely, something he didn't deserve from her, especially since he couldn't allow himself to return it. But he couldn't deny it either, not if he was being honest with himself. She hadn't said the words, but she loved him. He was sure of it, and it filled him with shame. He couldn't undo it or prevent the pain it would cause her.

"I'm so sorry, Carenza," he said uselessly, unable to come up with anything else.

"I'm not," she said, full of fierce determination, and walked out the door without him.

CHAPTER TWENTY-FOUR

AFTER SAYING GOODBYE to the earl and countess, Carenza went to find her mother. Lady Isabella would certainly have found out by now what the men were up to, and she didn't think that her mother would put up with defeat. The baroness was a warrior as much as the baron and had been by her husband's side during multiple naval engagements. She was also a masterful negotiator, working political alliances to the advantage of House de Vere behind the scenes to ensure her husband's success. While her relationship with her mother had never been easy, she knew Lady Isabella was her best hope of finding a way to save Daniel.

"Ah, Carenza! I was wondering how long it would be before you came to find me." Her mother opened the door of her receiving room. "I take it you've gotten wind of this ridiculous scheme our husbands have concocted?"

"Yes, and I'm furious," said Carenza, taking a seat on a silk-cushioned bench.

How could Daniel break his promise to allow her free will? This was what she got for allowing herself to fall in love. She should have expected this and never should have agreed to marry. Look where it had gotten her.

"Don't worry. I have a plan," Carenza said.

Her mother waved her hand dismissively. "Sit, Carenza. So do I."

With difficulty, she made herself comply.

"Men think they're the only ones who can possibly do anything useful at moments like this," her mother continued, "and they make poor decisions as a result. They left a loophole, and I plan to take full advantage. They're putting us on a ship to Aquitaine, but they never said we couldn't make stops along the way."

Carenza fought to contain a smile. Her mother did not disappoint. "I was thinking the same thing. In fact, I thought our first stop should be our next-door neighbor—Hastings."

Her mother smiled broadly and nodded in approval. "My plan exactly. I can give Countess Helisende a piece of my mind for her utter failure to support us in our time of need. She has a responsibility to us. Her husband is our liege lord, and Hastings has an obligation to come to our aid. I need to remind her of her oaths. If I can't cajole her into sending knights, then my name isn't Isabella de Vere." Her mother twisted her handkerchief as if wringing a neck.

"If that fails," Carenza said, "we should head to Calais and visit Papa's cousins. I'm sure I can persuade them to send aid as well."

"Good thinking."

Carenza allowed herself a moment to bask in the rare compliment from her mother.

"I'm only continuing on to Aquitaine if all else fails," her mother said, standing to pace. "It was a ridiculous scheme, insulting, really. I can't speak for Daniel, but I'm surprised at your father. He should know better after all these years!"

Carenza nodded as they laid out their plan together. It was a good one. It made her feel better to know they would act, not just let themselves be shipped off like delicate porcelain. "Have you heard anything about how our husbands plan to defend Winchelsea castle in our absence?"

"Ah, so that's what's troubling you," her mother said with a commiserating smile. "Yes, I worry about that too. Your father is an excellent naval strategist, but he has no experience fighting on land. The earl gave some helpful advice while he was here, and the castle's walls are strong. As long as they can keep the entrances defended, they can hold out for a long time, even with an inferior force. In the end, though, they need to defeat de Broase or make him retreat. They need more than a good defense, or the castle will be besieged."

"And how do they plan to do that?" Carenza asked skeptically.

"We've sent word to the king, but heaven only knows when there might be a response."

"And if that fails?"

Her mother gave a disappointed shrug. "They talk a lot about their fancy plans, but they have no idea. Your husband may be able to peel away some of his uncle's men and bring them to our side once they realize who he is, but it's a gamble. We have no idea how many might believe his claim or show him loyalty."

"I think he plans to go after Lord de Broase by himself," Carenza said, suddenly sure this was what Daniel intended.

"What? No! That's the stupidest thing I ever heard." Her mother stood abruptly and began pacing, herself. "First of all, it won't work. What's to stop his uncle from killing him and then continuing his attack? Second of all, what a ridiculous waste! Why are men always trying to die for love? Why can't they live for it?"

Carenza winced at the mention of the word "love." Her mother turned and loomed over her.

"What is it, Carenza?"

Carenza shook her head.

"Something is wrong. Don't play coy with me," her mother insisted.

She closed her eyes, wincing at the memory of what Daniel said in the boat. "Daniel isn't doing this for love, or at any rate not for love of me." It cost her greatly to admit this to her mother, but she could not hold it in any longer.

Her mother sat down next to her and patted her knee.

"Carenza dear, that man is completely in love with you. It's obvious to anyone who has eyes."

"But he said—"

"I don't care what he said. Men are fools. They say things they don't mean. Your Daniel has had a lot of pain in his life. Men don't know how to handle pain. They just bottle it all up and try to stuff it down in some deep corner of their soul, where it festers and infects everything until it feels like nothing else is left. Whatever he said, it was his pain speaking. Ignore it and listen to his heart. He loves you, Carenza. It's plain to see."

Carenza leaned her head back and closed her eyes. "It doesn't much matter one way or the other if he goes and dies a stupid death while I'm stuck on a ship."

"Yes, well, clearly, we'll need to find a way to prevent that." Her mother started straightening pillows with a vengeance. "Let's give it some thought. Let's meet again after dinner, and we'll come up with a plan."

Carenza rose and went in search of Elaine. She was gathering Carenza's belongings from her former bedchamber and moving them into the chambers she now shared with Daniel. "I need to speak to Gerard today, if possible. Can you arrange that?"

Elaine paused in her folding. "Of course. My Lady, if I may ask, what is this about?"

"It's about Daniel," she said, closing her eyes and touching her rosary. "I'm worried about him, and I think Gerard can help."

Elaine squeezed her shoulder. "Of course, my lady. I'll have him here within the hour. Don't you worry."

A short while later, Elaine took her down to the receiving room where Gerard was waiting. When she entered, he stood up and bowed.

"Lady de Broase, I am at your service."

It was jarring to hear her new name. For a moment, she thought he must mean someone else. "Please sit, Gerard. Make yourself comfortable." Elaine poured wine for all three of them. "First, I would like to congratulate you on your engagement to

Mistress Elaine. I'm very happy for you both."

"Thank you, Lady de Broase, we're both very happy. But I don't think you brought me here just to say that. Elaine mentioned something to do with Daniel—I mean, Lord de Broase?" He took a careful sip of his wine.

"I think he would prefer it if you continued to call him Daniel, given your relationship. Please don't stand on ceremony for my sake."

Gerard's smile was tight and uncertain. "Of course, my lady."

Carenza took a long sip of her wine to fortify herself for what she was about to say. "Gerard, I think Daniel is planning something foolish, and I'm hoping you can help me do something about it."

Gerard shook his head and stared into his cup. "He's hardly spoken to me since he went away to see his sister. In fact, he didn't even tell me he was going to see her. I thought he was going after his uncle. Next thing I know, he's back as Lord de Broase, living up here in the castle and marrying you. I used to think nothing under the firmament could convince him to take up that name. When he married Adele, he swore he'd left it behind forever. But here we are. I doubt there's anything I can do to help."

"Gerard!" Elaine reached out and pinched him hard. "You're being very rude to her ladyship!"

"Ever since her ladyship showed up, he's changed," Gerard said to Elaine, indicating Carenza. "The Daniel I knew fled from the name de Broase. He hated it down to his very bones, just like I do. Then she comes along, and suddenly, he doesn't mind being Lord de Broase. He's taken up the name of the man that killed my father and my sister. All these years, he's gone on and on about his love for Adele, and Lord knows the man needed to move on with his life. But how can he walk away so easily from who he was for seventeen years?"

"He hasn't," Carenza said. "He hates his uncle. He hates the name de Broase. As far as I can tell, he's still in love with Adele.

He seems to think he's going to go after his uncle alone to honor her memory by saving my family."

"And you," Gerard added, bitterness oozing from his voice. "The man lost his bloody mind over you."

"Gerard!" Elaine smacked his thigh. Gerard ignored her.

"He didn't touch a woman for six years," he said, gesticulating with his goblet. "Claimed he wasn't tempted after Adele. Then one day, you blunder into a warehouse, twist your ankle, and he sends me to sing you a bloody love song in front of my sister's murderer, who just happened to be your fiancé." He leaned toward Carenza, eyes narrowed. "What did you do to him? Why did you do this to him? He's a good man. He's the closest thing I have to a family since the other Lord de Broase murdered mine. What have you done to Daniel?"

Something in Carenza snapped. She stood up, raging at him, "I fell in love with him, Gerard! That's what I bloody well did to Daniel!" She turned her back to him and stared at the wall, shaking with fury and heartbreak.

Elaine came to put an arm around her. "My lady, I'm so sorry. I'll ask him to leave. And maybe kick him really hard on the way out."

"No, Elaine," Carenza said, composure returning. "I asked him here because I wanted to talk to him. I'm not done yet." She turned back to Gerard, determined. "Daniel has made clear to me that he doesn't love me, that he only married me to keep me safe. I haven't done anything to him other than to remind him a little too much of your sister. Unfortunately for me, I do love him. In the next few days, he's going to send me away to Aquitaine with my mother and sisters, supposedly for our safety. I need someone to watch him and make sure he doesn't do anything stupid while I'm gone. I'm going to try to come back as quickly as possible, but I don't trust him not to go after his uncle by himself while I'm away. Will you do it?"

Gerard closed his eyes with a long groan. "Daniel, you bloody idiot. Could you possibly have made a bigger mess?"

He shook his head and then looked up at Carenza.

"Fine, I'll talk to him." He sighed, pressing his fingers to his forehead. "And I'm sorry for what I said. It's him I'm angry at, not you. He and I need to have a little talk over a lot of ale." He stood up to leave but paused, realizing he hadn't been dismissed. "Is that everything, my lady?"

"Yes," answered Carenza.

Elaine grabbed his arm and grumbled sharply in his ear, "You and I also need to have a little talk over a lot of ale."

Gerard turned before the door. "My lady, for what it's worth, I don't think Daniel knows what he's about. He's turned Adele into some kind of angel or saint in his head. My sister wouldn't recognize herself in Daniel's Adele. And I'm quite certain he's fallen in love with you. I've had to watch it happen and believe me, it was agonizing. Whatever he might choose to call it, he cares for you." He offered a polite bow and then departed under a barrage of whispered abuse from Elaine.

THAT NIGHT, CARENZA tried to stay awake until Daniel came in. He was avoiding her. Yes, there were plans to be made, supplies to be secured, and men to be directed, but Daniel had little to contribute, given his lack of experience. He didn't need to let himself be kept away. He could be here with his bride, but he wasn't. She turned on her side, disappointed but resigned, trying to fend off sleep.

Late at night, at an unknown hour, he slipped carefully into bed beside her, trying not to wake her. But she needed to speak to him. She needed to tell him. "Daniel?"

"Yes?"

"I forgive you. I don't want to fight. We have too little time."

He pulled her against him and held her close. "Thank you," he whispered in her ear.

She thought as soon as she said the words, everything would be better, but as she lay against him, listening to his heartbeat, she realized that nothing had been solved at all.

CHAPTER TWENTY-FIVE

Daniel opened his eyes, hearing cocks crowing in the distance to greet the dawn. Carenza curled against him, perfectly peaceful. It took his breath away to look at her. When she slept, she looked vulnerable in a way she never did when awake. Her usual fire and curiosity gave way to the softness and warmth of repose.

She had to leave today, so he had to say goodbye and break the spell. It killed him to do it, but it had to be done.

She stirred against him, burrowing into his embrace and pulling his arm around her more tightly. The slow movement of her hips turned his usual morning arousal into something more urgent, and he nuzzled her neck as he pressed against her.

Eyes still closed, she smiled and murmured, "Mmm," drawing his hand downward to touch her between her legs. "I had a very good dream about you," she said softly as she guided his finger into her warm, wet cleft, gasping at his touch and filling him with aching, desperate need.

She shifted to her back, smiling, and caressed his cheek, blinking at him with drowsy eyes as he continued to stroke her. His heart was breaking at the beauty of her, at the tenderness of her touch, at the love in her gaze that he could never deserve.

He wanted to take things as slowly as he could, drawing out this final taste of her, savoring the pain and pleasure it brought him. Almost too soon, she shuddered in release, looking up at him with absolute adoration.

It was too much. He tried to pull away, but she brought him back with gentle hands. "Where do you think you're going?" she asked with a mischievous grin, taking him in hand and rubbing him up and down in tantalizing strokes. Then, she must have seen something in his face that gave her pause. "Daniel, what is it?"

"Carenza, I..." I love you. He couldn't do it. His mouth refused to form the words. "Carenza, I need you," he said instead, covering her body with his own, spreading her legs, and sinking home.

She has to be safe. Her heart is safer if you don't say the words. So he let his body speak for him. The intoxicating feel of her beneath him robbed him of sense and will, and he never wanted it to end.

He blinked back tears when she trembled beneath him in her final throes of ecstasy, leaving him in exquisite agony, unable to delay any longer the fruition that would bring the end of everything. The sensation was all the more powerful for the fact that it was torn from him against his will, leaving him bereft and empty as he braced himself for the pain of sending her away.

She lay beside him with her head resting on his heart, her legs and arms still entangled with his own. "Carenza, this is goodbye," he said at last.

With a sigh, she hugged him closer and tucked her head down so he couldn't see her face. "I know."

"I'm sorry, Carenza. It has to be this way."

"Mother said you'd say that. I was hoping she was wrong. I was hoping you'd come to your senses and change your mind. Have you already forgotten your promise to allow me free will?"

He had not forgotten, but her life was more important than a promise. He had to keep her safe.

After a long silence, a tear dripped down her cheek.

"You're really going to do it, aren't you? You're going to

break your promise and force me to go."

This was just one more way in which he'd failed to be the man she deserved. Somehow, her disappointment hurt even more than the fury he'd expected.

She picked up her rosary from the bedside table. She carefully twisted open the tiny golden circle that held the carved skull and handed it to him, placing it in his palm and closing her hand around his.

"Remember, Daniel, life should not be wasted. Death can come at any time, but you should not invite it by taking unnecessary risks. I'll be praying for you." She kissed him softly, then turned from him to dress and start packing her things.

Daniel was left speechless. She didn't seem to expect a response, for which he was grateful. He wasn't a man who was often at a loss for words, but this was beyond him. He suspected this was what had undone him the first time they met, now that he knew she, too, had suffered loss. It was the way she faced her grief and used it as inspiration to live. Daniel's grief had always been debilitating, something he ran from again and again. She'd found a way to welcome it, absorb it, use it to grow stronger.

Carenza was luminous in her grief, where he was broken, vibrant, and alive, where he was hard and withdrawn. He wanted to know her secret. He envied the way she seemed to draw vitality from pain. Even after this week with her, he felt so very far from understanding it, and he was humbled by her gift. Everything about this day was humbling. He would never deserve her.

The hours before the ladies' departure flew by. Just when he wanted time to stop, it seemed to slip through his hands like water. Blink. They were riding down to the docks. Blink. He was kissing her for the last time. Blink. The ship was gone over the horizon. It was done. She would be safe. She would live. He touched the skull that now hung beneath his shirt, on the chain with his rings, and prayed for their safe journey at sea.

As he stood staring out at the place where the ship disappeared over the horizon, Gerard came up and stood by his side.

"She's gone?" Gerard asked.

"She's gone." Daniel suddenly felt the full magnitude of his loss as he said the words. He was half a man with half a heart. He couldn't be whole without her. He needed her. But he'd sent her away. How had he ever let her go?

"Let me buy you a drink," Gerard said, pulling him away, looking more serious and grim than Daniel had ever seen him in his life.

Daniel raised an eyebrow. "Since when do you buy me drinks, Gerard?"

"Humor me. You've just sent your wife away. Besides, I want to speak to you."

Gerard led the way to the Juggler. Daniel could feel the stares of the townsfolk at his fancy garb. He'd always been so at home here. He'd always blended in, disappeared amongst the workers, but now he stuck out like a sore thumb. Everyone bowed and scraped as he passed, even some who knew him and should have known better. Daniel wished he could disappear back into his old anonymity, but he knew this was part of the sacrifice he made when he decided to take up his title. There was no going back.

Even Sir Percival watched him from a distance, licking his paws instead of greeting him and twining around his legs.

"My lord," Franny said, offering a curtsy as he entered. "What an unexpected honor!"

"I'm just plain Daniel, Franny," he said quietly.

She raised an eyebrow. "Whatever you say, my lord."

Gerard's eyes narrowed as he watched this exchange. "Two ales, please, Franny. Daniel and I need to have a little talk."

"Watch yourself, Gerard. You should know your place better than that," she admonished as she poured the ale.

Gerard just shook his head, plunked down some coins, and led the way to an empty table.

As they sat, Gerard raised his tankard in a toast. "To our dearly departed. May we never forget them."

Daniel raised his glass cautiously and drank, but he was worried. Gerard had never, in his recollection, toasted to the dead. Everything was a lark with Gerard, and he was every bit as skilled at avoiding his grief as Daniel. But at present, he was looking Daniel in the eye, a black and brooding expression on his face.

"Now," Gerard said in a low voice, leaning in, "I want to talk about how we're going to kill Raymond de Broase."

Daniel jerked back, but Gerard grabbed his arm.

"Don't pretend you aren't planning something. I know you too well. All I ask is that you let me help. I want him dead every bit as much as you do."

Daniel could hardly believe what he was hearing. "Gerard, what's gotten into you?"

Gerard's grip on his arm tightened. "What has gotten into me? You want to know what has gotten into me, Lord de Broase?"

"Don't you ever call me that, Gerard. You're family." His voice was ice even to his own ears.

"And why not? It's your name, isn't it? Suddenly, you don't mind being a de Broase so much since it lets you bed a de Vere."

Daniel had no awareness of rising from his seat. Suddenly, he'd pinned Gerard against the wall and was about to punch him. With great difficulty, he lowered his fist. He'd never hit Gerard, and he wasn't about to start.

"Raymond de Broase killed my family, Daniel," Gerard said, staring at him defiantly. "I want revenge. Is that so very hard to understand? Have you forgotten what he did to you? To me? To the people we loved? How do you justify using that name after what he did to Adele?"

Daniel pressed his forearm harder against his throat.

Franny came running over. "I'm sorry to interrupt, my lord, but might you be willing to take this outside? You're alarming the customers." Her words and tone were deferential, but her eyes were full of disapproval.

Daniel nodded, let go of Gerard, and turned to swiftly drain his tankard. Then he put it down on the table. "I'm sorry for making trouble, Franny. Might we have another round when you have a moment?" He hauled Gerard out the door and seated him against a barrel, leaning back against the wall of the Juggler.

"Mmmm. Good talk, Daniel," Gerard said, rubbing his neck where Daniel's arm had been pressing. The teasing tone in his voice was back, the tension broken.

"I'm sorry. I shouldn't have done that." Gerard had pushed too far, but every word was true. It was Daniel's own guilt that triggered his violent reaction.

"*Pffft.* I was provoking you. I would have worried more if you hadn't reacted." Gerard dropped his gaze for a moment, then he brought it back up. "I'm sorry for what I said about your wife. She's all right. I feel rather sorry for her, actually, being stuck with you."

Daniel found he couldn't disagree on that front. He knew very well that Carenza deserved better.

"And the rest of what you said?"

"I stand by it, though I hope you won't come at me again," he said, and a wave of chagrin crashed over Daniel when Gerard appeared to cringe. "Not sure the old windpipe could take much more." Franny came out, handed them their tankards, and gave them both a dirty look as she went back inside.

Daniel let out his breath in an exasperated hiss. "I won't. You're lucky I care about you."

Gerard smiled and took a deep drink. "I care about you too, Daniel. You still haven't answered my question, though. How are we going to kill Raymond de Broase?"

God knew Gerard deserved revenge as much as Daniel did, but the last thing Daniel wanted was for Gerard to put himself in harm's way.

Daniel shook his head. "It's too dangerous. I don't want to risk you."

"If you don't let me help you, I'll try on my own," Gerard said, crossing his skinny arms and raising his chin.

For the love of God, Gerard, be serious. You'll get yourself killed.

"No," Daniel said, alarm coursing through his veins. "Please. I may not be a knight, but at least I know a thing or two about how to fight. You don't even know that. Carenza would have a better chance of killing my uncle than you."

Gerard stood and stared him down, not a very impressive move as he was still a good head shorter than Daniel. "I don't care. I'm a grown man, and I need to do this."

Daniel's eyes narrowed. "What about Elaine?"

"What about Carenza?" Gerard asked with an impertinent shrug.

Daniel looked up at the sky and prayed for patience. Gerard wasn't going to let him out of this. Underneath all that insouciance, he was stubborn as a mule. If left to his own devices, Gerard might get himself hurt or worse, and Daniel couldn't allow that. "Fine," he mumbled at last.

"What was that?"

"Fine," he said more loudly. "If you must, I suppose I can't stop you. And I'd rather you stayed with me than went out on your own."

With a broad smile, Gerard clapped Daniel on the arm. "Excellent. I'm glad we've worked that out."

"Let's get back to the castle," Daniel said, shaking his head and turning to go. "You'll stay with me. I need to keep an eye on you. We've got to find you some armor."

And I pray to God that you'll never need it.

"As you wish, my lord," Gerard said with an overly elaborate bow.

"Don't call me that."

"Whatever you say, my lord."

CHAPTER TWENTY-SIX

"ISABELLA, I DON'T have any men to send. A third of my knights are off with my husband, traipsing around England with King Henry's court. The man seems to be allergic to staying put in London. A third of them are in Normandy, defending our holdings. I need the few that remain to defend Hastings."

While Carenza looked on, Countess Helisende of Hastings debated with her mother as a sumptuous feast was laid out. It felt all wrong to be feasting when Daniel was in danger, but what choice did she have? The countess was their best hope of sending swift help back to Winchelsea.

The great hall in Hastings dwarfed the one at home in Winchelsea. Carenza could hardly see the walls, as only the area immediately around the main table was lit. The table itself was as opulent as any she had ever seen, covered with a velvet runner, gilded serving ware, and delicacies she couldn't even name. The high-backed chairs were carved to look like cathedrals. The gilded candelabras were shaped like mermaids and mermen wearing ornate crowns that held the candles.

The opulence of the table was in direct contrast to the hard woman that sat at the end of it. The baroness was of an age with Lady Isabella, white just beginning to streak the golden hair peeking out from her veil. She wore a high-necked dress of rich brocade and a circlet of gold around her head with a single emerald in the front. There was nothing soft or forgiving about the countess. She was a powerful woman who frequently governed in her husband's stead while he served the king. She had the wary look of someone who could never afford the luxury of trust, even with allies.

"Besides, Isabella," the countess continued, "you chose to ally yourself with Lord de Broase. You tried to marry your daughter to Lord Raymond before you opted for this upstart Daniel. Both of them are de Broases. Either way, your alliance with Hastings falls by the wayside, and Hawkhurst takes over. I don't see why we should defend you when you've clearly changed your allegiance."

Her mother gritted her teeth and inhaled sharply. Mother has never been any good at controlling her temper. Carenza hoped she wouldn't offend Countess Helisende beyond repair. They needed her help to save Daniel from doing something foolish.

"My lady," her mother replied, with barely contained rage, "As I've told you repeatedly now, we would never have contemplated an alliance with any of the de Broases if you had only helped when our farmlands were flooded. You failed in your duty to us as vassals, my lady, and you forced our hand."

"It was an act of God. I don't understand what you expected me to do." Helisende cracked open a lobster with murderous strength.

Through clenched teeth, her mother responded, "As I said, you left us no choice. You think you can hold your lands together and keep your seat, my lady, if you let de Broase pick off Hastings' allies one by one? Do you think Raymond de Broase will be satisfied with bringing Winchelsea under his sway? Why would he stop with us when you've shown yourself to be so weak and fearful that you won't even bother to fight his first incursion? Hastings will be his next stop, and you know it." Her mother broke a lobster claw in half with a strange metal utensil Carenza had never seen before and sucked out the meat.

Countess Helisende narrowed her eyes. "I know Raymond de

Broase wants to expand his holdings, Isabella. I'm well aware of his intentions. I've raised my concerns with the crown. Are you threatening to mount a rebellion against me? Because that's what this sounds like." She used a tiny hammer to break open a crab.

Carenza clenched her jaw and swallowed hard in alarm at the direction the conversation was taking.

"I will do what I must to survive," her mother said in icy tones. "I would prefer to remain allied with you, but if you refuse to live up to your oath to protect us, I will do what I must." She cracked open a lobster tail with her hands and speared the flesh with a tiny knife.

"What of this Daniel de Broase? What makes you think he's any better than his uncle?"

"He's nothing like his uncle!" Carenza objected before his mother could respond. "Daniel doesn't want to expand his holdings. He only wants his uncle out of the way. Help us, and you have my word that my husband will never try to extend his influence over Hastings or any of its member towns."

"Carenza!" her mother warned, jabbing her elbow into her arm.

"No, I want to hear what she has to say," said the countess. "After all, if this upstart truly is Lord de Broase, your daughter outranks you." Carenza could feel her mother bristling with outrage beside her. "Well, Lady Carenza? What guarantee can you offer?"

What was the countess after?

"You have my word," Carenza replied carefully.

"Not good enough, my dear." Countess Helisende shook her head with a cold smile.

"What do you need, my lady?"

The countess smiled. It made Carenza's blood run cold. "I'll give you your knights, and you'll go with them as my emissary to your husband."

Thank you, Lord Jesus!

"You will remain with them," the countess continued, "for

your own safety, of course, until your husband signs an agreement of my devising. He will agree that Hawkhurst will come to my aid if I am ever attacked by invaders from abroad. He will promise never to attempt to extend his holdings to include Hastings. He will also agree to sell us grain at a reduced price. What we're currently paying to his uncle is extortion. It must stop. In addition, he will agree to repay us for the cost of the knights we send to defend Winchelsea castle."

Oh dear. She knew they would pay a price for the countess' help, but this was absurd. Still, a tiny ray of hope sprung up in her chest at the thought of seeing Daniel in the morning. They could sort out the consequences later.

"That's ridiculous," her mother said. "You're already obliged to—"

"Be quiet, Isabella. I'm not done," said Lady Helisende. "Lastly, he will agree to ally his family with mine through marriage. I have a nephew who needs a wife. I'm sure Lord Daniel has some female relative he can send my way, or perhaps one of Lady Carenza's sisters? I would find that acceptable as well." She turned her icy gaze on Alais and Iselda.

Don't you dare touch my sisters, Carenza wanted to scream.

"What's your nephew like?" asked Alais, wary.

Iselda shushed her, and her mother silenced Alais with a look.

"The important part is that I expect the dowry to be at least five hundred silver pieces, and she will be permanently settled here in Hastings so that I can keep an eye on her."

"Five hundred silver pieces," her mother exclaimed. "That's outrageous. You know we don't have that much!"

"Maybe not, but the Earl of Hawkhurst does," replied Lady Helisende.

"What happens if we lose to Lord Raymond?" Carenza asked. She had every intention of winning, but she needed to know.

"Oh, you don't want to lose, my dear. Your mother and sisters will stay here and keep me company while you go with my knights to see your husband. If I don't get my agreement back, they'll make an excellent peace offering to Lord Raymond."

Oh no. How dare she!

"You wouldn't," her mother gasped.

"I rather think I already have," Lady Helisende said with a smile that could freeze the ocean. "Don't look so shocked, Isabella. We all do what we must to survive. Dessert, anyone?"

The servants had just brought in a tray full of custards as Carenza seethed beneath a calm exterior. She couldn't let Lady Helisende see she'd gotten to her.

A young man Carenza didn't recognize entered with a lute.

"I insist," said the countess. "And I've brought entertainment. This is my newest acquisition, Peter de Luci. He's quite talented. I know how much you enjoy troubadour lyrics. I thought he might favor us with some verses as we conclude our repast. Peter?"

The man who stepped forward looked to be of a similar age to Daniel, with curly brown hair and blue eyes. He looked long and hard at her and then gave her a playful wink before launching into his song.

"I weave my wondrous words with song.

Lady, behold my unmatched skill!

My voice makes other men sound shrill.

My melody will make you long

For true love that I dare not speak.

She injures me with fits of pique,

Behaves as if I'd done her wrong.

I've heard it said her looks can kill.

I know that she wishes me ill,

But my love for her is too strong."

He had a clarion tenor voice, and his technique was exquisite. But Carenza couldn't be bothered to appreciate his skill, given the dissonance of his light and boastful song with the dark thoughts that filled her. He split his attention between his patroness and Carenza as he sang, and Carenza found herself blushing at the open flirtation in his look. Was he unaware of who she was and why she was here? Was this some kind of strange taunt from Helisende? Carenza didn't know what to make of it, and it only served to deepen the profound anxiety she already felt.

"My lady," Peter said to Carenza upon concluding his song, "Your reputation precedes you. From what I'm told, you have slain many dragons with your quick tongue and fearsome wit. I would like to observe your technique if you would be so kind as to demonstrate."

Carenza looked at Helisende and knew that the request was not a request any more than her plans for the morning were a rescue. "What did you have in mind, good sir?"

"A competition, perhaps? Just follow my lead."

Carenza nodded, wary, and for once feeling no inspiration whatsoever, but knowing that she could not afford to show weakness. She would make Helisende think twice about challenging her. She would gain some modicum of respect, even if she was entirely at the mercy of Helisende's steel.

"Of course," she said, standing and smoothing her skirts, then walking to stand beside Peter.

"We'll keep it short, and each take three turns. I'll start. Are you ready?"

Carenza simply nodded.

"Lady, your beauty fills me with despair

For I know I can never make you care.

You can't relieve my terrible affliction

Except by offering love's benediction.

Please don't leave all the suffering to me.

Could we at least split love's pain evenly?"

Carenza closed her eyes, glad that Daniel was not here to watch. She'd done this a hundred times before, but never had it felt so wrong.

"Friend, surely you exaggerate your pain.
What have I done to cause you to complain?
Before tonight, you've never even seen me.
Surely your words are meant to demean me.
I'll play this poet's game because I must,
But words of love fill my heart with mistrust."

Peter smiled at her, but it wasn't a friendly smile. There was a hunger behind it that made her squirm. She meant to rebuff, not enflame, but it seemed her words had done the opposite. This was supposed to be just a game, but she could see in his eyes that he wanted more.

"Lady, you wound me with your pointed verse.
Indifference is worse than a dark curse.
Don't you care at all that you made me fall,
That your words enthrall and leave me to crawl,
Robbing me of my breath and sanity
While you dismiss my love as vanity?"

Carenza felt ill. She wished she could stop. She couldn't help but think of the last time she'd done this. Daniel filled her heart and her mind. She didn't want to play this game with another.

"Friend, you must know that I love another.
He won my heart, and I will have no other.
For your misplaced love, you have my deep pity.
I like your verse. I even find it witty.
But I have had enough of your flirtation.
You cannot blame me for your own temptation."

She knew her blunt rebuff wasn't in keeping with the game

they were playing, but she was in no mood to playact at love while Daniel was facing mortal danger. At least there was only one more round before she was done.

"Lady, everyone knows love dies in marriage.
Give me a chance, and please do not disparage
The sweet love that I offer to you freely.
Are you so sure your husband loves you really?
I heard your husband sent you far away.
Let me give comfort to your heart today."

She tried not to wince at his words. He'd scored a hit with what he said about Daniel.

"Friend, you know that our song is at an end,
And, my good sir, I ask you to attend.
My heart and hand have been bestowed elsewhere.
Your professed love is hardly my affair.
Go bother someone else with songs of love,
While I pray for forgiveness from above."

It was done. The applause from Helisende was tepid. Peter had put on a good show, and Carenza had refused to play along. The lady was supposed to flirt, and she simply couldn't. Not under these circumstances. Still, she kept her composure and her wits throughout. It was a small victory, but a victory, nonetheless.

"My lady, it has been an honor to match wits with you," Peter said, pressing his lips to her hand. He held both her hand and her gaze a moment longer than was strictly proper.

Carenza stepped away quickly, anxious to separate herself from this man and his overly bold eyes. The countess watched them closely, obviously disappointed she'd failed to discomfit Carenza.

"Enough, Peter. I think we've shown our guests sufficient

hospitality for this evening. You may go." Peter retired with a final parting glance at Carenza. "And I believe it is time for you to be shown to your quarters. I wish you a pleasant sleep. Be ready to ride at dawn, Carenza. Do not be late."

She would not. The sooner she returned to Winchelsea, the better. Daniel needed her, no matter what foolish, overprotective notions might fill his head.

As they walked to their rooms, led by servants but followed by guards, Carenza whispered to her mother, "What do we do now?"

"We pray."

CHAPTER TWENTY-SEVEN

AN HOUR BEFORE dawn, Daniel pulled on his mail shirt and helm, grabbed his knives and axe, and snuck out of the room past Gerard's sleeping form. Gerard insisted on sleeping here, sure that Daniel was going to do something rash. And he wasn't wrong.

It was time to end this.

As he crept down the stairs, Carenza filled his heart and mind—her sweet face, the feeling of her body against his own, the love in her eyes he could never deserve. This was for her. He had to keep her safe.

Raymond de Broase had to die, and Daniel was going to see to it that he did.

If he succeeded, he could end this confrontation before it started. No one else needed to die. He had seen enough of death and couldn't bring himself to risk lives in a fight that was his alone.

If he failed, the knights would defend the castle. They would keep Winchelsea safe until the king's justice hopefully caught up with his uncle. Lord de Vere had sent a messenger to the king after Richard attacked Carenza. Daniel prayed that help would arrive quickly.

And no matter what, Carenza was out of his uncle's reach. The thought brought him peace and renewed resolution.

His uncle wouldn't be expecting trouble, at least not yet. There was no reason to think he had deviated from the plan he shared with John. His uncle was expecting to ride into Winchelsea Castle unopposed and then take it over from the inside.

Still, Uncle Raymond was a wary man. According to scouts, he was camped in the woods two miles outside of Winchelsea with twenty knights, no doubt sending his own spies into Winchelsea to assess the situation before his arrival.

Had his uncle learned of his presence yet, or his marriage to Carenza? Did he know about John's betrayal? Daniel didn't think so, or Uncle Raymond would already have taken action. Time was of the essence. Daniel had to attack before his uncle learned the truth and turned his full fury on Winchelsea Castle.

As Daniel crept out the door to the kitchen garden, he heard a sound.

He froze.

Was someone following him?

He hardly dared breathe.

A cat from the kitchens wandered by, rubbing against his leg, and he exhaled. It was nothing.

Resuming his previous course, he slipped past the guard house by the servants' entrance while the guard was looking the other way. Silently, he headed out into the foggy night.

He knew these woods well from hunting and trapping to supplement his meager income as a shipwright. The scout had given a detailed description of the location where his uncle and his men camped for the night. It was a simple matter of navigating to the right place—if walking into mortal peril could ever be called "simple."

As he made his way through the woods, his senses sharpened. He was aware of each beat of his heart. His blood roared in his ears as if to remind him how very alive he was, rebelling against his plan. Each step brought him closer to his fate. But with each step, his determination grew.

It was time to face death. It was time to be free. He kissed the skull Carenza gave him. Death can come at any time, and life should not be wasted.

A dying fire glowed eerily through the fog straight ahead. His uncle's camp. He arrived at last. In the quavering light, he could see the ghostly shadows of his uncle's men sleeping beneath their cloaks with two men standing watch.

Staying hidden in the trees, he crept forward, moving slowly to prevent his chain mail from rattling. There was only one tent. It was surrounded on three sides by sleeping knights. On the fourth side was a dense thicket shrouded in shadow. The entrance to the tent was opposite the thicket.

The two men on watch sat beside the fire near the entrance to his uncle's tent, playing dice.

Skirting the thicket and keeping in the shadows, Daniel drew out one of his knives.

A twig snapped beneath his foot.

One of the guards' heads swung in his direction, peering into the dark.

Daniel froze.

"Did you hear something?" the man said.

They both stared in the direction of Daniel for a long moment. He didn't dare breathe.

"Probably just an owl," said his companion at last.

Taking a deep breath, Daniel tried to calm the loud beating of his heart. The men went back to their gaming, and Daniel let out his breath slowly.

It was time. There would be no better moment.

Stepping cautiously past a large, sleeping knight, he made an incision in the canvas of the tent and drew his blade down, careful to make as little noise as possible. Parting the flaps of fabric, he entered.

Darkness enveloped him completely.

As his eyes adjusted to the deeper darkness, he could just see the long shadow of the man he loathed and hear his breathing.

Crouching down beside his uncle, he thought of all the people he loved who had died at this man's hands—his father, Adele, Ferdinand.

He brought his blade to his uncle's throat and—

"Coward," came a harsh whisper. "Just like your father, you hesitate at the crucial moment."

Hell and damnation. His uncle was awake.

"It's over, Uncle." Daniel began to draw the blade, piercing the skin.

Twisting away, his uncle hissed, "I don't think so."

His uncle jabbed a dagger in Daniel's leg. Pain lanced through him, momentarily blinding him to everything else, while his uncle escaped with nothing worse than a cut on his neck and cheek.

Damn it all, he'd been so close!

"Traitor," Uncle Raymond bellowed, scrambling off his cot and out of the tent.

Daniel pulled the dagger out of his leg and limped after his uncle, listening with a sinking heart to the singing sound of swords being drawn around him. He put away his knife, pulled his axe from where it was strapped to his back, and left the tent to face his doom.

It was time to test John's theory that his uncle's men would join him if he declared himself. It was his only hope. He was surrounded on all sides by bristling blades.

"I am Daniel de Broase," Daniel yelled to the surrounding knights. "Raymond de Broase murdered my father, Roger, and must pay for his crimes." For a moment, confusion stayed the hands of his uncle's men as his claim sank in.

His uncle's face was a hideous mask in the dying firelight. "This is the impostor I told you about who is trying to kill me." His uncle spat as he spoke. "End him!"

"No, wait! I can prove it. Here is my father's signet ring," Daniel said, pulling the chain up from around his neck. "And while I look nothing like the boy you remember, I look a great deal like my father. I—"

At that moment, a horseman came barreling through the camp, knocking men over and riding straight toward Daniel, breaking up the circle that surrounded him.

Who was it? Friend or foe? And then he got a look at the man's face.

"Gerard! What are you doing here?"

Daniel wheeled out of the way just as Gerard's horse galloped past. His heart lurched at the sight of his friend in his too-large chainmail, flailing at Hawkhurst men with a sword he could barely control.

"You didn't think I was going to let you sneak out and face him alone, did you?" Gerard yelled over his shoulder.

No, he didn't. That was why Daniel had been so careful not to wake him. Gerard coming here was beyond foolish. The man had never so much as thrown a punch, and this was certainly the first time he'd held a real sword. He was a court musician, for heaven's sake.

But Gerard didn't come alone. John and a dozen other knights on horseback followed behind him, taking the Hawkhurst men by surprise.

The fight was on.

Pulling out the battle axe strapped to his back, Daniel lurched into the fray. Chaos reigned. The fog was filled with shadows and groans.

Lunging forward after his uncle, Daniel barreled into a large, vicious-looking knight who took a swing at him. Apparently, he hadn't done enough to convince his uncle's men. He dodged, barely escaping the keen edge of the knight's broadsword.

Damnation. He'd lost sight of his uncle.

Daniel swung at the back of the man's knees with his axe, and the man crumpled to the ground, yelling in pain. Finishing the job, Daniel cut the man's throat with his knife, and the yelling went quiet.

Another knight immediately took over. This one had a familiar face. Could he have been one of his father's men?

The name floated to the surface of his mind. Claude. Yes, certainly one of his father's men. Could he kill a man whose only crime was following his liege lord?

There was no flicker of recognition in Claude's eye. Daniel wasn't surprised. He looked nothing like the youth who'd fled Hawkhurst so many years ago.

Claude swung his sword.

Daniel dodged just in time.

"Claude," Daniel panted as he defended himself from a vigorous onslaught. "You taught me archery when I was a boy. I don't want to kill you."

For a moment, Claude slowed his motions, and Daniel hoped he might have won a victory. Then fury washed over Claude's face.

"I don't know how you know my name, but I was a pallbearer at Daniel's funeral. How dare you desecrate his memory by claiming to be him!"

Taking deadly aim, Claude swung his sword. Daniel parried with his axe, feeling the reverberations all up his arms.

Of course, Claude didn't believe him. It was foolish to hope that anyone would believe his claim after all these years.

"I can prove it. Ask me something only the real Daniel would know."

A man fell to the ground beside him. One of his own. Another death. How many would die in his name before the end?

"I'm not playing your game, boy," Claude said, swinging again, this time aiming to cleave Daniel's head in two. It missed and bit into his shoulder instead, making him cry out in pain.

"I always shot a little to the left," Daniel said desperately as black flecks swam in his vision. "You corrected me over and over. Your daughter's name is Violet. She used to make us mud pies while we practiced."

Daniel raised his axe as best he could, waiting for the next blow, but it didn't come.

"Can it be? Is it truly you?"

"I swear on my father's grave what I'm saying is true, and my uncle is a murderer."

Claude looked at him long and hard, then nodded.

Thank God. Someone believed him at last. Perhaps there was still hope, even as he struggled to remain upright.

"I am at your service, Lord de Broase," Claude said, clutching his sword to his breast in salute. Then he turned toward the fray, ready to defend his lord.

"Tell anyone else who is still loyal to my father and stop this fighting," Daniel yelled after him. Claude paused to listen. "There's been enough death. This has to end. I must go after my uncle."

Turning back, Claude asked, "Would you like my help taking him down?"

"No. This is my fight. I must see it through." Only Daniel could end his uncle. Only he bore the weight of all those deaths. He wouldn't risk anyone else if he could help it.

"Are you certain, my lord? You're wounded."

Shoving aside his pain, Daniel drew himself up. "It has to be this way."

At that moment, a knight Daniel didn't recognize came charging out of the fog and swung his sword. Claude stepped in front of him and deflected the stroke.

"Go, Daniel," Claude yelled over his shoulder. "I'll fend him off."

Attempting to ignore his wounds, Daniel limped in the direction where he'd last seen his uncle.

Dawn was breaking, lending pale light to the raging battle.

Daniel spotted his uncle at last, cowering behind two knights. There was the man who was the cause of all this. Kill him, and the bloodshed could end.

Daniel would not fail or hesitate again.

He attacked. One of the knights peeled off to fight him. This one also looked vaguely familiar, though Daniel couldn't place him. Then it came to him. Bernard, whose son used to be one of his best friends.

Thrusting, Bernard narrowly missed Daniel's stomach.

"Bernard, your wife, Joan, was my nursemaid. She always wore her long auburn hair in a braid that I loved to yank when I was a toddler. I was friends with your son, Philip. He and I used to race each other on horseback every chance we got."

Pausing his attack, Bernard searched Daniel's face, then looked back at the other knight.

"And I always won," said the other knight as he stepped forward. "But we can have a rematch if you think you can take me, my lord."

"Philip! My God, is it you?"

His uncle cowered back in alarm as both men turned their weapons on him.

"You lied to us, Lord de Broase," Bernard growled at his uncle. "Daniel, would you like us to finish him?"

"No. It has to be me."

The world narrowed to his uncle and him. At last, he could end this.

Just as he lunged at his uncle, he heard a familiar voice yelling for help in the distance. It took a moment for the sound to reach his conscious awareness.

His uncle ran for the protection of the trees as Gerard came riding toward them on a horse, awkwardly batting at three Hawkhurst knights with a sword, barely staying clear of injury. "Help," Gerard yelled. "I can't fend them off."

God's wounds!

Daniel turned to his friend, abandoning his uncle for the moment. Bernard and Philip spun with him.

Seeing Bernard and Philip raising their swords against them, two of the three knights paused in confusion.

"Run, Gerard! Run now!" Daniel bellowed. But it was too late. Gerard made an unearthly sound as the third knight's sword sliced into his leg, and he nearly fell off his horse as it ran straight toward Daniel. Grabbing the reins, Daniel halted the horse as

Philip and Bernard engaged the knight that injured Gerard. Daniel shoved his barely conscious friend back into the saddle, smacking the horse's flank to send him off at a gallop. "Run, Gerard! Go back to the castle!" he shouted, praying that his best friend, his brother in all but blood, could escape alive.

Suddenly, sharp, searing pain bloomed in his unarmored left thigh, the same leg his uncle had stabbed, and he looked down to see a sword protruding from it.

Hell and damnation.

Daniel felt the pain, but somehow, it was divorced from his consciousness, which floated above it all, guiding his axe hand with rage and fury. The knight who had stabbed him didn't stand a chance.

As the knight's body dropped to the ground, darkness crept into the corners of Daniel's vision and threatened to squeeze out the last of his awareness, but he resisted. He had to get to his uncle before he passed out. There was so little time.

Philip ran up to support him as he limped forward, each step bringing a jolt of excruciating pain, fighting the dizziness that threatened to overtake him as blood streamed down his leg and into his boot. With the last reserve of his strength, he stood up straight and stepped away from Philip. He had to go it alone. This was his fight.

His vision swam, and his balance began to fail. He was losing focus. It was getting harder to stay aware of what was behind him as he stumbled forward. His uncle came into view just ahead, attempting to hide behind a tree. Daniel swung with all his might, aiming to cleave the man's head in two. His uncle flinched back, escaping the deadly stroke.

"You always were a coward, Uncle," Daniel said, black creeping into the edges of his vision.

"And you were always a fool. A lucky one, but a fool, nonetheless. Well, today, your luck runs out."

It was getting harder and harder to focus. Daniel swung wildly with his axe as they inched farther and farther from the main fighting. His uncle cowered behind his shield, deflecting his strokes again and again. They were alone in a forest clearing, surrounded by thick fog.

Shaking his head to clear it, Daniel swung at his uncle's neck.

His uncle stumbled back, catching himself just before he fell. When the stroke missed, his uncle laughed.

"You're too soft, boy, just like your father. You can't land a deadly stroke when it matters most."

His uncle lashed out with his sword. The blade bit into his right shoulder, despite the mail, deepening the wound from Claude.

Daniel's axe dropped to the ground, and he lurched forward onto his face. Darkness took him, and all he could think was I'm sorry, Carenza. I tried.

CHAPTER TWENTY-EIGHT

"My lady, I understand your orders and will obey," said an older man who looked surprisingly like Peter, Lady Helisende's troubadour. He stood before Lady Helisende. But instead of Peter's curls, his hair was short and cropped and streaked with gray. His blue eyes were the same as the singer's, if much colder in their expression. "I'll see that no harm comes to her."

"Do. The consequences for Hastings would be dire should you fail," Countess Helisende said in a flat tone, then turned and went back into the castle without a backward glance.

"My lady, my name is Thomas de Luci, commander of the baroness' knights. Please do me the honor of riding with me." He bowed and invited her to mount.

Carenza was well aware that she had no choice in the matter. She chose to behave as if she was in control and was merely allowing him to attend her. If she acted like a prisoner, it would only encourage him to treat her as one. So she inclined her head slightly in acknowledgment of his bow. "Thank you, Commander. I would like to leave immediately. My family's danger is great, and we must make haste."

He mounted his destrier and motioned for her to follow him, the first light of dawn creeping over the horizon. She squared her shoulders and put on her most regal and haughty face, staring straight ahead as if her escort was beneath her notice. Never mind that her heart was ready to beat out of her chest with worry for Daniel.

They rode to the head of the column of men that Lady Helisende had assembled to join the defense of the Winchelsea castle. It was a formidable force, despite Lady Helisende's complaint that all her men had gone to court with her husband. Surely, this group was more than sufficient to defeat de Broase when combined with her father's men and Daniel's hired knights.

Carenza had little time to decide how to proceed. The journey to Winchelsea was a mere eight miles. She needed to find a way to turn Lady Helisende's men to her advantage, but Daniel must not sign that ridiculous agreement. She was certain Lady Helisende would have ordered her men not to engage until the agreement was signed, but perhaps they didn't need to join the fight to have their intended effect. Perhaps their mere presence would be sufficient to tilt the balance of power. Or perhaps she could find a way to goad them into participating regardless of the agreement.

"You look concerned, my lady," Thomas said as they rode briskly along the well-worn road built by the Romans centuries ago. "I have sworn to my mistress that I will protect you. While it is never safe when there is violence, I will ensure that you are well-defended. You need not fear."

She gave him a cold look. "I do not fear for my safety, Commander, but for my family's."

He smiled. "You're very brave, or perhaps foolish."

"Death can come at any time, and life should not be wasted. I know my duty to my people. I do what I must." She turned and looked at him. "As you will do what you must for Countess Helisende."

"Yes," he answered.

They rode in silence for several minutes before curiosity got the better of her. "By any chance, are you related to the troubadour, Peter, that I met at dinner last night?"

Thomas narrowed his eyes and ground his teeth. "He's my son," he said at last, "though I can't say I approve of how he spends his time."

"Despite his talent?" She knew she shouldn't antagonize this man, but she couldn't help standing up for a troubadour, even one she didn't like much.

His eyes narrowed as he glanced in her direction. "You must be concerned for your husband, my lady," he said, obviously avoiding her question.

She cleared her throat. "I pray that he is safe and victorious."

"Of course, my lady. We will find him for you, whatever course the fight may have taken." He gave her a grave nod.

Finding him was not the same as finding him safe and victorious. She closed her eyes and said a silent prayer for Daniel.

"Why don't you approve of your son's poetry?" She couldn't help needling him after his lack of concern for Daniel.

"It's immoral."

"Oh?" She privately agreed that troubadours and their notions of courtly love weren't exactly virtuous, but she wasn't going to say so in present company.

"The Bible says thou shalt not covet thy neighbor's wife. But my son goes around saying true love cannot exist in marriage and that marriage to another should not be an impediment to love. It's disgusting and immoral. This romantic love they speak of—" he spat on the ground in disgust—"is the invention of Satan and has no place in or out of marriage."

Carenza bit her lips together to hold back a sharp retort. She agreed with most of what he said, but suggesting that love in marriage was an invention of Satan was a step too far. Love in marriage was a blessing, or it was when it was shared, she thought with a pang.

"Adultery, fornication, lust." The man seemed lost in his own fury, unable to recall his company. "Man and woman are joined in holy matrimony for the purpose of procreation. There should be no longing, no burning, unless it be in the fires of hell for the sinners that forget that God Himself is the only worthy object of our love and admiration."

Her heart ached at the thought of the sacred joy she had shared with her husband in the short time after their marriage. Their union was not imperfect because of love but because of the lack of it.

"My lord," she said, doing her best to convince herself that she was Lady Helisende's equal and could stand up to this old goat. "You go too far. I could cite dozens of Bible verses that speak of marriage in reverent terms, even going so far as to compare Christ to a bridegroom with the Church as his bride. Does Paul not say in his letter to the Ephesians, 'Husbands, love your wives, even as Christ also loved the church, and gave himself for it.' And may I remind you that the countess invited your son to perform?"

Oh, how she pitied this man's wife.

He cleared his throat. "My apologies, my lady." His eyes darted to hers in grudging contrition, and he rode ahead, apparently to avoid her company.

She was relieved that he left her to her own thoughts until the walls of Winchelsea Castle came into view. The short ride seemed to take an eternity as she churned through all the terrible possibilities that could await her at its end. The castle might have already fallen into the hands of the false Lord de Broase. Daniel or her father could have been injured or captured, or dead. She prayed that the enemy had not yet begun his attack or that he had already been defeated, even as she made herself picture each possibility in vivid detail, preparing herself for the worst. All the while, she strove to convince herself that they were fine and there was nothing to worry about so that she would have the courage to continue. For all her irritation with Thomas, she developed a grudging appreciation of his refusal to give false hope or false promises. This was not safe for anyone, and she must face whatever was to come, however painful.

As she looked up at the castle, she saw de Vere banners flying high in the wind. Surely, that was a promising sign. Either the false earl had not yet arrived, or they had succeeded beyond her hopes. What awaited her at home? A small group of armed men on horseback carrying the de Vere banner approached and asked to speak. The knights from Winchelsea would surely recognize Helisende's banner, but they approached with caution. Rightly so, Carenza thought.

"Who goes there?" the de Vere men shouted as soon as they were within range to be heard.

"We come from Hastings to aid in the defense of Winchelsea castle," Thomas shouted back. "We bring the Lady Carenza de Broase with us as proof of our good faith."

As the men rode closer, Carenza recognized her father among them.

"Then you are most welcome! Join us, please!" her father shouted, pausing for the head of Hastings' column to reach him. He fell in line beside her after exchanging a brief greeting with Thomas. In a low voice, he asked, "Carenza, how can this be? You were supposed to be on a ship to Aquitaine. Please tell me your mother and sisters didn't come, too?"

"They are in Hastings," she said, hesitating to reveal any more in present company. "I have much to tell you, but first, please tell me what is happening. I need to know."

Her father looked pained. "Lord de Broase is here. His men arrived yesterday and camped in the woods. I expected an attack today, but Daniel snuck off by himself to confront his uncle this morning before dawn. Gerard led Daniel's men to rescue him, but they haven't returned. I fear the worst."

Carenza swallowed. She had prepared for this. She had imagined this. Nonetheless, she felt as if she was drowning, tugged down to the bottom of the ocean by inexorable forces, unable to breathe, light diminishing to a pinprick in the distance. No. It was only shock. She had to fight her way back. She couldn't give in. There was uncertainty, which meant there was hope. She had to hold on, she had to be strong while there was hope. She grounded herself in the sensation of her own body on her horse, forcing herself to breathe deeply and return to the present. Shaking herself, she squared her shoulders. "We have to go help him."

"We'll discuss it inside," her father said, shaking his head.

"There's no time. We have to go now!"

Thomas rode forward, interrupting her.

"Lord de Vere," Thomas said, "Lady Helisende has heard your plea for aid against Lord de Broase and has sent us to be of assistance. There are, however, certain conditions for that assistance, and I must be assured they are met before we can join the fight. I believe Lady Carenza has been made privy to the conditions?"

She pulled out the parchment for the treaty she had received from the baroness and handed it to her father, who read it silently, his brow furrowing more and more deeply as he went. He stared at her and then at Thomas. He turned back to the parchment. It was an outrageous proposal, and it was clear her father agreed with her assessment.

His face beet red and his mustache trembling, he said in a low voice, "Am I to understand that my wife and my daughters are being held until this...this..." He stopped and took a deep breath. "Until Daniel agrees to this?"

Thomas looked at him levelly. "Your wife and your daughters are my lady's guests until such time as she deems it safe for them to return. Lady Carenza is under my personal protection. I will see that no harm comes to her."

"But she is not free to leave with me." Carenza had never seen such fury in her father's eyes.

Thomas returned a stony gaze. "No, she is not. But you have my word that I will keep her safer than you could if I released her into your care."

"She's my daughter."

"And I will keep her safe." The two men glared at each other. Thomas was the first to break eye contact, much to Carenza's surprise.

They rode through the castle gates and dismounted in the front courtyard, the horses' hooves clattering on the cobblestones.

"Where is Daniel de Broase?" Thomas asked, looking around.

"I don't know," her father responded, giving Thomas a look of irritation.

Just then, her father's marshal came running up. "Lord de Vere, Gerard returned a short while ago with an injured leg. He says we need to send help," he panted and then stopped short, seeing Carenza and the stranger. "How did you get here, my lady?"

"I brought knights. There are strings attached, but never mind that. We have to go now."

Her father nodded and remounted his horse. Thomas gave him a dubious look. "You let your daughter give orders?"

Her father narrowed his eyes in challenge. "She's a countess, and I owe her fealty. Besides, do you have anything better to propose?"

Thomas grumbled. "No. I suppose it is in Hastings' best interests for me to go along with this. The countess would rather work with Lord Daniel than Lord Raymond. What's your plan?"

The men conferred briefly, and they set off at a gallop for the forest. Ignoring her father's protests, Carenza followed behind. Then she noticed a skinny horseman tagging along behind with a bandaged leg. Gerard.

She dropped back to speak to him.

"What are you doing? You're injured. You should stay at the castle."

"Not while he's in danger."

"But—"

"I love him like a brother. I'm not letting him go."

She sized him up with new respect.

"Me neither. Let's catch up."

Together, they rode toward the forest, uncertain of what they would find.

CHAPTER TWENTY-NINE

LIGHTNING STRUCK DANIEL'S boat, setting it aflame and splitting it in two. He struggled to keep his head above the punishing waves, grasping at pieces of wood to stay afloat. Purple and green clouds circled in the sky above him as the unnatural storm created swells as big as leviathans to pummel him, sinking him beneath the roiling surface. This was the end. There was no hope. The last of his breath was squeezed from his lungs, and he swallowed the sea in great gulps.

Then, a glowing light appeared in the water ahead, growing closer and larger until it encompassed him. He was suspended, filled with the light, miraculously able to breathe even in this deep place. The pressure and weight of the water was gone, as was the cold. He could see the waters churning all around him, but within this bubble, he felt nothing but warmth and peace.

"Bring me home, Adele. I'm ready," he whispered into the light.

"No," Adele's voice answered, achingly familiar even after all these years.

"Please, Adele. Let me rest. I want to go home."

"Your home isn't with me anymore. I'm gone." Her voice was gentle but firm. "Let go, Daniel. Let go and live."

An unseen hand took his, warm and alive and familiar. Loving arms embraced him. A soft voice whispered in his ear, "Live."

"Carenza," he murmured.

A sharp pain in his shoulder brought him abruptly back to consciousness as someone repositioned him where he lay. Daniel opened his eyes slowly to see his uncle hovering over him with a knife to his throat. He'd lost. His vision swam. At least Carenza was safe. He prayed Gerard was, too.

"Don't move, or he dies," his uncle hissed.

Daniel blinked until his vision cleared enough to see what was around him. A small cadre of knights stood surrounding him and his uncle in a standoff with a much larger group of knights wearing a mix of Winchelsea and Hawkhurst colors. One of his uncle's men had a crossbow aimed at John.

His heart swelled at the sight. Most of the Hawkhurst men believed him. He'd won if only he could survive.

But his uncle would see to it that he didn't. The odds of his coming out of this alive were extremely low as long as his uncle was holding a blade to his neck.

Instead, the thud of hooves pierced his consciousness.

"Daniel!" It was Carenza's voice. There was no mistaking it. Horror and pain washed over him far beyond what he'd felt being wounded and captured. Everything he'd worked to accomplish was undone by her presence. She was supposed to be safe.

"Stay back, Carenza," Lord de Vere said sharply. Between the knights' legs, father and daughter came into view as they dismounted. Lord de Vere tugged on Carenza's arm to hold her back as she tried to break free to reach Daniel. Her eyes were wide, and her usually composed face a portrait of distress. A large group of unfamiliar knights, far outnumbering his uncle's men, was arrayed behind them.

"How touching," his uncle said in frosty tones. "A lovers' reunion. You're just in time to watch him die. Martin, aim the crossbow at her. Shoot if anyone tries anything."

Daniel watched with horror as Martin adjusted his aim.

Carenza froze, staring at Daniel, eyes wide. "Carenza," Daniel said as calmly as he could manage, "Let me go. Back away and leave. It's me he wants, not you."

She stood firm and defiant. "I'm not backing down. I brought knights with me from Hastings." She glanced back at a knight wearing the crest of House Hastings. The man gave no acknowledgment but stared straight at Uncle Raymond.

Standing unsteadily next to him was Gerard. Stubborn ass. What was he doing here, wounded as he was?

"We have him outnumbered and surrounded, though by the looks of it, he's already lost," she continued, now looking Uncle Raymond in the eye. "It's over, Lord de Broase. Surrender yourself to your liege lord, and pray he has more mercy on you than you ever did on him."

"I disagree, my lady," said his uncle, glancing around with the crazed look of a cornered animal. "My so-called 'liege lord' is still my prisoner, and your life hangs by a thread. I admit my position is somewhat precarious, but I'm far from ready to admit defeat. I might be willing to consider an exchange that leaves us both intact, however. If he legally renounces his false claims, you can have him back, and I will withdraw. Know that I will kill him and you, though, rather than bend a knee to this sorry oaf." He pressed the blade into Daniel's neck, drawing a bead of blood to punctuate his point.

Daniel wanted to laugh. Wasn't this, in fact, all he'd ever wanted—to be free of the de Broase name and associated burdens?

But he knew his uncle would never relent. At best, it would be a temporary detente, and then the assassins would come after him once again—as well as Carenza. They would never be safe while his uncle lived.

No. He had to end this stand-off. But how? He didn't care about himself, but there was no way he could extricate Carenza from his uncle's clutches without help. Solving this alone was not an option.

"Martin," Daniel said, trying to remember what he knew of the man holding the crossbow. "We grew up together. Your father trained me in swordsmanship. I know we never got along, but you don't want to do this."

As he spoke, he caught John's eye and glanced up at the tree branch above him. John nodded and whispered something in Claude's ear. Claude backed away and disappeared, coming back moments later with his bow and arrow, then disappearing behind the tree.

"It's cowardly to kill a woman," Daniel continued loudly to distract attention from Claude, who reappeared moments later in the branches of the tree. "Not to mention that the king doesn't look kindly on men who kill noblewomen in cold blood."

"Quiet," his uncle hissed.

"Or what? You'll kill me? I'm the only leverage you have."

All of Daniel's attention was focused on the crossbow. Nothing could happen to Carenza. He couldn't allow it. She was everything to him. Somehow, he had to talk the man into surrendering. Claude might be able to shoot him down, but not before Martin got off a shot at Carenza.

"Martin, I am the true Earl of Hawkhurst, and she is my wife. Do you truly want to risk killing a countess and being complicit in the death of your liege lord?"

"You aren't the true earl," Martin grumbled.

Ah, so he didn't believe.

"John," Daniel called out. "Who am I?"

"You are Daniel de Broase, son and heir to Roger de Broase, and the true Earl of Hawkhurst. Your uncle poisoned your father and ordered your death. I rescued you and took you to live in disguise as a commoner. I watched you grow up from afar and am proud to finally help you claim your birthright. Martin, you've known me your whole life. I am not a liar or a coward. And you're a better man than this. Lower that crossbow."

For a tense moment, no one moved.

Then, ever so slowly, Martin complied.

Relief flooded Daniel as Lord de Vere yanked Carenza behind him.

Taking advantage of the momentary distraction and throwing caution to the wind, Daniel grabbed his uncle's wrist and twisted out of his clutches. If his uncle slit his throat, so be it. Carenza was safe. That was all that mattered.

The knife grazed his throat but failed to cut deeply. Daniel wrenched himself over and pinned his uncle to the ground, drawing the blade across his throat before he could fight back.

"It's over, Uncle."

The old man's face was a mask of pain, eyes wide, throat gurgling with blood. But then a smile spread across his face. "At least I've had my revenge," he rasped.

Daniel ignored him. The man must be raving.

Seeing the battle was lost and their lord defeated, the remaining Hawkhurst knights lowered their blades and surrendered to the overwhelming force that surrounded them.

Daniel yelled for Gerard, who staggered over.

"Let's finish this."

Gerard nodded. "For my father and sister," he said in a low voice breaking with fury.

"For my father and my wife," Daniel added in a rough voice, filled with grief. He nodded, and Daniel plunged his dagger into his uncle's neck as Gerard stabbed him in the heart.

His uncle's body twitched, then was still, cold eyes staring, lifeless, up at the clouds.

No one spoke. No one moved.

At last, John stepped forward and pronounced, "Raymond de Broase the usurper is dead. Long live Daniel de Broase, the true Earl of Hawkhurst!"

Claude and several other men took up the cheer. "Long live Lord Daniel de Broase!" Then more joined. They rallied around Daniel, cheering him on. It was finished. At long last, it was finished. Daniel could never repay his debt of gratitude to those loyal to him. His uncle could trouble him no more. He could live a long and happy life with Carenza. He could give her all the love and joy she deserved.

His eyes met hers, and he reached out for his beloved wife. Then his vision swam. The world tilted, and his knees buckled. The ground rose up to meet him as everything went black.

CHAPTER THIRTY

CARENZA DROPPED TO the grass beside Daniel as he fell, her hands shaking and her heart pounding. Were his wounds more serious than they appeared? She couldn't find anything besides the injuries to his leg and shoulder.

"He's lost a lot of blood, but I think there's something else wrong," John said, bending over his lord. "His wounds aren't severe enough to explain his loss of consciousness. We need to get him back to the castle and bring a healer immediately."

Her father, standing beside them, barked orders to his nearby men, and soon Daniel was on a litter being carried back to the castle with Carenza by his side. Thomas was right behind her.

"Commander, what are you doing?" she demanded as Thomas continued to dog her steps.

"My mistress' orders were clear. You are to remain under my protection until the treaty is signed. The situation here is still dangerous. With your husband's health in question, everything you've gained could fall to pieces at any moment. I must ensure your safety."

Carenza turned to face him. "Such concern from the man whose mistress is holding my family prisoner!"

Daniel, regaining consciousness, raised his head and groaned, "Who are you, and why are you bothering my wife?"

She glared at Thomas. It was one thing for him to bother her but something else entirely for him to upset Daniel, especially since he was injured.

Thomas looked down at Daniel, his face devoid of sympathy. "I'm Thomas de Luci, commander of the army sent by Baroness of Hastings. When you're well enough, there are a number of things we must discuss. In the meantime, I am under orders to keep your wife safe."

"I'll keep her safe," Daniel grunted.

"From a litter? You can't walk," Thomas responded, his lip curling into an unpleasant sneer.

"I have more men than you." Daniel pointed behind the man at the combined strength of Winchelsea and Hawkhurst.

"My lord, Countess Helisende has Carenza's mother and sisters under guard in Hastings. Are you willing to risk her ire under such delicate circumstances?"

Daniel tried to rise but fell back, groaning in pain.

"Commander." Carenza admonished, leaning into her fury to give her an air of authority to match Lady Helisende's. "Surely this conversation can wait until my husband's wounds have been properly tended. You have my permission to see to my safety, within reason. Upon our return to the castle, you may post guards by our chambers if you must, but otherwise, you are to leave us in peace until my husband is well enough to speak with you. Is that clear?" Carenza glared at him.

"Yes, my lady," Thomas said, blinking and stepping back several paces.

The journey back to the castle proceeded without further incidents, aside from Daniel muttering fevered curses under his breath the whole way.

Finally, after Carenza got Daniel into bed and sent for a healer, she had a few moments alone with her husband.

They were safe at last. Raymond de Broase was no more. They had won the day!

She knelt beside him and pressed her lips gently to his. He raised his head ever so slightly to invite more. He moaned as she deepened her kiss, letting all her hopes and fears pass between them in wordless speech. She ached for more, for what came after the kisses, and she could feel that he did, too. But that would have to wait. First, he must heal. First, the danger must pass. She took his hand and kissed it, then held it against her cheek as she murmured a prayer, head bowed beside him.

"Carenza, I thought you were gone. I thought you were safe. You promised." His voice was ragged. A fever chill shook him, and sweat trickled down his brow.

Foolish man, thinking she could ever stay away while he was in danger. And look what had happened while she was away! Her heart ached at the sight of him. Nothing could keep her from his side, not even his own stubbornness.

"I promised to get on the ship. I never promised to stay on it." She continued to hold his hand to her cheek, her eyes closed. "How could I promise the impossible?"

Dear Lord in heaven, she loved this man!

He tried to raise his head but was forced to let it fall back down with a groan. "I needed you to be safe. I couldn't live with myself if something happened to you." A twinge of irritation prickled her at his words, even as she nuzzled and kissed his hand. Here he was lying in bed wounded, and he was worried about keeping her safe? "And now you're here, and I can't protect you. That man you came with, Lady Helisende's man. He's not going to leave you in peace. You aren't safe."

She took a deep breath, summoning patience. The man outside the door was of no import. What mattered was the man before her. "He's no match for me, and right now, neither are you. Stop trying to defend me as if I was some delicate seashell. I'm Countess de Broase of Hawkhurst, and I'm perfectly capable of taking care of myself. And you, too."

He shook his head weakly. "You don't understand the danger—"

"Do you think so little of me?" she interrupted, unable to refrain from standing up for herself. "Do you truly think I'm incapable of matching wits with that pompous, pious prick Helisende sent after me?"

Daniel's eyes went wide. "Did you just call him a—?"

"I'm your countess, and I'm fairly certain I have a better idea of what dangers we face than you do." She was tired of being underestimated.

"Carenza, be reasonable." He took her hand and squeezed it, but she wasn't ready to be placated. Words kept tumbling out. He'd broken her heart when he sent her away. Didn't he understand that?

"While you were off playing with boats—"

"Ships," he corrected with a wince.

"My parents were teaching me how to govern," she persevered, determined to make her point. "They didn't send me to the abbey because they wanted me to become a nun. They sent me so that I could study in their library. Where else could I learn the histories of Athens and Rome, read Socrates and Cicero? They knew that one day, I would be wedded to a man with power and would need all my wits to navigate the deadly currents of courtly life. I've trained my whole life for this. I'm not going to let you put your life at risk trying to save me from dangers I know far better than you." If only he would see reason and let her take care of him instead of trying to fight her battles for her!

He reached for her with his uninjured arm and pulled one of her hands free, then kissed it. "I sent you away for your safety, and you came back at the head of an army. I was a fool to underestimate you. I won't do it again. All I ask is that you be careful. I don't trust that man."

She gasped. He'd acknowledged she was right? His words left her momentarily speechless. Was it possible she was lucky enough to have married a man who could truly respect her after all?

He closed his eyes and gritted his teeth. "I'm not feeling well. I need to rest."

Suddenly, all she wanted was to have him healthy and whole

in her arms. "I'm sorry for upsetting you, my love. I'll let you rest."

Daniel tensed at the word "love." His eyes flew open and grew round and fearful. "Yes, Daniel, I love you," she said, closing her eyes to avoid the heartbreaking truth in his.

"I know you don't love me," she said, her heart shattering into a thousand pieces as she spoke the words. "You sent me away to ease your conscience, but I couldn't let you go so easily. Pathetic fool that I am, I couldn't give you up. I had to come back to save you—from yourself. I'm selfish, Daniel. You can try to push me away all you want. Ignore my wishes. Put me on a ship. It doesn't matter. I will always come back. I love you too much to let you go."

He murmured her name. She hurt too much to look at him. He could still die, and there was nothing she could do. How could she fight his injuries? No army could help her now. "Do you remember what you said the day we met? 'Death can come at any time, and you should not invite it.' If you feel anything for me, if you pity me at all, don't invite death. I need you. I love you. Please fight this. Please live."

He murmured her name again, and then his eyes rolled back in his head as he lost consciousness. She stood and looked down at the man she loved beyond all reason. His face was pale and drawn. He radiated heat. She eased him out of his battle-stained clothes and into clean braies with loving hands. Then she gently cleaned around his wounds with a cloth dipped in cool water from the basin, wiping away crusted blood and dirt. Her eyes filled with tears at the sight. She blinked them away, offering silent prayers and touching her rosary for comfort.

At last, the healer came. "I'm sorry for the delay, my lady. I came as soon as I could."

Carenza nodded and stood back to let him work.

After a careful examination, he looked up at her. "I won't lie to you, my lady. His condition is serious. The wounds themselves pose no danger to him, but I believe one of the blades may have been poisoned."

"Poisoned?"

Dear Lord in heaven, please no!

"Based on his symptoms, I would say belladonna. But, my lady, all hope is not lost. If he has lasted this long, he may not have received a fatal dose. Only time will tell."

Grasping her rosary, she sent a silent prayer to heaven. God had given her this beautiful, brave man to love. Surely, He would not take him away so soon.

"I am going to clean and dress his wounds," the healer said, continuing his examination. "After that, we must wait and see. I have remedies to help with the pain and lower his fever, but his recovery is in God's hands. I recommend you find somewhere else to wait while I treat him, my lady."

She shook her head vehemently. "I'm not leaving him."

The healer gave her a long look and decided against arguing. "Is there a servant that can fetch hot water, honey, and clean cotton cloth?"

She ran to the door and called for Elaine, who ran up and wrapped her in a hug. "My lady, I was so worried. I can't tell you how glad I am to see you safe."

"You too, Elaine," she said, returning the hug.

"Have you seen Gerard?" Her voice shook as she spoke.

Carenza nodded. "He's injured but safe," she said, pressing Elaine's hands.

"Oh, thank you, Jesus!"

"But Daniel is in danger. He may have been injured by a poisoned blade. The healer needs hot water, honey, and some clean cotton cloths as quickly as you can get them."

"Of course, my lady." Elaine took off at a run.

Carenza returned and sat on the bed, taking Daniel's hand in hers while the healer took over cleaning the wounds with water. Elaine returned promptly, with another servant carrying the requested items. She gave Carenza's hand a quick squeeze and left, and the healer set to work.

First, he bathed the wounds on Daniel's right leg in hot water. Then he applied lavender oil, followed by large dollops of honey, oozing over the torn and damaged flesh. Finally, he wrapped the leg in the clean cloth and tied it tightly to keep the wounds closed as they healed. He repeated the procedure with Daniel's shoulder.

Carenza watched the man at work, determined not to flinch. She had to be strong for Daniel. She had to hang on. She needed him to feel her presence, pulling him back from the brink. If she let go or even looked away, he would slip away forever. She would tie him to life, will him to live. She wasn't letting him go without a fight.

"It's done," the healer said. "I'm leaving white willow bark, which you can make into a tea to ease the pain and fever. See that he drinks some every few hours. You'll need to have his dressings changed daily, reapplying honey until the wounds close. He's young. He's strong. He has as good a chance as any of recovering, but it's in God's hands now."

Carenza nodded and thanked him. When he was gone, she made Daniel tea from the remaining hot water and the willow bark, and she touched it to his lips, offering sip after sip until the cup was empty. Then she curled up in the bed beside him, needing to see his chest rise and fall, to feel the warmth of his hand in hers. She whispered prayers and murmured words of love to his sleeping form. There was nothing more she could do but wait and watch.

CHAPTER THIRTY-ONE

DANIEL STOOD IN the familiar garden of Winchelsea's castle, holding a bloody dagger. Somewhere out of sight, he heard a woman weeping. The flowers and trees crowded in, overripe and overgrown, a tinge of rot mixing with the customary sweetness. He wandered down familiar paths that led to unfamiliar places, the garden becoming labyrinthian as he followed the sound of weeping. The wind was still, and the air hot and stifling. There was no birdsong. The distant percussion of the waves was missing. The only sound was the weeping, always just around the corner.

He began to run, sweat pouring off him as a hostile sun shimmered overhead, beating down with oppressive heat. There were no clouds in the sky, which had an odd orange tinge. The flowers and trees grew mouths and teeth that snapped and tore at him as he tried to run, impeding his progress toward the woman he sought. There was something familiar in the voice. She was someone he knew, someone he loved, someone he could not live without. But who? He couldn't remember. He tried to call to mind his own name and couldn't remember that, either. All he knew was that he had to find her. There was something he had to make right.

The attacking plants grew more aggressive, twining around his legs, tearing his clothes. He hacked at them with his dagger to little avail, still wondering whose blood was on it. The sun bore down on him, growing in size and heat until it seemed to fill the whole sky. Tree limbs enfolded him, trapping him in place. He couldn't move. He couldn't escape. The woman was so close. There had to be a way. He struggled and jerked, trying to pull free as the sun boiled his blood and sharp-toothed roses pierced his skin.

A knight approached, shoving a woman before him, a dagger at her throat. It was the woman he sought, tears streaming down her face, blood dripping from a wound over her heart.

Carenza. His heart stopped. No. She couldn't be here. She was safe. She was far away. The trees tightened their hold, strangling the breath from him. The knight behind her gave a malevolent laugh.

"Nephew, look what you've done. I was going to kill her, but you beat me to it. Bravo, my boy. Now it's time to finish your work. Tear her heart out. End it."

The thorny plants shoved him forward, forcing his hand toward Carenza.

"No!" he cried and tried to drop the dagger, but thorny vines tied it to his hand to prevent him.

The commander from Hastings appeared in full armor, yanking Daniel's arm away and pushing him to the ground, impervious to the writhing thorns. The man grabbed Carenza out of reach. "Look what you've done. She isn't safe with you. You'll only hurt her. I'll protect her. I'll lock her in a castle tower far from here where you'll never find her, not you, not anyone." He grabbed her and pulled her away. She collapsed, limp in his arms.

Daniel lunged forward, ripping free from the vines that tore at his skin and plunged his dagger through the commander's throat. He collapsed to the ground, and Carenza fell with him. Daniel rushed to her, enfolding her in his arms.

"Why, Daniel? Why?" She looked down at the bleeding wound in her chest, her head lolling to the side.

The sun came closer still, sizzling the treetops, setting fire to the branches. "How do I make it right, Carenza? Please!" He pulled off his helm, which was burning his skin as the sun's flames licked closer and closer.

"Live," she said as the sun crushed them, and they were both turned to ashes.

Daniel woke with a start to find himself in bed, drenched in sweat. Carenza was sound asleep, kneeling on the floor beside him with one arm lying across him, clutching her rosary and her face buried in the mattress beside him. The fever had broken at last. He was sure of it. While he felt hollowed out and completely sapped of strength, the putrid heat was gone.

"Carenza," he whispered, caressing the arm that lay across him. She shifted slightly, then settled back down. "Carenza," he whispered again. Still, she did not wake. He began to sing to her quietly:

"Songbird, take flight

And leave tonight

To a land far away

Where my lady waits for day.

Find her and remind her

How my subtle words entwined her.

Don't let her forget she's in my sway."

She raised her head at last. Her eyes were bloodshot, and her hair was mussed. There was an imprint on her cheek from a crease in the bed's coverlet. To Daniel, she'd never been more beautiful. When she said his name, the music of her voice filled him with transcendent joy.

"I love you, Carenza, with all that I am. I'm sorry that I was so blind." He'd done as she asked. He'd lived. And at last, he was ready to reveal the truth of his own heart, which he had kept hidden for so long. She needed to know it, too. He had to tell her. He'd hurt her, and he needed to make it right.

She lifted herself to sit on the edge of the bed beside him, blinking, concerned. "Is the fever worse?" She felt his forehead and then gently explored beneath the edges of the bandage on his shoulder. Her breath caught. "It's gone. Daniel, the fever is gone. You're going to live. Oh, thank you, Jesus!" She kissed her rosary and clasped her hands in prayer.

"Carenza, please get off the floor and come up here with me. I have things I need to say, and that can't possibly be comfortable." She rose with difficulty, her legs hardly supporting her after who knows how many hours spent kneeling on the hard stone floor. Climbing onto the bed with none of her usual grace, she collapsed beside him in exhaustion and relief.

"How long have I been asleep?" he asked.

"Three days," she murmured in his ear.

"Three days! Have you slept?"

"Barely," she said, stifling a yawn. "I was too worried to sleep. I had to hang onto you, make sure you didn't slip away while I napped."

"Then rest, my love. Let me guard your sleep as you have guarded mine. Rest while I find the right words to tell you how very much I love you."

She looked sad and exhausted. "Please don't say things you don't mean, Daniel. It hurts too much. Please just let me sleep."

Daniel winced. Of course, she didn't believe him. What cause did she have to trust him? She needed rest, and it would be selfish to keep her awake just to relieve his own conscience. He let her drift off beside him while his mind whirred with words, arranging and rearranging them as he watched her deep and steady breathing.

When she awoke, he was ready. He waited patiently as she changed his dressings, prepared his willow bark tea, washed her own face, and combed the tangles from her ink-black hair and wove it into a simple braid.

"Carenza, come sit with me, please. There are things I need to say." She sat at the foot of the bed, facing him, eyes wary as he took her hand and brought it to his lips. He lingered, tasting and caressing her fingers with his lips. She gave a small, shuddering sigh as she softened at his touch, but the sadness in her eyes remained.

"I must ask for your forgiveness for the pain I have caused you. You've given me your hand. You've given me your heart without asking anything in return. I don't deserve your love, and yet you've given it to me freely. I insulted you. I sent you away. In the name of protecting you, I hurt you with my words and actions." She looked down, avoiding his gaze. He gave her hand a gentle squeeze, and she looked up at him again, so sad and so vulnerable.

"There's nothing to forgive," she said with a tired sigh.

"Yes, there is. Forgive me for taking so long to speak of what is in my heart, for fighting what should have been clear to me from the first time we met. I've been such a fool. And a coward. I was so afraid of what you made me feel. That first day, when you stepped out of the shadows in the warehouse and asked if I wrote that song, I was lost. I'd hidden for so long. I kept everyone at a safe distance for fear of the consequences for them and for me. I never let anyone in except Gerard. I never let anyone see me. But you saw. With the first words you spoke, you pierced my armor. You stripped me bare. I was at your mercy."

He held her gaze, deliberately lowering his guard and allowing all the love and fear and hope and pain to shine through, everything he'd kept locked away and hidden from everyone for years. He let her see him unmasked, unarmed. Her eyes shone with love, tenderness, and warmth, welcoming him and inviting him to continue.

"And then you injured your ankle, and my heart stopped. Hardly knowing you, I would have given anything to take your pain away. Even then, my heart knew, though I didn't. I couldn't stand to see you harmed in any way."

He reached out and brushed her cheek. She sat spellbound, lips parted, eyes round and moist, locked on his. She was listening. Thank God she was listening. Saying these things made him feel bare and raw, but they were necessary things. The tie between them strengthened with each word.

"And then I touched you. I held you, so warm and alive in my arms. I smelled the sweet spice and almond cake scent of you, felt the fluttering beat of your heart against my chest. I hadn't allowed myself so close to a woman since I lost Adele. It was like holding fire. You scorched me with your heat. You melted me. I could hardly breathe after I put you down. I was so enflamed by your touch."

"So was I," she whispered.

"I was terrified, Carenza. You made me feel so many things I had locked away, sworn I would never let myself feel again. You must understand, my uncle broke me. He killed everyone I loved, making me think my love was a death sentence. I was petrified by the feelings you awakened. When I learned who you were, a part of me was relieved to find you utterly beyond my reach. How could I be tempted when it was impossible for me to ever see you again?"

"It only took you a day to change your mind and reach out, though," she said with a smile.

"Very true. But the thing that moved me most of all that day, the thing that shook my very soul, was when you told me that death could come at any time, and life should not be wasted. For so many years, I fled death, hid from it. The grief and pain of my losses overwhelmed me, buried me. And here you were telling me that you'd accepted it, that you'd found a way to transmute grief into vitality, that grief inspired you to live. I wanted your magic. I had to learn your alchemy. I needed the impossible lesson you taught me, with that skull nestled where I hardly dared look. And it's only now that I've finally begun to understand.

"Carenza, my heart is yours. You've taught me how to live again. You've taught me how to love. I am yours, Carenza, all yours. My love for you is beyond words. Please believe me. Please forgive me."

She sat absolutely still before him, searching his face for some final clue.

"Say something, please." He held her hand, waiting.

"I believe you," she whispered. And then she touched her lips to his, and moments later, her body covered his. He surrendered himself completely to her fierce love.

CHAPTER THIRTY-TWO

IT WAS STIFLING inside the carriage bumping along the road to Hastings. Carenza envied her father, riding his horse in the open air where the sea breeze could reach him. The reason for her current discomfort sat across from her, trying not to grimace at each bump in the road. Daniel's wounds had begun to heal, but he still wasn't anywhere near strong enough to ride, so she had insisted on the carriage for herself, giving him the excuse to join her.

Thomas and what remained of the Hastings knights trailed along the road behind them. He'd sent most of his men back to Hastings two weeks ago when it became clear they would not see battle at Winchelsea. Thomas remained with a small contingent of knights, however, to remind them of their unfinished business with Helisende. Carenza couldn't wait to be rid of him and his dour, disapproving looks.

She smiled at Daniel as he gazed fixedly out the carriage window, no doubt absorbed in plotting out how he would approach Helisende. Sweat ran down his furrowed brow, and he was gritting his teeth against each jolt of the carriage. He needed a distraction, she decided.

"Amuse me, Daniel.
This coach is too slow.

The trip makes me weary,
And you look a bit dreary."

He looked at her, and one corner of his mouth curled in a
mischievous grin.

"Amuse you, my lady?
Let's find somewhere shady.
I know what to do
Out of view with just you."

She returned his smile with a smirk.

"And abandon the others
To rescue poor mother
While you and I dally
In some shady valley?"

He waved away her objection.

"Never mind about her.
Let me make you purr.
I'll make you moan and gasp
As you lie in my grasp."

She shook her head in mock outrage.

"I'm a dutiful daughter!
Don't make this coach hotter
By setting a flame
That you can't hope to tame."

He closed the shades on the windows. Then he reached
across and slowly and deliberately ran a hand up her skirt, starting
at her ankle, tickling and caressing his way up to the center of her

warmth as he spoke. At his touch, fire spread through her body.

"My dear, is that a dare?
You haven't a prayer.
You can't resist temptation.
I'll start a conflagration."

His hand reached its destination, and blinding heat obliterated her senses. Some small corner of her mind tried to remind her about duty and decorum. "Someone might hear!" she whimpered before surrendering utterly to him.

"Then you'll just have to see how quiet you can be," he said with a wicked grin as she squirmed against him. "I want to watch my wife." He shifted to the bench beside her, and she breathed him in, melting against him. "While I touch her," he said as she clapped a hand over her mouth to stifle a moan. "And make her tremble." He pressed a finger into her, sending lightning straight through her core. "I want to see you. The most beautiful thing I've ever seen. My beautiful wife who loves me. And the way you look when I touch you."

At his words, a thousand sparks exploded. Thinking became impossible. There was only the white-hot connection between them. He transformed her, made her new, a vessel of pure light in the midst of the dim inferno of the carriage. She trembled head to toe as she shattered into a million pieces and collapsed against him, utterly spent.

"Oh, my love," he murmured into her hair. "That was beautiful beyond words."

All she could manage was, "Mmm."

When they emerged from the carriage in Hastings, they had made themselves presentable again. Thomas cast a disapproving look in their direction, but she couldn't tell if it was any different from his usual demeanor.

Lady Helisende's welcome was as frosty as expected despite the heat of the summer day. She grudgingly shared bread and salt with them upon arrival, offering only water to drink rather than wine. Then she left Daniel, Carenza, and Lord de Vere in a modest receiving room to wait for over an hour. Clearly, her intention was to belittle and insult, perhaps hoping it would lead the inexperienced Daniel to make mistakes out of anger. From what Carenza had seen of her husband in action so far, however, she was sure Lady Helisende would come to rue taking this approach. Just last week, Daniel had deftly maneuvered his cocky and outraged cousin, Raymond II, Raymond de Broase's heir, into surrendering his claims and swearing fealty.

Despite his years of living as a commoner, Daniel had a presence and authority that could not be denied. He knew how to bend people to his will as skillfully as he once shaped wood into seaworthy vessels and set sails to the wind, though manipulating people wasn't something in which he took pleasure. He played the part of Lord de Broase as only someone born to it could. Only she, and perhaps Gerard, knew what it cost Daniel to do so. He'd taken up the name and the title. He'd wrested it back from his uncle. There was no going back now. And yet, for his sake, she wished there was a way for him to surrender it, to extricate himself from the tainted legacy he'd embraced for her sake.

"I think it's time we take a walk and find our host," Daniel announced, rising and heading for the door. When he opened it, he found Lady Helisende standing just outside, whispering with Thomas.

"My lady, I was just going to look for you. I'm sure you have urgent matters to discuss with your commander, but I think you'll find a conversation with me even more beneficial to the peace and safety of Hastings."

The countess' shrewd eyes sharpened. "You think so, do you?"

Daniel gestured to invite her into her own receiving room since she was making no move to join them. "Hastings is surrounded by de Broase land. My cousin Edmund has New Romney, and I have Winchelsea and Hawkhurst. Our combined strength at sea is considerable as well. Even greater, I daresay, than that of Hastings."

She gave a little huff of irritation, came in, and sat down. "How kind of you to remind me that you can attack me from every side."

"Did I say anything about attacking?" He smiled. "I'm here to discuss our mutual interests, my lady."

"You may have Hastings surrounded, but you're sitting in my castle right now, surrounded by my guards and knights, and I have members of your family locked away." Carenza laid a hand on her father's arm as he flinched in his seat. Lady Helisende showed her teeth. That was the best way Carenza could describe it because the expression certainly wasn't a smile. "For their own safety, of course," Lady Helisende added.

"Of course," Daniel answered, his smile gone. "I should tell you that my commander is very concerned for my safety and that of my family. If we aren't all back in Winchelsea safe and sound by nightfall, he's going to come looking for us."

Lady Helisende tilted her head to the side, a touch of fear breaking through the irritation if Carenza wasn't mistaken. "I assume if he comes, your knights come too?"

Daniel leaned toward her, and she leaned away ever so slightly. "What commander travels without his knights, especially when his liege lord's safety is in question?" He leaned back and made a tent with his fingers.

Lady Helisende cleared her throat and said nothing.

"I would like to see my wife and daughters and be assured of their safety," Lord de Vere said when the silence had become truly agonizing.

Carenza was starting to enjoy herself. The idea of threatening that John would bring his knights if they didn't return on time was hers, and she was more than a little bit proud of how well it worked.

Lady Helisende pinned her with a look as if she suspected her role in this. Carenza just smiled. Daniel was so much more than anyone ever expected.

"I'm a practical woman," the countess said at last. "I will always do what I must to keep Hastings safe and prosperous. Before I return Lady de Vere and her daughters, I'd like to know what you're hoping to accomplish here today. Let me be frank. Do you have designs on Hastings?"

Daniel's eyebrows shot up. "No, I do not."

She stared him down, eyes narrowed, and he looked right back, commanding and firm. A silent battle took place between them as the others looked on anxiously. At last, Lady Helisende nodded.

Daniel nodded in return. "I'm here to negotiate an agreement. But it's going to be quite different from the one you sent me. You utterly failed in your responsibility toward Winchelsea, my lady, and you have lost any claim to their loyalty. We are going to renegotiate our agreement with the Cinque Ports, and you, Lady Helisende, are going to pay for the damage caused by this little conflict. You will also find an appropriate family member to either send along with me as my ward or to marry into my family. Either way, they will become a part of my household in perpetuity. I promise they will be well treated."

He leaned forward.

"Unlike you," Daniel continued, "I'm not interested in extortion. I only want Winchelsea to be left alone in peace. In return, I promise to leave, not to attempt any incursions into your sphere of influence. As we've already discussed, my family's territory surrounds yours on three sides, and our combined naval power exceeds yours. Don't provoke me, and I'll leave you alone. Do we understand each other?"

Lady Helisende looked at him, assessing. "That's a remarkably fair agreement under the circumstances. I confess I was expecting you to be less reasonable. Perhaps we can work together after all." She smiled coolly, allowing a grudging respect. "I'll summon wine and refreshments. Then we can work through the details like civilized people."

Daniel held up his hand. "Before we do anything else, I'd like to see Lady de Vere and her daughters to be assured they are safe and sound."

She gave him an odd look. "Your mother-in-law? Are you sure?"

"Very," he said in a voice that brooked no dissent.

Lady Helisende shrugged. "Lucky woman. Most men I've met would pay me to keep their mothers-in-law away from them. But if you're sure...." She walked to the door and opened it, ordering an unseen servant just outside to bring Lady de Vere and her daughters and fetch refreshments.

Several silent, awkward minutes later, Lady de Vere, Alais, and Iselda were ushered in. An enormous weight lifted from Carenza's shoulders as Lord de Vere rushed to greet them. "Isabella, I was so worried. Are you all right? How are the girls? Have you been mistreated?"

"We're quite all right, Martin. You know I can handle myself. And we've been well treated, for prisoners." She gave the countess a pointed look.

"Carenza, did you defeat Daniel's awful uncle single-handed?" Alais bubbled, grabbing Carenza's arm.

"Not single-handed. No," she answered, laughing. "But he is dead, and his men surrendered to Daniel. It's safe to go home now."

"Good, because Lady Helisende keeps threatening to marry me off to some awful nephew of hers when he gets back from Spain."

The countess cracked a half-smile, and this time, it seemed genuine. "It's a shame. You'd be an excellent match. Lord de Vere, when you're ready to find her a husband, I hope you'll keep my nephew in mind."

Alais hid behind Carenza, and Lord de Vere gave her a reassuring pat on the shoulder.

"And Iselda, how have you fared?" Carenza asked.

"Quite well," she said with a shy grin. "Lady Helisende has an excellent library. I found some fascinating medical texts I haven't read before."

"I think that may be the most words she's ever said in my presence," Lady Helisende observed in dry tones.

The refreshments arrived, and after helping themselves, Daniel, Lady Helisende, and Lord de Vere went to another room to complete the treaty negotiations. Carenza stayed with her mother and sisters, exchanging stories.

"Daniel was poisoned?" Iselda asked with a bit too much interest. "I've been reading about treatments. Most texts say the patient must be bled to remove the foul humors, but I can't help but think that would weaken the patient when they most need their strength. Did the healer bleed Daniel?"

"No, he did not. He'd already lost too much blood from his wounds, and fortunately, he got better without it. But since when have you been so interested in medicine?" Carenza nudged Iselda with her elbow.

Iselda blushed. "A long time, actually, but people don't ask me what I'm reading very often."

"I'll have to ask you more." She patted Iselda on the knee.

"And Mother, I assume you've been conducting reconnaissance and have a wealth of information to share about the politics in Hastings?"

"Of course! Just wait 'til I tell you about how she's been playing Dover and Sandwich off each other."

LATER THAT NIGHT, after an uncomfortable journey home with five in the hot carriage instead of two, Carenza rested in her husband's arms. Daniel had taken her twice upon their return to the castle to celebrate their triumph against Lady Helisende.

"Daniel?" she murmured to his chest.

"Mmm?" he answered, stroking her hair.

"We're free now. We won. Everyone is home and safe. What happens next?"

He hugged her close and kissed the top of her head. "I was just thinking about that. I have some ideas."

CHAPTER THIRTY-THREE

THE RAMPARTS OF Hawkhurst loomed in the distance, and Daniel took no joy in the sight of his childhood home. Two nested walls encircled the familiar spires of the castle, which jabbed like poignards at the clouds. Hawkhurst had none of the delicacy and light of Winchelsea. While his memories of his family were fond, his memories of the place itself were not. Hawkhurst was all-consuming, an obsession without end for his parents. It was a place of power, not beauty, built for the sake of defense, not comfort. He hoped this would be his last visit.

"It's huge," said Carenza, riding beside him and staring ahead at the fortress. "Are you sure you want to do this?"

He nodded. "More than ever. That place killed my father."

"Your uncle killed your father."

He shook his head. "That place drove him to it. It poisons people."

"You're a better and stronger man than your uncle." The love and pride in her eyes made him smile.

"Our children deserve better than this," he said. "I don't want them plotting against each other for this looming hunk of rock."

Carenza nodded. There was temptation in her eyes. Hawkhurst was hard to resist. He understood its lure better than most, but he also knew the price of trying to hold it. He'd already lost one family to this place. He would not lose another.

They wended their way through verdant fields and up into the over-large, spiky fortress. His cousin, Raymond II, greeted them in the courtyard along with his wife.

"Welcome to Hawkhurst, my liege. I invite you to rest and refresh yourselves from your journey, and then we have much to discuss."

Daniel inclined his head in acknowledgment. "I thank you for your hospitality, and I look forward to a productive conversation."

His cousin's wife led Carenza off for a tour of the castle.

Soon, Daniel was seated at the head of a large trestle table with his cousin on his right. John, now commander of Daniel's knights, sat to his left. Daniel had also brought a lawyer and a notary so that he could carry out his plan on the spot, provided his cousin agreed. His cousin also brought an array of functionaries that Daniel greeted and then ignored.

"Cousin, I believe you will be pleased when you hear what I have to say," Daniel began. "I'm sure you were expecting me to come and take up residence, but I have something else in mind. After much consideration, I have decided to relinquish my claim to Hawkhurst in your favor. I have written to the king, and he has agreed to establish a new earldom in my name."

Raymond stared in silence at his cousin for a long moment. "You can't be serious," he said at last.

"I assure you I am. I have never had any wish to govern Hawkhurst, and I have no wish to breed ill will by taking away what you have always considered your birthright."

John's expression changed to a brief look of disappointment and resignation. Daniel had talked this through with him, but John couldn't help hoping he might have a change of heart. The moment passed, and John returned to the hard and impassive expression he had worn before.

Raymond laughed in disbelief.

"I have certain conditions," Daniel continued. "They are all laid out in the documents I had prepared for our meeting today.

The proposal has the blessing of the crown." He signaled his lawyer to hand them over. "I would like to lay claim to all the de Broase land from the border with Hastings over to the walls of Petit Iham and east to Icklesham as part of a new domain of Winchelsea. I plan to stay in Winchelsea and make that my seat. Everything else, I surrender to you."

"Done," said Raymond eagerly. He motioned to one of the seated functionaries. "Draw up a map."

Daniel's lawyer interjected, "We already have one, my lord." He pointed it out amongst the documents he had handed over.

"What else?" Raymond asked, examining the map.

"I ask for your written commitment that you and your descendants will never interfere with Winchelsea again. I would like to stay out of Hawkhurst's business, and I expect you to stay out of mine."

Raymond shrugged and nodded.

"I plan to retain John in my service as well as any other knights that wish to join me. I don't imagine it will deplete your defensive capabilities too greatly."

Raymond cocked his head. "John betrayed my father. While I may not grieve the old coot, there are those who do. I'd probably be forced to execute John if he stayed. Take him."

"You can read the rest of the detail," he said, signaling his lawyer to hand over the remainder of the documents. "I'd like favorable prices on wheat and iron. I'd like to request certain family heirlooms and a modest sum of money. I think you will find it all quite reasonable. Take your time to review it."

"My lord, why are you doing this?" Raymond looked wary, waiting for the catch. Certainly, this must seem too good to be true.

Daniel looked at his cousin and then at John before responding, "It always seemed to me that the burdens of leading Hawkhurst far outweighed the benefits, even before my father's death. I never wanted this. I'm not prepared for it. And I don't want to watch this place poison my children as it poisoned our fathers. If you want it, you can have it. There's nothing for me here."

Raymond shook his head in disbelief. "What a fool my father was. All those years he chased you, and you didn't even want Hawkhurst."

"No, I didn't. I don't even want to be a de Broase. In fact, I'm planning to change my surname to Rossignol."

"Rossignol?" Raymond raised a dubious eyebrow.

Daniel smiled. "I thought 'nightingale' would make a good family name for a couple of poets, don't you think?"

"Suit yourself," Raymond said, looking at him like he was one wheel shy of a full cart.

"If you will excuse me, I'd like to visit my mother's grave. I've never been able to pay my respects, and I don't plan to visit here again once I leave. We can finalize and sign everything this evening. I leave for home tomorrow morning." Daniel stood to leave, and John followed.

As they made their way to the cemetery, a thousand memories flooded back to him. This place never had a hold on him like it did on his father. It was the people he loved that he held in his heart, not Hawkhurst itself. He thought of his mother, who'd perished before he could see her again. What would she have thought of the man he'd become?

"Your parents would be very proud of you," John said, as if reading his thoughts.

Daniel paused. "But you were disappointed."

"You would have been a great leader, better by far than your cousin. But I understand. As the Proverbs say, 'When pride comes, then comes disgrace, but with the humble is wisdom.' You followed the path of humility. I respect that."

John stopped and let him approach his mother's grave alone, respecting his privacy. He laid a bouquet of lavender against the headstone. It was her favorite flower. She always said it reminded her of her home in France.

A tear trickled down his cheek as he said a silent prayer.

"The nightmare is over, Mama," he murmured. "Maggie and I are safe from Uncle Raymond at last. I'm so sorry you aren't here with us."

A starling landed on the headstone and chirped, cocking its head as if listening.

Daniel wiped his cheek and laughed. "Or maybe you are here. You always did love starlings."

He smiled at the tiny bird.

"I got married, Mama. My wife's name is Carenza. I think you'd like her. She's a poet, if you can believe it. A good one, too. I know how much you loved poetry."

Pulling a parchment scroll from his pocket, he laid it beside the flowers. "I wrote you something. I hope you like it. You always liked my compositions. Well, I never gave it up. I'm still your little nightingale."

The starling chirped and flew away.

"I love you, Mama. Rest in peace," he said and walked back to the castle.

That night, in their strange bedchamber, Daniel held Carenza close. "We're free," he murmured into her hair.

"We're free," she whispered into his chest.

At long last, he was rid of his legacy and able to start fresh. Even here, within the heavy walls of Hawkhurst, he felt light, buoyant, ready for a future he'd always feared to contemplate. His life was his own at last. Death could come at any time; that was true. But life should not be wasted. And he would not waste it.

CHAPTER THIRTY-FOUR

TWO MONTHS LATER, Daniel walked along Fish Street, past sailors, merchants, and dock workers going about their business, holding a sheaf of parchment in his hand. He stepped into a familiar warehouse that, as of this morning, he now owned. He greeted his old friends, stripped to the waist, took an ax, and set to work. He'd missed this. His new life didn't give him as many excuses as he would have liked for working up an honest sweat and building something meant to last. Lords were supposed to be warriors, but in his heart, Daniel was a maker. He practiced the arts of war because it was expected of him, and he appreciated the physical and mental challenge, but he never felt a sense of accomplishment at the end of his training in arms. He needed to do something productive.

Carenza had suggested this. Daniel suspected she was trying to get him out of her way while she dealt with the day-to-day administration of their holdings. He had been delighted by her talent and affinity for the work. She managed most everything in his name and only brought him in when he was needed or for things that he particularly enjoyed, such as agriculture and public works. He supposed that she was right to insist that he find something productive to do with his time besides looking over her shoulder. He would feel a great deal less restless if he could spend even one day a week doing this.

He worked through the afternoon and hardly noticed as the sun dipped in the sky and the other men departed. At twilight, a familiar silhouette appeared in the door. Carenza stood, leaning against the doorframe with crossed arms, with a look of pride and profound love on her face as she watched him in silence. He nodded his head, inviting her in. She perched on a barrel, reminding him of the day they first met.

That day so long ago, he found their meeting uncomfortable, unsettling. He couldn't allow himself to acknowledge the heat between them or the strength of his own need. He had been desperate for her and in total denial. And she had still been convinced she wanted to be a nun. What a mess they had made of it all!

But now, she was patient, assured, and so was he. There was love and desire, but there was no hurry, no desperation. She liked to look at him. He liked that she liked to look at him. He liked to look at her, too. He continued his work for another ten minutes, finishing off the board he was working on as he basked in her unabashed gaze. Her eyes kindled something within him. He let it grow slowly, without taking any action, knowing she was his and that he could be with her when he wanted. There was no rush. He could enjoy a slow build.

Out of the corner of his eye, he saw her bite her lip as he changed from his axe to a chisel for some detail work. A flash of desire surged through him at that tiny movement. He picked up the board and leaned against the warehouse wall, then raised his eyes to meet hers. The heat in her gaze matched his own. Her mouth was slightly open, and her breathing grew uneven as he locked eyes with her.

Slowly, methodically, he picked up his tools and hung them on the wall. Then he caught her gaze again and approached the barrel where she was perched.

He leaned in, letting the sparks between them build to a bonfire as he stood inches away but not yet touching her. Her face was tilted toward his, sultry and flushed, her mouth raised in invitation. Her eyes burned and flashed, crackling with the heat of her need. He prolonged the moment as long as he could stand, her ragged breath whispering against his lips. He placed his hands on either side of her and leaned in, not quite touching her. She shivered despite the heat and moaned quietly. His lips just touched hers, the softest of brushes. Lightning ran through him with that brief contact. He backed away just an inch and let out a low, hungry "Mmm."

She reached up and tickled his chin through his beard and gave a gentle tug, pulling him into a fierce kiss. "We should go back to the castle," she said as she released him, trailing fingers down his bare chest.

"You like to watch me work," he observed with a wicked grin.

"Yes, I do," she mused, sliding off the barrel so that the full length of her was pressing against him, her enticing spice and almond scent tickling his nostrils. It was heaven to hold her so close and know that soon he would hold her closer still. "I think I might have to make regular visits, inspect your work, and keep an eye on our investment."

"I think you should. It's only prudent." He nibbled her ear and nuzzled her neck. "Any special commissions, my lady?"

Her expression changed. Where moments ago he saw smoldering desire to match his own, now he saw something tremulous and joyful in her eyes. She took a deep breath and gave him the sweetest smile. It absolutely melted him.

"Actually, yes," she said, reaching one hand up to caress his curls. "We need a bigger boat."

"Oh?"

"The Adele only fits two." She took his hand and placed it on her belly.

His heart skipped a beat as he absorbed her meaning. "You're...?"

"Ensuring the succession. Yes," she said lightly with a wry smile.

Joy blossomed within him, a joy that was beyond any he had felt since he was a child himself. He was going to be a father! Carenza's belly would swell with their precious little one, and he would have a family once again. The thought nearly brought him to his knees. A family. His family. A future he hardly dared dream of for so many years. And it was all thanks to the amazing woman that stood before him. Thank heavens she'd stumbled into this very warehouse that day. She had utterly transformed his life.

He grinned ear to ear and pulled Carenza into an embrace, his hand on her middle as if he could feel the magic within her. "Have I told you how much I love you?"

"You're always welcome to tell me again."

He swept her into his arms and carried her out to her horse, gently easing her into her saddle, and then he mounted behind her, wisps of her ink-black hair tickling his face. "Let's go home," he said, kissing her neck and guiding the horse up Castle Street.

EPILOGUE

My beloved Daniel,

A year ago today, you asked me what words I would use to describe the act of love. Today, I'm ready to tell you. Happy anniversary!

Love,
Your Poetess

You had the key to me, my love
Unlocking joys I'd never known.
With words and whispers, you alone
Could give me pleasures undreamt of.
Before you touched me, I was lost
Each verse a kiss that sparked a flame.
Your voice set fires I could not tame.
I fell for you despite the cost.
And then you touched your lips to mine.
You swept away my last defense.
The taste of you robbed me of sense
Intoxicating me like wine.
Then you came back a nobleman.
You wooed with words as you caressed

And pressed the ardor you confessed
Our vows blessed by a clergyman.
When nighttime fell, you opened me
With taste and touch, you tantalized,
Such tender torture you devised
To tutor me in ecstasy.
Within me and enveloping
Our bodies fit and move entwined
No longer by our flesh confined
We soared, our bodies trembling.
Two hearts as one, two halves a whole,
An alchemy of flesh and bone
No longer wandering alone
With sweet touch you seduced my soul.

About the Author

Leslie Vollard has a longstanding passion for the Middle Ages. Her obsession with all things medieval dates back to college when she dug through archives at the Bibliothèque Nationale in Paris to study the 12th century troubadour, Arnaut Daniel. In her work, she brings courtly love, chivalry, and the troubadour tradition to life. Romance reigns supreme in her steamy novels about how love conquers all.

Leslie lives in Long Island with her delightfully nerdy husband and two cats. She loves gardening, baking, and reading love poems in dead languages.

www.ingramcontent.com/pod-product-compliance
Lightning Source LLC
Chambersburg PA
CBHW070533310726
48976CB00002BA/610

9 781963 585209